THE FOREIGN HUSBAND

CLIVE COLLINS

THE FOREIGN HUSBAND

A Novel

Marion Boyars

London · New York

Published in Great Britain and the United States
in 1989 by Marion Boyars Publishers
24 Lacy Road, London SW15 1NL
26 East 33rd Street, New York, NY 10016

Distributed in the United States by
Kampmann & Co, New York

Distributed in Canada by
Book Center Inc, Montreal

Distributed in Australia by
Wild & Woolley, Glebe, NSW

© Clive Collins 1989

British Library Cataloguing in Publication Data
Collins, Clive
    The foreign husband.
    I. Title
    823'.914[F]

Library of Congress Cataloging-in-Publication Data
Collins, Clive, 1948–
    The foreign husband.
    I. Title
PR6053.042486F6   1989   823'.914   88–7373

ISBN 0-7145-2893-5 Cloth

Typeset in Baskerville 10½ on 12½ and Optima by
Ann Buchan (Typesetters), Shepperton
Printed and bound in Great Britain by
Biddles Ltd, Guildford, Surrey

for Walter Allen
novelist, man of letters, teacher

'It's a mudswamp much more frightening than what the Christians call hell —
this Japan. No matter what shoots one tries
to transplant here from another country,
they all wither and die, or else bear a flower
and a fruit that only resemble the real ones.'
                    Endo Shusaku, *The Golden Country*

Admit it,
this is what we have made,
this ragged place, an order
gone to seed, the battered plants
slump in the tangled rows,
their stems and damp rope sagging.
Our blunted fingers,
our mouths taste
of the same earth, bitter and deep.
                    Margaret Atwood, *Nothing New Here*

PROLOGUE

S he said it was like waking deep in the ocean. The world was blue, and this made her very happy for she had imagined that afterwards it would be all darkness. Now she felt safe, and knew that what she had done was right.

Something drifted past her just as she was beginning to enjoy her new world, moving upwards along one of the shafts of filtered light that reached through the waters. She decided to follow, and it was only when she understood that the shape before her was her own body that she realized she was involved in a desperate pursuit. She called, but there was no answer; she reached out with hands she did not have towards hands she no longer possessed. She could not catch the elusive form, she could only follow, pulled along by a growing sense that she must stop the ascent.

It was no use. The light grew stronger and she could hear human voices shouting her name. She tried to go back, to reach down again into the blue world where she had, for a moment, felt safe and happy, but the voices grew more urgent now, compelling her to rise towards them. The light and the noise closed about her like a net; she was a tiny silver fish, meshed by the gills and already beginning to drown.

She was very close to her body now, and so near the surface of the water she could see the shifting forms of the fishermen. Their voices were loud, and they kept calling to her, telling her to wake up, but she wasn't asleep. Whatever else it was, this state in which she had found herself, it wasn't sleep.

Hands reached down to her body and seized it. She wanted to shout, to tell the men to let it go, but she was suddenly afraid. She knew that if she opened her mouth she would choke on the water. It would rush into her, violating all her spaces. She had somehow betrayed her sea-world and it was giving her up, rejecting her.

The hands began to shake the body they had grasped, heaving and twirling it in the water like a piece of washing. There was a terrible pressure in her head and chest, and she knew she must breathe, but to breathe would mean that she could never hope to find the blue-shadowed spaces below the water again.

Someone hit her, once, and then again, across the face, hurting her. The pain told her she had lost. Her mother was there, weeping, repeating her name over and over. A voice said she was going to vomit, and she felt her head being forced over a bright metal bowl. The light glaring from its refracted surface hurt her eyes, and she wanted to turn away, but with the compliance of the defeated she allowed a bitter stream to flow through her mouth, spattering the polished basin.

TOKYO

David Kennedy followed the tourists along Millbank and up the white steps of the Tate Gallery. They seemed to come earlier each year now, like birds in a ceaseless migration. As the little groups paused just inside the doors, bemused suddenly by the possibility of not having to buy a ticket, the half-expected threat of bag- and body-searches, David moved past them, into the smell of floor-wax and dust and paintings. He was a tourist himself now, more or less; in the months since he had come to London this time he had done almost nothing, been almost nowhere, only when he knew he was to leave had he begun his headlong journey around the city's museums and the galleries, to peer at the stored booty of other people's pasts.

He walked straight to the place he always went to here, the ill-lit area on the left where a few items from the gallery's British collection were hung, almost in apology. The two Lucien Freuds were there, where he had grown accustomed to finding them, *Girl With a White Dog* and *Two Plants*. He looked at the girl, her eyes so far away from the painter as she sat with her cold, pale breast slipped from the dressing-gown. They were never present in the paintings, the people, the subjects, only their bodies were on the canvas, the flesh cold and dead. Still lives, *nature morte*. David admired the technique.

On the opposite wall was a painting by Victor Pasmore, *The Inland Sea*. He had looked at it before, remembered the swirled gold, the peacock shades, the utter flatness. Usually he passed with little more than a glance. Today he stopped in front of the picture, its title helping him to see it for the first time. As he ran his eye over the work a group of anxious Japanese hurried past, their lack of interest making an ironic commentary on the pretensions of the European mind. For them there was no 'Inland Sea', it was simply another invention of the foreigner, as irrelevant as a comic opera mikado. David guessed they were making for the Pre-Raphaelite collection, or possibly the Turners. The Japanese were the new barbarians, looting with their cameras where once the English had stolen with their hands. He watched them go, the violence of their passing moving about the gallery like a wind. Soon he would follow them, not to pay obeisance to Rossetti and Burne-Jones, but to their homeland. Soon he would be the barbarian.

He was to travel to Tokyo to take up a position as a teacher of English at one of Japan's most prestigious private universities, a place described to him by his predecessor as the Vassar of the Orient, 'or at least, that's how they like to think of it. As you'll see when you've been in the place for a couple of weeks, the reality's a wee bit different.' He had met the man through the British Council, which had recruited for the post, and together they went to a tourist pub near Trafalgar Square, all scrubbed plank-tables and sawdust, and flat beer in mock-Tudor tankards. The man was from Edinburgh, and he and David got on well together, sharing the tenuous security of having once lived in the same town, walked the same streets.

The job seemed almost too good to be real: for only eleven hours of teaching each week he would receive almost twenty thousand pounds a year, and free accommodation.

'Then there'll be the part-time jobs,' the Scot had said. 'Once word gets around that there's a new *gaijin* — foreigner — about the place, the offers will come in. You'll not need to be short of cash.'

David had wondered as he sat with this bringer of good news, why the man should quit such a post to return to Britain and a future with nothing more certain in it than an MA course, but had said nothing. It was a gift horse that had been too long in coming.

More than three years earlier he had walked out of his emptied apartment in Fez and driven to Casablanca to take the plane back to Britain. He had known he was going to certain unemployment, but there was nothing he could do; the aid agreement under which the British government paid his salary at the University of Fez had been ended. He had seen it coming, tried to find other work, failed. Jean, his wife, was waiting for him in Edinburgh. She had never been happy in North Africa and when they knew the job in Morocco would end, said she would spend that last year in Scotland at her parents' house. She would look for a place for them to live, get a home ready for them when David was back. She hoped to enrol in a post-graduate course at the University, then, by the time David returned, she might be working and so be able to support them while he applied for another post.

In the September before he went out to Fez for the last year, David handed over most of the money he had saved from five years teaching, and received in return the mortgage on a dark, four-roomed apartment in a little street off the Lothian Road. It was over a butcher's shop, the smell of offal pervaded the place. His wife became a student again, and he returned to Morocco.

He came home, finally, regretfully, to a country of circuses but no bread. A prince's wedding, a short and bloody war: expensive entertainments to divert the mind from the gutted hearts of dying cities, the ritual slaughterings in the damp fields and cold streets of Ulster, three million unemployed. Four million, some said, if those who were not registered were taken into account. David did not register: he was ineligible for benefit and so did not see the point.

The first summer passed pleasantly enough; there were things to do to the apartment, furniture to buy, walls to be painted. Jean had camped in the place during the winter and spring, but now she seemed eager to put together the home she had promised to make for him while he was away. They spent money easily: carpets, tables, chairs, a television and stereo. David acquiesced in everything, but somehow it seemed as if it was all happening to someone else. He was like a swimmer moving awkwardly in heavy water, going through with each stroke only because not to do so meant he must drown. He knew they were preparing themselves for a life they could not afford; the repayments on the mortgage would soon erode the final three months' salary from Fez, the separation allowance and the sum he had received from cashing in his insurance scheme, but he said nothing.

Autumn came, and the trees in the Castle Gardens wore crowns of gold and russet. Jean went back to university, where she was enrolled as a doctoral candidate. Sometimes she would leave the library early to walk with David in the New Town, watching the white smoke from afternoon drawing-room fires eddy down into the Georgian squares, mixing its sharper scent with the fragrance of burning leaves. Or they would wander across The Meadows, among the dogs and the old men, before crossing George Square to find their way to the teashop in the Canongate which always smelt of lavender and dry toast. Jean would talk about her work, or her friends at the university. David listened, or pretended to. He had nothing to talk about, except his worries. When he had spoken before of what would happen when the money they had was gone it was Jean who said nothing. So he kept his silence, and his fears became serpents that fed on his heart.

Autumn faded into winter, and winter into a cold, cruel spring that coaxed green buds from the trees only to snap them off with sudden, vicious frosts. David lived between intervals of newspapers, gutting the vacancies columns as soon as he got his hands on them. He applied for any kind of job now — he was interviewed for a place on a training course for prospective managers of an American fried-chicken franchise that was opening in Britain. Nothing came of it; the Americans felt he was over-qualified.

He filled the hours when he was not typing out his resumé or completing application forms by cleaning the apartment, so that soon it came to look as if no one actually lived in it. He read the newspapers from end to end, listened to the radio throughout the morning, all the time drinking cup after cup of instant coffee, until the smell of milk heating in a pan sickened him. In the afternoons he would sleep, furtively, for he was afraid Jean might return early and find him. He was an adulterer, with a mistress called despair.

In the evenings, when Jean was with him in the apartment, and at the week-ends, he worked on the book he had begun in Morocco, a critical biography of the Austrian painter Egon Schiele, but he knew it was all a pretence, and felt, from the looks he sometimes caught Jean giving him, that she knew as well as he the project would never be finished.

When June came, the money in their bank account was low enough for David to claim supplementary benefit, and so he went to sign on as unemployed. The end followed very quickly after that; by the middle of the second autumn it was all gone, the money, the apartment, everything.

One warm evening in July David had talked with Jean about their situation. He told her that, no matter what they did, they would have to sell the apartment before the end of October. She said she understood, and they made their decisions: the flat must be sold. They could pay off their other debts with whatever was left to them after settling the loan from the building society. Then he told her he had decided to move to London. He thought he could probably find work in one of the private language schools there, and he was sure he would stand a better chance of getting interviews once he was living in the south. Then, at least, the accountants who now ran the universities and education authorities could not hold the cost of a rail fare from Scotland against him. Jean again said she understood, that she knew of a room to let in a flat with other postgraduates for the coming autumn term, and that she would try to get it. She said she would rather not move back to her mother's house in Leith.

He left Edinburgh in the second week of November, stopping off to spend the weekend with his parents in Loxley before completing the journey south. He had some luck then: Harry, the friend he had arranged to stay with in London while he looked for a place of his own, heard of someone who needed a flat-sitter for a year. David moved to Bayswater in early December and Jean came down for Christmas. They spent some of the money they had managed to keep from the sale of the apartment on a trip to Venice, where they wandered the cold and deserted squares on New Year's Day. A squally wind swept over the Lagoon, peppering the air with tiny pellets of ice.

Alone in London again, he remained without work. He spent an unhappy week in one of the language schools that had sprung up since he had last been in England, but they existed by exploiting new graduates, the first of a generation for whom a degree was, literally, worth nothing more than the paper it was printed on. For a few pounds these educated paupers, in fraying, washed-out clothes, were willing to stand before the sniggering girls from Rotterdam and Lille, the ever-uncomprehending tribes of Arabs, whose thoughts were never far away from what their money could buy them next — English clothes, English houses, English women. David walked out of his class-room on the Friday afternoon and never went back.

When February came and he still had nothing, he accepted that he would never find work in Britain, and began applying for posts abroad. He told Jean one Sunday over the 'phone; she said she understood.

And so his life lapsed into the pattern it had followed in Scotland: the papers, the coffee, the afternoon naps and the endless reiterations of who he was: *Name* — David Brendan Kennedy, *Age* — 35, *Marital Status* — Married, no children, *Education* — The City Grammar School, Loxley, the universities of Edinburgh and London (the Institute of Education and the Courtauld Institute), Ph.D. (Applied Linguistics), PGCE (TESL), BA (Fine Arts), *Present Post* — Presently unemployed.

At the end of the month, on impulse, he joined a gym and began to lift weights. He had never been attracted to sports at school, but he enjoyed the mindlessness of these exercises, and the easy friendships in the gym. Almost everyone there was like him, without a job, paying their fees off each week with a few pence from their dole. He had stopped going to pubs and parties with Harry because the people he met always asked him what he did. In the gym no one asked that question. Soon he was training every afternoon except Sunday, when the place was closed. He bought a pair of track shoes and began to run, early in the morning when the streets were empty except for milkmen and paperboys, moving through the dawn-grey city, skipping between the piles of ravaged trash and the dog-shit.

He stopped smoking and drinking, grew muscles that surprised him each time he caught sight of himself in the locker-room mirrors. He was fitter than he had ever been, yet he could not quite get rid of the feeling that he was somehow punishing himself for not having found work, like a flagellant, tearing his flesh for its sins.

It was Easter when he heard he had been offered the job in Tokyo. The news came with another offer, an administrative post with the University of Stirling. It was for two years in the first instance, and with a salary of under six thousand pounds. Both offers arrived on the day he left London to spend the holiday

in Edinburgh with Jean. She had written to say she had the loan
of a house; it belonged to a lecturer she knew who would be in
New York for most of the vacation. That night David sat with his
wife in a bare and austerely re-modelled Edwardian terraced
house, uncomfortable on a harsh wire chair, and showed her the
two letters. Jean said he should take the one in Japan, that it
would mean another year's separation, but after she had
completed the six terms residency she needed for her doctorate,
she would join him and finish her thesis in Tokyo. David felt he
could stop swimming.

The British Airways flight from Heathrow to Tokyo's new
airport at Narita travels through time as well as space, delivering
its passengers some nine hours into the future. As David was
carried north towards the Pole in the early part of May it seemed
to him that he was truly moving to another dimension, a point
where he would enter a new life in a new world. He felt as if he
had just woken from some dreadful sleep, as lifeless as the great
frozen ocean over which he was now passing, as lifeless as the
golden waves of the Inland Sea in the painting he had admired in
the Tate.

Yet he was disappointed when he landed at Narita, for it was
like any other airport in the Western World, and, for all its
newness, already going to seed. It was at Anchorage, on the far
north-western rim of the Americas, where the flight stopped for
refuelling, that David felt he had arrived in Asia: Japanese was
being spoken all around him, and there were ideogrammed signs
and notices everywhere. In the duty-free shopping area the very
press of elegant, expensively-dressed Japanese women fighting to
get their orders for bottles of whisky and packets of deep-frozen
steak taken, the urgency with which they thrust well-manicured
fists full of money at the cashiers, suggested the oriental
market-place.

He did not have long to nurse his disappointment, however,
for he was very quickly in a car with two Japanese, speeding
away from the airport along a highway towards Tokyo. He had
come from the Customs Hall and found himself face to face with a
large number of people with placards, each bearing the name of
an expected passenger. One of the placards had his name on it,

and when the man holding it saw the sudden shock of recognition on David's face, he had stepped forward and introduced himself, telling David to wait where he was, before he plunged into the crowd, returning moments later with another Japanese.

Both men were lecturers at the university where David would teach, and they had been sent to meet him. David, not having expected this, was suddenly confused, and meekly followed the two men and his luggage through the crowded concourse toward the exit.

He found himself dozing on the journey into the city, unable to follow the men as they chatted together, sometimes in English and sometimes in their own language. They were an odd pair: Asano, the one who had first spotted David, was a small, perfectly round man, with a schoolboy's face which he had tried to hide behind a thin moustache, and topped with an unruly fringe of heavy, rather greasy hair. The effect was to make of him an oriental Oliver Hardy.

The other, David had not caught his name when they were introduced, was absurdly handsome and his English, which was much better than Asano's, was spoken in a deep, rich voice, a voice that should have been selling Scotch or cigarettes, casually convincing us that our lives can be better if only we will try.

At one point a sudden little peal of bells came from the dashboard, playing the tune 'Greensleeves', and David asked what it was.

Asano, giggling, said, 'He is breaking the law. The music tells that he drives too quickly.'

'I've disconnected the alarm on my own car,' the other man said, 'but this belongs to Kokujo — the university in which you will be teaching. They're confounded nuisances really!'

'He is a very wicked fellow,' Asano said, still smirking.

'Yes, I'm a bad lot all together, I'm afraid. I can say that, "a bad lot"?'

David, his head hanging heavily, agreed that he could.

Accommodation for the night, like everything else it seemed, had been arranged for him and, at a little after five-thirty in the afternoon, he sat with Asano in the coffee shop of the Westport Hotel, drinking tea and looking out across the hotel gardens towards the moat of the Imperial Palace. David and his companion were the only men in the narrow, glass-fronted cafeteria. All the other customers were women, elegantly dressed for the warm spring day and engaged in animated conversations as they toyed with plates of overly-rich cakes. It seemed to David Tokyo was a city of parks and women, for that was all he had seen so far.

'Would you like to walk in the gardens?' Asano asked, pulling David's attention away from the women that surrounded them.

They left the coffee shop and walked through the lobby into the sunshine. David expected Asano to turn into the gardens that ran along the side of the hotel, but instead he crossed the driveway and made for the road, leading the way through the heavy stream of traffic and into a tree-lined corridor which skirted the moat.

'Are we allowed in here?' David asked, but then realized that the paths threading between the trees were filled with joggers. The runners kept together in packs, each group dressed in identical running gear, following a leader who would bellow and evoke a shouted response from those behind. One group followed a man with a small flag inserted into a pocket between the shoulders of his running vest. When David pointed this out to Asano, he giggled and said something David could not quite hear.

The sun had set, and the day was beginning to gather itself inward before they turned to begin the walk back to the hotel, but David's eye had been caught by an enormous bronze arch that rose into the evening sky from another smaller park across the road from where they were standing.

'It is for the Japanese war dead,' Asano said. He seemed to be embarrassed. 'This is a place of ghosts where we have put you. I am sorry.'

The lights were on in the lobby of the hotel when they got back, and David was beginning to feel again the effects of the long flight from London: his head ached in an odd sort of way and he felt detached from his surroundings. At the entrance, he paused to say goodbye to Asano. More than anything he wanted to get to his room to bathe, and eat something before trying to sleep.

Onizuka, the other Japanese who had met him at the airport, had said goodbye as soon as they arrived at the hotel. While Asano saw David's luggage safely into the charge of a porter,

Onizuka had said he had another appointment and must leave, and then taken out his wallet. For one absurd moment David had thought he was about to offer him money and began to explain that he had some Japanese notes as well as his travellers' cheques. But it was not money Onizuka was to give him, it was a small, exquisitely printed business card, in Japanese and English.

'This is called *meishi*,' Onizuka had said. 'They are very important here. Without them we do not know who we have been talking to.' Then he laughed, and said, 'see you', before pulling the car door closed and driving out into the traffic.

Asano was not to leave so easily. 'Do you eat Japanese food?' he asked in reply to David's thanking him for all he had done. A short while later the two men were being shown to a table in a restaurant in the hotel basement by a pretty girl wrapped tightly in a pink kimono. The table was by a window through which could be seen an austere, floodlit garden, with a waterfall that emptied into a pond. Carp swam in the crystal waters.

'It is very beautiful,' Asano said, gesturing towards the garden. David nodded, but his eyes were upon the girls who worked in the restaurant. He had never seen women in kimono before. The swaddled cloth completely effaced their figures, but the necks and faces that emerged above the stiff expanse of the *obi*-belts were beautiful, and below the hem of the garment itself, tiny feet were decked in immaculate white socks like spats. He watched as one of the girls served a group of men seated on a raised dias at a low table. She knelt before the men and David's eyes fell upon the silk stretched tightly across her buttocks. The clothes were immensely sensual, each woman an extravagant present waiting to be unwrapped.

His attention was recalled by Asano, who asked about Jean. He wanted to know when she would be coming to Tokyo. David faltered in his reply, explaining that it would be at least a year before she could leave Edinburgh because of her work. The Japanese nodded as David smiled at him, but said nothing.

It was almost eleven-thirty before Asano finally left. When David went up to his room he was drunk with fatigue and the whisky Asano's polite insistence had forced on him. The whisky sat uneasily in his stomach, for he had eaten little of the food in the restaurant. The lacquered tray placed before him had been exquisite to look at, with its half-dozen separate bowls and dishes, each holding a carefully arranged morsel, it seemed as if he had been given a tiny gallery of paintings. The waitress laughed as she set the tray down, putting her hand to her mouth, and David had looked up from his food to see the hand flutter before her lips, like a butterfly about to alight on the scarlet petals of some exotic flower.

But he had not been able to eat. Much of the food was raw and, unused to the sensation of uncooked flesh in his mouth, he had swallowed it only with mouthfuls of the beer that had formed the somewhat coarse accompaniment to the meal. When Asano was gone, David had asked at the front desk for sandwiches and milk to be sent up to his room, but it was too late for the kitchens were closed.

The telephone in his room began to ring as he fumbled with the door, and in his rush to answer it he was unable to find the light-switch. He lifted the receiver in the darkness to hear a voice saying, 'Hello David, I'm Jack Stevens. Welcome to Japan.'

In his tiredness David was unable to make any sort of reply, and the voice at the other end of the line began again, 'I know you must be tired, but I'm the other full-time British teacher at the university and I wanted to give you my telephone number as soon as possible. Have you got a pen and paper?'

He managed to turn on the lamp by the telephone, and saw that there was a small pad of paper and a pen. He copied down the number his unexpected caller gave him.

'Mr Asano will be taking you to your apartment tomorrow, I think. Give me a ring tomorrow night and we can arrange where to meet on Thursday.'

Utterly confused, David said, 'I'm sorry, but what's happening on Thursday?'

'Oh, you didn't get Duckham's letter? It's most probably at school, so you'll get it tomorrow. You're invited to dinner with a bloke called Richard Duckham on Thursday evening. He's the English Language Officer with the British Council here, and is someone you should definitely get to know. My wife and I are also invited and Duckham asked us to meet you and take you along to his house.'

There was another silence before Jack Stevens said, 'I'm sure you must be tired so I'll let you go. Call me tomorrow evening, all right?'

David said he would, and put the telephone down.

He slept fitfully during the night, waking once from a dream in which he was choking to find his mouth rank with the taste of blood. His nose had bled, and there was a small but deeply stained patch of blood on the pillow-case. He got up to rinse his mouth in the bathroom, and then went back to bed searching once more for sleep.

He was up and showered by seven o'clock the next morning. He had found himself suddenly awake, with sunshine bright against the drawn window-blinds. He ordered breakfast in his room: oatmeal, an omelette with bacon and sausage, toast, preserves and coffee. He ate while he sat, dressed in the soft white cotton gown he had found folded beautifully upon his bed the night before, and watched television.

Asano was already in the lobby when David got down there a little before nine o'clock. They went into the coffee shop where they had sat the day before because Asano had left his home so early he had had nothing to eat or drink. This morning the place was deserted.

'You are very handsome, Mr Kennedy,' Asano said as they sat down. 'You dress like a film star. The girls will all be in love with you.'

David smiled, not knowing how else to acknowledge the compliment. He had bought the light, fawn-coloured suit he was wearing from Simpsons, along with another, blue suit, and several shirts, ties and pairs of slacks, justifying their purchase on the grounds that he would need them for his new position. However, the guilt he continued to feel made him uneasy in the clothes. It had always been like this with him. Jean once said he had all the instincts of a dandy, but none of the convictions. He was a good-looking man who, when he could, dressed expensively, but somehow always with an air of hoping that no one would notice. Asano had, and David was embarrassed.

He checked out of the hotel, leaving his bags with the porters until the evening when, Asano had told him, they would return to the Westport and go by taxi from there to the apartment the university had taken for him.

'It was your predecessor's and is small by European standards perhaps, but we hope it will be satisfactory for some time,' Asano said as they walked out into a street still choked with traffic from the morning rush-hour. 'Perhaps when your wife comes to Japan you will find somewhere else.'

At six-thirty that evening the taxi in which David and Asano had crossed the city pulled up outside a corner house on a quiet side road. David had no idea where he was. It had taken longer to get from the hotel to where they were now than the journey into town from the airport yesterday. Traffic had been thick, even on the elevated roadways that crossed the city. During the journey his idea of Tokyo had changed dramatically. It was, for the most part, a sprawling monotony of ugliness. Once the area around the Imperial Palace was left behind, it seemed that one part of the city looked like any other.

The taxi-driver turned to Asano and admitted, as Asano translated to David with a grin, that he was lost. It took an hour of grimly circling endless, identical backstreets and alleyways before Asano, who had visited the apartment before, recognized the house. Getting out of the taxi while Asano paid the driver, David felt profoundly depressed. It was dark, but the light from an erratic street-lamp spasmodically illuminated a pile of rubbish waiting for collection against the outside wall of the house, and the flaking paint of the gate with its five letter-boxes.

The day had largely consisted of David following Asano around, like Alice and the Rabbit. They too began by going down a hole in the ground. In the Tokyo subway system they had changed from a blue train to an orange train, and then, emerging from a tunnel into the daylight high above a huge intersection where cars and trains and people went their ways, each group on its own elevated routeway, had pulled into the largest, most complex and crowded railway station David had ever seen. Asano laughed when David remarked upon the crush of people, and said it was much worse during the morning and evening rush-hours. From this station they had taken one last train to the university.

The National Women's University had been set up in 1954 on the site of a former agricultural college. The buildings of the college had been destroyed during the war, but somehow the gardens survived the bombing and, as David had walked with Asano through the great wooden gates that morning, he had fancied himself in a kind of wonderland. There were banks of flowering azaleas everywhere, reds and whites and pinks and, rising from behind the bushes, set among the great yew trees and the cedars, were buildings that seemed to have been copied from an old Hollywood movie of collegiate life. If the style of architecture had had a name it would have been Paramount Gothic. As they were passing down one of the azalea-lined walks, a clock somewhere on the campus began to chime.

'It is the end of the second teaching period,' Asano said, and as he spoke the campus was suddenly flush with girls, wave after wave of chattering, running, laughing black-haired girls bursting from the buildings into the narrow, flowered paths. Asano had turned into the lobby of a building and begun to mount the stairs, and David almost lost him as he paused to look back at the girls in the sun-filled, blossom-bright day outside.

All of that seemed farther away than London now as he followed Asano, the little man struggling with David's heaviest suitcase which he had insisted on carrying up a spiral set of iron steps to a door on the first floor of the building. David was about to come home.

A small Japanese woman in her late middle-age answered the door and made a great fuss when she saw the two men, backed into the apartment, all the time bowing deeply from the waist. David followed Asano inside, colliding with him as the Japanese paused in the small hallway to kick off his shoes.

'Please,' Asano said to David, indicating his feet, 'we never wear shoes in the house.'

David, annoyed with himself for forgetting one of the few things he knew about Japan, knelt and untied his laces as Asano introduced him to his landlady. Somehow he got one of his Japanese words onto his tongue, and the women smiled as he acknowledged her introduction with '*Hajimemashite*'.

The landlady gestured for the two men to sit at a large table covered with a plastic cloth. She was plainly intent on feeding them and spoke incessantly to Asano as she produced, first, a two-litre bottle of beer, and then a paper bucket of Kentucky Fried Chicken. Asano asked if there was Kentucky Fried Chicken in Britain, and David nodded. He thought of telling Asano that he had once tried to work for the company, but checked himself. One thing he had learned today from meeting his colleagues was that the Japanese university teachers, the *sensei*, took themselves and their work very seriously.

He stared at the greasy chicken and the doughy white roll he had been given. He had no appetite. At lunch-time he had eaten in his departmental staff-room. Lunch had been ordered for him, and he was given a black lacquered box inside which were small compartments each filled with various pieces of cold food. He had eaten a large shrimp, deep-fried in batter, using his fingers after he failed to get it anywhere near his mouth with the chopsticks that had come with the box.

There had also been a kind of Japanese spaghetti called, he was told, *soba*. Cold like everything else, David had tried to eat it following Asano's example, dipping the noodles into a tiny cup of thin soy sauce before putting them into his mouth. But the taste and texture had been far from pleasant. A papery seaweed had been sprinkled over the *soba*, and the strong, briny flavour of this combined with the cold ooze of the noodles to make his gorge rise. Somehow he had got the mouthful down his throat, but then quietly put the lid back on the pretty box and set it on a table.

The nausea the food had induced was not lessened by the noises coming from the other diners. It was something David had noticed in the restaurant the night before. He could not understand how these people, almost impossibly formal in every other social action, could eat with all the delicacy of pigs at the trough.

Asano was slurping and chomping now, his mouth open, grease and a crumb of half-chewed chicken on his fat chin. The landlady stood behind the men, darting to the table from time to time to refill the beer-glasses, or place more chicken on Asano's plate. David was uncomfortably aware of her presence and felt inhibited from looking around him. The little he could see of the apartment did not afford him much joy. It was small, much smaller than he had imagined from Asano's description, and furnished with cheap Western fittings.

In the guide book he had bought just before leaving Britain he had read that it was still possible to find traditional wooden houses in Tokyo, and that such accommodation was cheap, the Japanese preferring concrete 'mansion' blocks. He had not known then that the university had already retained his predecessor's apartment for him and so imagined himself, in the cold spring days he had spent gathering together the things he would take with him to Japan, in a place of paper walls and painted doors that opened onto a stone garden. Where he now found himself was all so different.

Asano swilled the last of the bread and chicken from his mouth with a swallow of beer, put his empty glass down on the heavily-embossed table cloth, belched slightly and then began to vigorously scrub his chin with a paper napkin. He said that he must go soon, but before he did he wanted to show David around the apartment and then explain how to get to the university next day when he would have his first classes. He stood up, and with the nervous, chattering landlady in close attendance, began taking David around the small apartment.

It took but a matter of moments, the short, narrow corridor off the living space which housed a sink and a single gas-burner for cooking, the tiny cupboard into which was fitted a deep but otherwise cramped Japanese bath, a lavatory, and, separated from the rest of the apartment by sliding, wood-veneered doors, a small wardrobe and a bed, were all quickly seen and then David was out in the night again, walking with Asano the short distance to the railway station.

David's spirits were lifted by the walk, and as he made his way back towards the apartment he jingled the key in his pocket. The area in which he was to live was called Nakano, and its station was a major centre through which ran two of the most important overground train lines in Tokyo, as well as a subway. As Asano had walked with him towards the station he had repeatedly said how convenient David would find this place. The station stood in a large square which lay off a major road. Asano pointed out a McDonald's and a large department store. They would be, he said, relishing the word, convenient.

David crossed the road at the pedestrian crossing and turned up a small alley-like path. It was this and the other similar route he had to follow back to his room that had cheered him. The alleys were lined with small shops, still open in spite of the relative lateness of the hour, cafés filled with men and women, and bars. As he walked by one bar the owner, dressed in a short, kimono-like jacket over tight, blue trousers and with a towel banded around his forehead, was busy hanging a large red lantern outside his door. There were lanterns hanging where, in Britain, the street lamps would have been, and gay branches of plastic leaves and blossom sprouted from the iron poles that carried the web of overhead powerlines and telephone cabling. The little streets seemed dressed for a carnival. Close to his apartment David passed a fruit-shop, its wares displayed in the open beneath bright, naked bulbs, and a flower-shop filled with chrysanthemums and white, almost waxen, lilies.

Set between these was a store whose windows contained only one article, a silken kimono of dove grey with a pattern of storks shimmered somehow into the weave, and creamy cherry-blossoms patched onto the collar and sleeves. The whole garment was spread over a black stand which curved at the top like the monumental arch for the war dead he had seen the day before. He stood in front of the window for some minutes before taking up his way again.

In the short time it had taken to get to the station and back the landlady had tidied away the remains of the meal and left. She lived next door, something David was unhappy about, and kept a key to the apartment: for emergencies, Asano had said. It was built over the garage of a three-storey family house, to which this and another bed-sitting room adjacent to the second storey had been attached as a profitable afterthought. Asano had said that the monthly rental for the apartment was equivalent to almost three hundred pounds; looking at the lime-green, rather shabby carpet, the dirty orange drapes, the scarred chairs and other pieces of furniture crowded into the inadequate space, David felt the price was high.

Unhappy again, he decided to call Jack Stevens. A woman answered the telephone, speaking Japanese and confusing him. Then, in English, she asked if he wanted her husband. David heard her put the receiver down and call 'Jack'. A few moments later Stevens himself came to the telephone. He had not noticed it the first time they had spoken, but Jack Stevens had a marked London accent.

He seemed pleased to hear David's voice and asked how his first full day had been in Tokyo, how he liked his apartment. David was non-committal, saying that things were all right.

'About tomorrow,' Stevens said, 'I take it you got Duckham's invitation, yes? Well, do you think you can get yourself to a station called Takadanobaba? You're in Nakano, so you take the blue subway line. Takadanobaba is just two stops away from Nakano. Stay on the platform and I'll find you.'

David wrote the name of the subway line and the station into his diary, and asked Stevens how he would recognize him.

'Well, every other bugger down there will have black hair and slanting eyes, but if you like I'll wear a red carnation and carry a copy of *The Times*.'

David felt stupid and, looking down at his feet he also realized he still had his shoes on. Scuffing them off while Stevens talked, he kicked them over into the little tiled hallway by the door.

When he put the telephone down a great sense of loneliness came over him. He walked into the tiny kitchen and looked around it. His landlady had loaned him an odd assortment of crockery and other utensils. In the refrigerator he found another large bottle of beer, a carton of what looked like corn soup, a litre of milk and the remains of the fried chicken, which had been packed away into its stiff paper bucket. There was also a small piece of cheese wrapped in plastic, and a packet of butter. Sitting on top of the refrigerator were a packet of tea-bags, a small pot of jam and some tiny sachets of sugar.

He thought about trying to buy some bread and cereal for breakfast in the morning. The landlady had left him a rough map of the district with grocery stores and supermarkets marked in English, he could see one of the stores from the kitchen window, but he felt unable to go across to it. He would have to enter the Japanese world alone for the first time soon enough. When he was through the trial of getting to the university there would be time enough for shopping.

It was almost nine-thirty when he began to unpack; half an hour later, with clothes and books strewn around on the bed and the floor he decided to make tea, searched, without success, for a kettle, and ended up boiling some water in a tiny aluminum saucepan. He found a copy of a tourist newspaper he had picked up in the hotel. There was a piece in it on how to make overseas calls; it seemed that in the world's most technologically advanced society a direct dialling facility for international telephone calls was to be had only by special request. David dialled the number for the international operator and said, in slow and precise English, that he wanted to reach the United Kingdom. He gave his parents' number, and then his own. He was told to hang up, and a few moments afterwards the receiver trilled softly. His call was ready. There was a long silence followed by a whirr of static before he heard a ringing tone. His father answered in his slow — after all the years he had lived in England — Irish voice. 'Hello, Daddy,' David said.

After he had spoken to his father and mother David thought about calling Jean, but it was early afternoon in Britain and she would be at the university. He tried to think what day it was and remembered it was Wednesday. She usually visited her mother on Wednesday evenings, he might be able to catch her there. He drank some of the tea he had made, and spread a little of the jam on one of the rolls left over from earlier in the evening. It was so sweet he spat it into the rubbish-bin and scrubbed his teeth at the small sink in the bathroom.

He was awake at six the next morning and immediately alert. He dialled the number for overseas calls again and asked for a person-to-person call to Jean Kennedy, giving her mother's number in Leith. The call had already been connected when he picked up the receiver again and he heard Jean saying, 'David? David, is that you? I thought you might 'phone tonight so I stayed on a bit at Mum's.'

She asked all the usual questions of those who have stayed at home to those who have left: how was the journey, how was he, how was Japan. He answered her succinctly, coldly.

'You sound a long way away, David,' she said, sadly.

'I am.'

'No, I don't mean the miles, I mean —'

He cut her off sharply, 'Well, what do you expect?' There was a silence between them punctuated only by the sounds of the technology that lifted their voices up into the blackness of space, exchanged them and cast them down again upon the earth.

'Look, Jean,' he said, 'have you decided anything yet?'

'David, I can't talk here. My mother's in the other room just — I'll write to you. Can you give me an address?'

He read her his address from the slip of paper where Asano had put it, together with the instructions for getting across Tokyo in the morning.

'David,' she said when he had finished, 'I'm so sorry for all of this. I wouldn't have had it happen for the world. I didn't mean to do this to you. Look, this call must be costing a fortune, I'd best go. I'll write, I promise. Take care, David.'

He walked into the kitchen and looked out of the window into the road below. It had rained in the night, the street was wet and mirror-like with light. The house opposite had been roofed with blue tiles of an odd, undulating shape, and with the gloss of the rain still on them they looked like the waves of some frozen sea flung into the air.

A girl walked in the street, in spite of the early hour. She wore a yellow skirt and held a pink umbrella. To David's eye she seemed a stem of blossom blown along by the morning breeze. There was something else too, something he had not noticed the night before on his walk; dominating the little houses and alleyways was a tall tower-block, with darkened windows and matt-black cladding. It stood sinisterly on the skyline, like a mark of censure over the wet street and the shining blue roof and the girl with the yellow skirt and pink umbrella.

He turned from the window and ran some water into the saucepan for tea, then picked up a towel from the mess of his possessions that still covered the floor of the apartment. He wondered what would happen now, not now, in the day before him, that was all arranged, but in his marriage. For David Kennedy, in the week before he left Britain to begin his new life in Japan, had discovered that his wife was unfaithful to him.

SUMMER

In July a lugubrious heat fell upon the city. David Kennedy moved through it as a swimmer under water, a sleeper woken unwillingly in the dawn. He took shelter during each necessary excursion in the frigid, smoke-filled atmosphere of coffee shops and cheap cafés. Here he would sit, drinking impossibly sweet iced tea amidst the swirls of tobacco-smoke and banter of blue-suited office workers.

In the ten weeks he had been in Japan David had slowly come to shed the carapace of fear and move out into his new and alien world, comforted by the cloak of invisibility his almost complete incomprehension of the Japanese language afforded him. Like the Jesus of the plaque that hung in his parents' home, he was the unseen guest at every meal, the silent presence at every conversation. The cloak was turned aside only to order something or acknowledge his change, otherwise the flow of Japanese life swept on untroubled by the foreigner in its midst.

Looking back on that time, he would say it was like a troubled dream that was not quite a nightmare. The roads he walked along then, the stations where he became entrapped, unable to find the one exit he needed from the dozens that he might try, the places he visited, had all the distanced immediacy of a dream, they were not the same streets and stations he later moved through with such contemptuous familiarity. Waiting for a train once on the long space of the platform at Takadanobaba Station he tried to recall it as it had been that first time he waited there for Jack Stevens, and could not. The place, the characters on the platform, seemed entirely other now. The things that had happened, the things he had done, were fragments, half-forgotten, from a story whose ending he could not remember.

Jack Stevens was a man in his early forties who at some time, possibly when he was still quite young, had willed austerity upon himself. His black curly hair was scraped back from his face, emphasizing the erosions time had made upon his hairline, and he wore severe steel-framed spectacles over eyes that were dark and with the sheen of polished coal. Once he might have had about him the luxuriant beauty of an Elizabethan courtier, one of the dandies Hillier painted; now it was gone, driven away by a reasoned discipline, an act of mind.

Stevens was the university's foreign celebrity. In the mid-1960s he had been one of the coming men in English poetry, a member of the so-called Islington Group of writers. His work appeared in *The London Magazine* and *Stand*, and his first collection of verse, *A Blind Horse* won the W.H. Smith award for Poetry. David remembered *The New Statesman* articles he had read in the sixth form, memories of growing up in London during the 1950s, and he had seen him once at the Commonwealth Institute, reading with Dannie Abse and the Nigerians, Wole Soyinka and Christopher Okigbo. David had had no idea that the Jack Stevens he had seen then and the man who telephoned him on his first night in Japan were the same person.

The first time David met him he was wearing a white carnation, pinned to the lapel of the crumpled, stained jacket he had on over an unironed, collarless shirt, 'Tottenham took the U.E.F.A. Cup on penalites,' he said, explaining the flower.

He led David up some stairs and out of the subway to the drab, badly-lit main concourse of the National Railways station, and a woman of David's age, with a cascade of blond hair that reached down past her waist, like a young girl's. Jack Stevens introduced his wife, Nicky.

The Stevenses went swiftly through the station, pulling David along in their wake. He remembered nothing from the confusion of the journey except for the sound of a lonely siren by a crossing where their train cut over a road, the signal lights flashing red in the darkness. When, after the dinner, they left him to find his own way into the subway that would take him back to Nakano, he felt abandoned, and floundered, plunging this way and that about the station until a Japanese, sensing his distress, spoke to him in broken, school-book English and asked him where he wanted to go.

Richard Duckham, the British Council man, was another Londoner, younger than either David or the Stevenses, and irredeemably vulgar. After the meal he held court in the sitting-room of his large house, seated in an enormous, overstuffed chair, a heavy, outsized crystal balloon of cognac in one hand, a panatella in the other, and set the world of English teaching in Japan to rights. He was interrupted frequently by Nicky Stevens, who seemed to find it necessary to say the word 'fuck' loudly and often. During dinner she had described at some length her experiences of being felt up on trains, 'I shout "fuck off" as loudly as I can. I don't think they actually understand but it seems to do the trick.'

Mrs Duckham, who wore a constant expression of surprise on her face as if she could not quite believe the large house she inhabited was actually hers, was clearly upset by it and pointedly ignored the Japanese girl who leant across David to ask her what 'fuck off' meant. Now Nicky was telling her about a party she had once organized for a group of B.B.C. men, 'and well, I mean, I didn't know who the fuck any of them were, and when one of them started coming on as if he owned the place I said, "and who the fuck do you think you are?"'

A week afterwards, late in the afternoon, Nicky Stevens had telephoned David to ask if he wanted to meet her and Jack that night. 'We were thinking of getting something to eat and then going for a drink. Do you want to come along?'

He met them by a flower stall in a station close to where they lived. He had imagined that they would have a favourite restaurant they wanted to take him to, but they did not and so the three foreigners began what became a prolonged tramp through dark streets looking for a place to eat.

'This would all be a lot easier if Jack would spend some of the money he's stashing away over here,' Nicky Stevens said. 'He just disguises his generally tight-wad approach to life as the, quote, Search for the Perfect Little Hole-in-the-Wall Japanese Restaurant, end quote. So far all we've come up with have been holes.

'I for one,' she said, turning from David to her husband, 'have sore fucking feet, Jack.'

'All right,' Jack said, sounding unconvinced, 'we'll try the next place we come to.'

They ate *ramen*, a broad, flat noodle served in a soup of chicken and leeks, together with large steamed dumplings stuffed with minced pork and vegetables. Jack ordered the food in what to David was impressive Japanese.

'This is the only thing he can order,' Nicky said. 'Usually we have to take the bloke outside and point to the plastic stuff in the showcase.'

'Well, you both do a lot better than me. You really threw me that first time I telephoned and you answered in Japanese.'

'Yeah, one of these days she'll do that to a native, then she'll be in trouble. "*Moshi-moshi*" is the whole extent of Nicky's vocabulary.'

'Fuck you, Jack,' Nicky said disdainfully, as she swallowed a mouthful of her beer. Jack Stevens ignored her and asked David what he had thought of Richard Duckham. David hesitated in making his reply.

'Jack, of course, thinks the sun shines out of his arsehole,' Nicky said.

'That's right,' Jack said. 'I watch it come up every morning.'

Nicky leaned across and kissed her husband. 'You looked a bit worried for a moment there, David. The repartee Jack and I sometimes engage in doesn't mean anything. You can answer his question now if you want to.'

Still David hesitated, 'Well, I think it's rather difficult to judge a person that quickly. I know that my own first impressions usually turn out to be wrong. It's just that generally I've found the British Council to be — what — not altogether a good thing for outsiders to get involved with. I knew a few people in Morocco who worked as sort of volunteers, and in each case when they needed the Council's help they were treated very shabbily. Personally, I'm just not interested in having that much to do with the Council here at any level.'

Jack Stevens spread himself in his chair. 'Yeah, well, I do a fair bit for them, but it's all in my own interest. And I know exactly where Duckham is coming from. Somebody described him as an intellectual thug once. I'd only question the use of the word "intellectual".'

Just after nine o'clock they left the *ramen*-shop to go to a nearby bar where the Stevenses sometimes drank. As he was passing out of the little restaurant with its glaring light and harsh formica tables, David heard Jack ask his wife to stop swearing so much.

The bar was a thin space that had somehow been wedged in between a Japanese McDonald's and a hostess club. To get inside David had to slip between a case of plastic hamburgers and french fries, and a board displaying photographs of the girls whose company was for hire in the club. It seemed that everything on sale in this city, food or drink or women, was offered in replica on the street, tempting the customer in to buy.

A counter ran the entire length of the narrow corridor, the row of stools set before it was unoccupied except for a man sitting in the half-darkness by the far wall of the building who raised his hand in greeting as Jack and Nicky followed David into the bar. 'Peter, hello,' Nicky Stevens called out, 'how are you?'

Peter Morizawa was an American of Japanese descent, who seemed almost to be trying to hide his almond-shaped eyes behind the fringe of thick black hair he allowed to fall over them. 'So Peter, what's new?' Nicky said, while Jack called their order to the barman.

'Oh, you know, more of the usual. Today it was some guy in Shinjuku Station looking for the Marunouchi line. When I said I didn't speak Japanese very well he looked at me like he could have punched my lights out.'

Nicky turned to David, 'If you're ever feeling bad about your situation here, just give a thought to poor old Peter. Because he looks like the genuine article people get confused and rather upset when he can't speak Japanese.'

'Really,' Peter Morizawa added. 'It's like I'm kidding around with them or something.'

They drank and talked. Peter Morizawa wanted to know what David's feelings were about Japan. When he said how much he found to admire the others laughed, sharing the communion of the disenchanted.

'The first couple of weeks are all right,' Jack Stevens said, 'but you begin to get more than slightly pissed off when people keep asking the same questions. You know, "How do you like Japan?", "How are Japanese students?", "Do you find it strange being in a country where people actually take a bath every day?", "Can you use chop-sticks?".'

'I ask them if they know how to use a knife and fork,' Nicky said.

'Tell me about your life,' Nicky said.

'She's doing a doctorate in Edinburgh —'

'I said your life, not your wife. Have you been married for a long time?'

'Nearly twelve years.'

'That's a long time. Jack and I have been married for three but there are days when it seems like forever.'

David asked how she and Jack had met.

'It was in London. I was divorced, living with my two children. A couple of friends had a friend who was running for the local council in Islington and they took me along one night to an election meeting. The friend was Jack, of course. After the meeting we all went to a pub and, well, he was a fast worker in those days.

'When I think about it now, Jesus! I mean, Jack didn't have a regular job; he'd been made redundant and was working as a supply teacher during the day with some classes for the W.E.A. at night. I suppose we were just both right for it, although I swore after my first marriage never again.'

David asked if her children were in Japan, and she laughed, 'God no, much to the embarrassment of Jack and the comrades, Sarah and Daniel are at schools in England. And very expensive they are too, which is why, after we were married, Jack pulled a lot of rather dusty strings to get this job. It was the only way we could keep up the fees, their father not unreasonably declining to continue paying once I was living with another man.

'I pass the time teaching English, in the same school as that terminally dreary woman Deborah Duckham, as a matter of fact. The money's useful, if nothing else. But tell me about yourself, Jack said you have a degree in Fine Art.'

'No,' David said, 'I have a first degree in Fine Arts. I was at the

Courtauld for three years. I was going to be a radical art historian but, for various reasons, that didn't work out. I still enjoy looking at painting and sculpture, and I have friends who are artists.Why did you ask? Did you think it strange that I should be out here teaching English?'

Nicky unpinned her hair, shaking out the long heavy skeins onto her shoulders. It suddenly seemed to David that everything about her, her name, her clothes, her hair, were too young. Girlish affectations that did not sit well on a body already moving towards middle-age.

She answered his question by saying, 'Not at all, it's just that I was at St Martin's when I met my first husband. I just —'

'Did you finish your degree?' David asked.

'No, no, I didn't. We were so short of money I decided I should leave and get some sort of a job. Anyway, at the time I thought having a degree wasn't going to make me an artist, all that sort of thing.'

'What were you doing, painting?'

'Yes, I still do. I go to a life class in Ogikubo once every two weeks. Some Japanese chap we met in here told me about it. He started talking to us because he wanted me to model for him, but Jack wasn't very happy about that. Anyway, I told him that I painted and he asked me along to meet his little group. Jack looks benignly upon it all as one of the little woman's foibles.'

At the station where the four of them waited for their trains, Nicky kissed David goodbye, but afterwards he saw little of her or her husband for a long time. It seemed as if Jack Stevens had done all he felt he should for the newcomer and so withdrew back into his own life.

David saw much more of his Japanese colleagues in those first few weeks. He was taken out almost every day after his classes finished: by the women teachers to discreetly elegant cafés with carpets poured upon the floor as thickly as the cream in the coffee, and Mozart playing quietly above the subdued hush of feminine conversation. The male staff offered more robust entertainment. They favoured ersatz German beer halls, the word for once seemed absolutely appropriate, where plump-faced Tokyo girls masqueraded as Bavarian *Mädchen*, and the 'Horst Wessel' echoed in the smoky air. David sat entranced as his companions fed knackwurst into their mouths with chopsticks, and slowly lowered their carmine faces to the table as the emptied steins of Hokkaido beer piled up around them.

Asano was a constant companion, and David found himself warming towards the Japanese, ashamed of the first impression he had formed of him. He had been to Asano's house to meet his wife and child, a pretty girl of six or seven whose English was better than her father's. Then, on the last weekend before the summer break, he found himself on a bus with them, journeying towards the lakes and mountains of Kawaguchiko. He sat by Keiko, the little girl, and shared the child's excitement as they broke from the dreary sprawl of the city into a countryside which felt no shame as it effortlessly copied the idealized panoramas of painted screens and *ukiyo-e*. The vision faded, too quickly for David, and the bus pulled into a scruffy little town that held uneasily to its identity as a place where people might live, aware of what its presence did to the landscape in which it was set. David had seen places like this before, spread across the American south-west, guilty afterthoughts of the bus companies that had opened the land and left the wounds of their passing unhealed. So it did not surprise him that the first two Japanese he saw after he got down from the bus should be wearing high-heeled boots and stetsons.

David and the Asanos were to take a taxi to their hotel, but first Asano had something to show him. He led David to the edge of the car-park where the bus had left them, giving his wife and Keiko the care of the luggage they had brought with them.

'There,' he said to David, gesturing with his hand, 'now you will see Japan.'

David looked. In front of him was an enormous amusement park. From its heart, rising up into the sky in two steel loops, was a huge roller-coaster. Through the air came the distant screams of the people in the little cars that rattled about the defiant arcs. David wondered what he was supposed to say and turned to Asano. As he did so he understood that there was something else out there, something that Asano could see and he could not. Perhaps, it came to him, it was the only thing Asano could see. He looked again. As if he had shifted the focus on a camera lense he suddenly saw, beyond the steel loops, and the screams, the snow-smeared cone of Fujiyama reared up in the thinly clouded sky.

In the hotel bar that night David asked Asano how anyone could have been allowed to build an amusement park across the face of such a mountain. Asano seemed surprised at the question, and so David said, 'At the very least, it ruins the view. There wouldn't seem to be any other reason to come except to see Fuji-san.'

Asano smiled into his tumbler of whisky-flavoured water. 'What you must understand is that we Japanese know what we should look for. We feel that what we look for is what we will see.'

David arrived back at the house in Nakano late on the Sunday evening. He had stopped at a small restaurant in Shinjuku and was drunk on Japanese beer. In his room he read again the first letter Jean had sent him. She had written:

I don't have your address yet so I don't know where I'm sending this letter to. I was really nervous around two o'clock today thinking about you landing in Tokyo, and I've been wondering ever since how you are getting on and what's happening. It's pointless speculating, of course, I'm sure you'll let me know how everything is when you telephone.

I'm feeling very sad and lost — nothing to how you're feeling, I'm sure. I expect it will take us both a while to adjust after the trauma of last week. I'm sure you must feel you never will recover — or maybe what I mean is that I wonder if I will ever recover.

I hope there are some nice people there who will make you feel welcome. I remember arriving in Morocco and how awful those first few days were — that nightmare journey up to Fez from Casablanca. I always felt it would all have been so much worse if we hadn't been together.

This is crazy. I should wait until I hear from you before I write any more. I'm doing what I'm always telling you not to do — worrying about the unknown.

David, I've just finished talking to you, and now I don't know what to say. I haven't come to any decision. You always see things so clearly, so definitely. The world isn't like that for me, it isn't so simple. I can't choose, I can't decide one way or the other.

You'll say I'm being selfish and cruel, I know, but I remember you telling me, the night we had that terrible scene at the end of my last year in Fez, that I wasn't being selfish enough. Perhaps now, when I'm trying to put my life in a new perspective I have to be completely selfish. You said before you left that I wasn't looking at things from your point of view. I do understand your side of things, David, and I suffer for you, but I need my own point of view. I need to work things out for myself.

I've been thinking a lot about those last few days we were together, and all the things you said. When you first found that letter I was very distressed and my immediate reaction was that I ought never to see Cairns again; that I should quit my research and come with you to Japan. I wanted to heal the hurt I'd caused. I feel so much for you, David — compassion, love — I'm not sure which is the strongest. I'm so confused. I don't seem able to sort out one emotion from another these days.

This is making me feel incredibly sad. David, I can't stop seeing Cairns, but at the same time I don't want to lose our marriage. I'd still like to come out to Tokyo in August, but if you'd rather I didn't I'll understand. I think I'm completely screwing up my life and I don't understand why I'm doing it. It just seems I have to see this thing with Cairns through to the end, whatever that might be. I know I'm risking losing you, but I have to take that risk. I can't expect you to understand or blame you if you don't. I suppose what I'm asking you for is time. If you can't give that to me, if it's too much to ask, then we'd better separate I suppose, I mean divorce. You probably won't believe this, but I love you.

Again he could not put words on to paper, but in the night he produced thousands in his head. He tossed from side to side in the empty spaces of his bed, getting up for water, to piss, to curse. When he had given up all thought of sleep he fell into a series of troubled dreams, waking early with the memory of just one of them — sitting in the room he had occupied as a student in London, before he had known Jean, while she, placed there with the anarchy of the unconscious, had packed a bag and was leaving him. All the words of pleading fell from him with that memory. He got up, taking a sheet of paper, and wrote, 'Thank you for the sympathy, I deserve it. No, I don't think you should come here. Yes, I do think we should get a divorce.'

He gave his last class of the term late on the afternoon of the second Friday in July. All over Japan colleges and schools were closing as the heat of summer eddied down from the cloudless skies. In his ten weeks in Tokyo David had fallen gratefully into the order imposed by his work. He taught for only eleven hours each week, yet somehow every other hour seemed to be filled. When not in the classroom he prepared his lessons and corrected written exercises by the students, then there were the Japanese lessons he took at a school in the Shinjuku area of the city. And always there remained the other, more menial, tasks involved in the life of a man living alone and caring for himself: shopping, the visits to the launderette. Each busied minute was a comfort, it was the empty hours of the night he dreaded, when his soul leaked the bitter distillation of his hatred and self-pity. When the vacation came and even the Japanese classes withered in the heat, all the hours were empty and David ceased to know peace entirely.

He tried to force a routine upon himself, a morning of domestic chores, an outing each afternoon, work or reading in the evenings. He pulled out the file of notes he had made on Egon Schiele, hoping, intending, to begin the task of writing again. He did not. He could not bring a pattern to his days. He now slept so little each night he begrudged disturbing the rest that did come to him and so took to staying in his bed until ten or eleven each day, sometimes later. Once, long after midday, he pulled back the curtain from the kitchen window to see his landlady staring up at him from the yard below, the disapproval on her face banished by the sudden bow she made to him in acknowledgement of his presence.

Marooned in the squalid little apartment by his sloth, he became increasingly the slave of television. He sat hour after hour hunched over the huge screen, constantly changing channels, switching between the unending motion of the figures he conjured to appear before him: the samurai, the women wrestlers, the faceless avengers of the children's programmes, the endless screaming wheels and pistol shots of dubbed American films. He watched in total silence, on through the afternoons and the short summer evenings until the electronic shadows lit up his face, bathing his features in their violet light.

Late, late in the night he watched the 'wide' shows, each station had its own, but they were all the same. An elderly man with grey hair, a dignified man, a man of the world, sat in the studio with a pretty girl by his side and introduced in sober tones a succession of pimps, men in dark glasses and baseball caps who pushed cameras and microphones into the faces of bar-hostesses, or porno-stars, inciting them to pull their skirts over their heads, or offer a breast to the camera. One show had a section dubbed The Tissue Time, where a girl would writhe in a bath, simulating the ecstacy of masturbation while a clock counted down the seconds remaining for the imagined audience to reach their own climax. David saw quiz shows in which women shed their clothes for each wrong answer given by their partners, a dice game in which girls in fashionable bars were undressed down to their panties, and suffered their breasts to be pawed by the celebrity host. Once two girls were stripped and trussed like chickens, then hoisted over a beam, and their naked breasts lashed with roses. And all the while the dignified, grey-haired man in the studio offered neither smile nor condemnation, but discussed all that happened in polite, meaningless words, and his pretty companion bowed her head from time to time in acknowledgement of all this wisdom, this familiarity with life, and did not blush for her own sex or the indignities enacted upon it. And all the while David watched, through the long hours, caught up, even while repulsed, in this repetitive delirium of blood and sex and death.

But sometimes he managed to get out into the heat, following the trail ordained by his guide book, and always, inevitably, becoming lost in the city without end.

In the streets and stations he fed his hungry eyes on the beauty of women, but it was no nourishment to his heart. Once he watched a schoolgirl dance before a mirror in a subway station, unaware of his gaze. In a crowded café, open to the street, he sat alone and looked on as a plain girl was transfigured before him into a talisman of his desire when she stood and the light exposed the brief silhouette of her panties beneath her clothing, the thin material barely cupping the half-moons of her buttocks. In a cinema David watched a foreign man, an American perhaps, and his girlfriend. The girl wore the shortest of skirts and, as the lights were dimmed, he could not help but see the man's hand edge beneath its hem. From every encounter, whether sacred or profane, he turned away, his loneliness keener than ever before.

One day a girl, an English girl, tall and strong-limbed, spoke to him. She had seen the confusion on his face and offered help. Grateful, David invited her for iced coffee in a nearby café. She accepted, they talked, exchanged names and telephone numbers. She left, saying she was late for an appointment but promising to call and arrange another meeting for a drink. She never did. Once, three weeks after meeting her, he dialled the number she had given him; there was no answer.

That August the temperature rose higher than for sixty years in Tokyo. David's apartment was equipped with an air-conditioner and he now kept it on all the time, incapable of caring about the cost. Towards the end of the second week of that hot month he answered the telephone and heard the voice of Nicky Stevens. She said she was close by and wanted to visit. With a certain reluctance he told her how to find his apartment, and then, putting down the receiver, moved across to the kitchen window to watch the street. In a few minutes he saw her swinging past the little shops, making towards the house.

She stood before him at the open door in a loose, striped shift of some cottony material that held the fullness of her figure. She had coiled her long hair up on her head, and as she went past David into the apartment he saw that her neck and arms were glossed with a film of sweat.

'My God, you actually use your air-conditioner. Jack thinks it's immoral to cool the inside of a house, or so he says. Actually, he's just fucking mean. So how are you? Isn't the summer here absolutely shitty?'

She moved around the room, inspecting it, 'Yes, this place is a dump. I thought it was, the way you were so non-committal about it when Jack asked. Would you have a towel? I just felt chill, and I need to dry off a little.'

David pulled a clean towel from the black sports bag he used for carrying his washing to the launderette. He had been the day before, but the clothes he had washed were still in the bag, knotted and twisted together from the drier.

Nicky rubbed her face and neck, and then patted beneath her arms. When she had finished she folded the towel slowly and neatly before putting it onto a chair. The care with which she performed these actions surprised David: he had not associated such thoughtfulness and precision with her.

'How have you been managing? I feel guilty that we haven't seen you for so long. It's easy for a wife to blame things on her husband, but truly, since we moved here Jack has turned into a near-recluse. I mean, okay, we do have a nice house, but these days the only time Jack ever moves outside the door is when he goes to work at the Council. Which, by the way, is where he is now.'

David asked what he was doing there, affecting more interest than he felt. The sudden presence of Nicky in his room made him uneasy. He wondered what she wanted.

'Who knows? Working his arse off, I suppose. When he gets home in the evenings he's so tired he just eats and then goes to sleep. We have such a fulfilling life together. Could I have something to drink?'

He moved towards the kitchen, but Nicky Stevens cut him off, saying she would get it herself. She opened the refrigerator, disappearing behind the door.

'Good God, David! What are you on, the *Playboy diet-of-the-month* or something? I've never seen so much fried chicken. Do you live on the stuff?'

She stood up, holding a bottle of Coca-Cola, 'Opener? When is your wife coming out? You look like you need some help around here. Wasn't she supposed to be spending the summer with you?'

He said what he always said when people asked about Jean, and added that she had decided to stay on in Edinburgh for the summer, working in the library while it was empty of undergraduates.

He could feel Nicky Stevens watching him while he spoke and then she said, 'You know, that sounded as if you'd rehearsed it a thousand times. Are the Japanese going on at you because your wife isn't here? Their friendly question-and-answer sessions can become a little wearing after a while. I could never work out whether they were really interested or just taking the piss all the time. No need to tell you which point of view Jack subscribes to.'

She sat down on one of the hard chairs by the table, 'You must be wondering why I showed up all of a sudden. Well, the fact of the matter is, Jack is in a bit of a fix and thought you might be able to pull him out of the mire. The second Saturday in September he's going to a Council literature seminar, which means he won't be able to be at the *Mainichi* newspaper's English speech contest, where he was supposed to be one of the judges — famous English poet and all that sort of thing, you know?

'Anyway, he thought you might substitute for him. He has cleared it with the people at *Mainichi Shimbun*, so there's no problem there. The fee for this is very good, thirty thousand yen. What do you think?'

It was after four in the afternoon by the time Nicky Stevens left. She and David had eaten lunch together in a small noodle shop, and then sat and talked over coffee. When he finally got back to his room he was glad to be rid of his visitor. His head ached from her incessant conversation. She seemed possessed of some great, abundant energy which, lacking any direction, had resolved itself into an unfocussed discontent. She troubled and disturbed the very air about her.

He had agreed to substitute for Jack, saying yes mostly to be rid of Nicky for he had little need of the money. Since coming to Tokyo he had more money than he had ever had before and no one to spend it on except himself. Now, however, alone in his room, he wondered what he had done. It was a commitment of time he was unwilling to make. His actions often conflicted with his actual desires, and throughout his life he had made decisions he almost at once came to regret. He was a man held to ransom by his charity.

Obon came, the day of the dead. People flooded out of the city on holiday, or simply to go back to their birthplaces where they might more properly await the returning souls of their parents and grandparents. It was one of the great festivals of Japan, a time to feast and to dance with ghosts. A time to realize the power of the past, the interdict against forgetting. David Kennedy, marooned by the holiday in his room, remembered his own dead marriage.

During the years in Morocco he and Jean had watched as relationships foundered all around them. There seemed to be a grim inevitability about adultery among the expatriates in Fez. With the heat and the drink, the boredom of empty days, women took up infidelity much as they did tennis. Yet through it all he had never thought that any of this applied to his marriage. He and Jean were different. They were the couple the others came to, for confession, for help, sometimes for shelter. Now he found himself wondering exactly how Jean had passed the long afternoons, what she had done those summers she had gone home alone. He had known Jean was unhappy, had felt their marriage had got out of Fez as one of the walking wounded, but perhaps after all it had been dead already, a zombie waiting for its final end. David did not know, could not understand.

He stood by the kitchen window looking out at the deserted street. A fine mist of warm rain was falling, each drop of rain carrying with it one of the returning souls. The memory came of Sundays they had spent in the flat in Edinburgh. It was always a slow day, the papers, Jean washing her hair, bathing, endless cups of coffee, huge sandwiches for lunch. The day smelt of coffee and the soapy steam that misted the windows. Sometimes in the afternoon they would go to bed, and afterwards Jean would get up to begin making dinner, an extravagant departure from their normal frugality, while he stayed on to sleep. At night, when the food and wine were finished, when it was time to sleep again, it always felt to him like the death of the week.

At lunchtime on the last day of the holiday Nicky Stevens telephoned. She said she was in the neighbourhood again and asked if she might stop by to see him. David put the phone down and went to wash his face.

The day was hot and fiercely humid. He had just got back from the university where he had gone to prepare some material for classes the next day. On the trains the old men fell into the seats, looking like half-drowned frogs, and the frantic whirl of the overhead fans could do nothing to dispel the miasma of the city in the heat of summer, perspiring bodies and naptha, and rotted, half-metallic mouths. David had stood surreptitiously reading the nonsense on a girl's tee-shirt on his way home, 'Have you eat me not yet, although I am done brown and seemed delicious.' He was drowning himself, but it was not air he needed to save him.

Nicky Stevens had brought lunch with her, and soon she sat with David as they ate prawns and salad and still warm, crusty rolls. They drank wine, too much, David felt, for the time of day and people who were still almost strangers to one another. Afterwards Nicky wanted to talk. The wine she had drunk had gone to her head, and for the first time it seemed that she was not wearing the mask of hip insouciance she usually affected. Intoxicated, Nicky Stevens was simply a charming woman who wanted for a time to forget the bacteria of dislike she carried within herself. He found he was suddenly attracted to her.

'Listen,' she said, as they cleared away the remains of the food, 'would you let me do something about this place? I can't stand the thought of you living like this. Perhaps if we re-organized things a little it might be better.'

Soon she had begun moving furniture around, taking down curtains to be washed, cleaning lightshades, removing the plastic cloths and covers on every surface. In less than an hour she had transformed the drab little apartment and made of it a space in which it might be possible to live.

'Do you have any posters or art cards or something?' she asked. 'You know, stuff we could put on the walls?'

He went over to the blue cabin trunk that had carried most of his belongings to Japan and pulled from it a large folder and a shoe box.

'God, these are beautiful,' Nicky said as David took the drawings from the folder. 'Who did them?'

'A friend. His name is Martin Cassidy, he teaches at the Ulster Polytechnic, near Belfast. We met when we were both students in London.'

'How does he do it? How does he get so much out of so few lines? God, it's like he makes the paper luminous or something. Do you have anything else of his?'

David opened the shoe box and took out an object heavily wrapped in tissue. Removing the paper he set it on the carpet by the drawings.

Slowly, like a child touching a gift that seems too rich, Nicky Stevens put her fingers around a small lump of granite set into a worked bronze container. Along the top of the stone a deep incision had been made, shaped like the mark a caress might leave on skin, and filled with more of the bronze.

Nicky put the sculpture down and turned again to the drawings, 'Who was the model — she looks Japanese?'

'She was Chinese. She and Martin lived together in London. Her name was Lynne.'

'She's beautiful. Are they still together?'

David shook his head, 'No. Lynne died, leukaemia. It's six years ago now. I was in Fez and Martin called me. We — my wife and I — had seen them earlier in the summer, you know. We had no idea there was anything wrong, although she'd been ill for a couple of years. They never told anyone about it, or at least, the people around them knew she had to keep going to hospital but nothing else. It took me a long time to really believe she was gone. The last time I saw her, when we said goodbye, she'd seemed so alive and then there was Martin telling me that she wasn't.'

'And he gave you the drawings?'

'Yes, he gave them to me just before I came here. I went over to see him for a few days. He used to draw Lynne all the time, he always said he never felt comfortable with another model, but after she died he destroyed everything. He found these three in an old folder the week I was there. He said he wanted me to have them, to take them to Asia with me. He thought it would be like taking her home.'

'Did they have children?'

David shook his head. The afternoon became silent then.

They drank tea in a café close to the station, 'Can I ask you a personal question?' Nicky said.

David shrugged. They had consumed another bottle of wine during the afternoon and at that moment he found himself unable to care what Nicky Stevens asked him.

'This really isn't any of my business, but you seem to spend a lot of time away from your wife. Do you have one of these open marriages one reads so much about?'

He stirred his tea. 'She seems to, I don't.'

He could have turned back from there had he really wanted to, simply by saying nothing else, but he did not. Afterwards all that concerned him was how quickly the secret was told, how few words it took to reveal the facts of his situation. The deceit, the humiliation, the anger and desire for revenge seemed so banal in the telling.

'You are at least fortunate in that you don't have children,' Nicky said when he had finished. 'They keep bad marriages together and the parents in a tandem of mutual loathing. I'd have left my first husband years before I did if it wasn't for my two. In fact, there are days when I sometimes feel that if it wasn't for the kids I'd walk out on Jack as well.'

Later, when he was alone again in the night, he knew he had done something stupid in telling Nicky Stevens about his marriage. Like the fisherman in the Arabian tale, he had let a genie out into the world, but not one that could ever be duped back into some green bottle.

NO
CONTINUING
CITY

'So,' Nicky Stevens said, 'here comes the big question. After six months here, what do you think?'

David closed his eyes and smiled. He had drunk enough wine with the dinner Nicky had prepared to know what he was saying, but not care very much about its effect. 'I think,' he said 'just having a job is great. And having a job in Tokyo is more than great.'

Nicky looked across the table at her husband and made a face, one of the secret signs of the married. 'I told you, Jack. A lost fucking cause.'

It was a warm night in mid-October. The awful heat of summer had been tempered by mornings that were all but frosty, and it was a welcome sun that warmed the air at noon. The afternoons were long and filled with yellow light, the evenings, like this evening, made for sitting with friends by an open window, drinking and talking. He was at the Stevenses' house in Mitaka, one of the inner suburbs of the city, at the end of the Sobu and Tozai train-lines. The room was small, the floor covered with straw *tatami* matting, the ceiling wooden. Except for the low table around which the three of them sat, and a tall chest set against one of the walls, it was unfurnished. The setting was so completely Japanese, David found the venom that infected the

Stevenses' attitude to the country jarring. But it could not sour the feeling of contentment that was upon him that evening.

Perhaps it is impossible for anyone to be as completely unhappy as he had been for very long. In the end must come an accommodation with sorrow, an acceptance, a regulating. When the new term began he found himself forced into the routine of his teaching and obliged to wear a public face again, masking the realities of his life. Over the days of September that face itself began to take on an equal reality, balancing, even modifying, his other emotions. In this he was helped by Jack and Nicky. Perhaps Nicky had told her husband about David's situation, but that autumn the Stevenses spent time with him as they had not chosen to do before. David's new timetable had him teaching on the same days of the week as Jack, and they fell into the habit of having lunch together at a small restaurant across the street from the university. Once Nicky sent her husband to school with a picnic the two men shared on a seat in the small piazza at the centre of the campus, their presence causing much stifled laughter amongst the students who passed them there.

The more time David spent with Jack Stevens the more he found in him to like. He was a good man, whose gentleness of heart was belied by the harshness of his tongue. It saddened David that he gave so much of his energy to cursing the city in which he found himself, and that he gave so much of his time to the British Council. David had seen him there on one of his own rare visits to the Council's offices, an abused servant of unworthy masters.

He began to see him outside work regularly again. Often Nicky would call to invite him to a film with them, and afterwards they would go for coffee and cheesecake to a large, noisy cafeteria Jack liked because it reminded him of London.

He spent a lot of time with Nicky as well. He did not work on Tuesdays, and twice he went over to have lunch with her while Jack was busy on a project for the British Council. The first time David saw the house in Mitaka, crouched behind its overgrown garden as if waiting to jump out and surprise someone, saw the tiny, wooden rooms with their straw-matted floors, floors so delicate that even the soft felt house-slippers were forbidden, his envy was extreme. Reading his thoughts, Nicky had laughed and said, 'Yes, it's pretty right now, but you cook in the summer and freeze your arse off from November to April.'

She showed him her work. It was undirected and ill-disciplined, but there was an energy about it he found difficult not to admire. Nicky was pleased when he praised it and urged her to go back to art school when she could. She took out a folder of work from the life class she attended. The line was strong and sure, more focussed than in her painting. He left thinking she had a real talent.

'But why do you two dislike it so much?' David asked, aware suddenly of Jack and Nicky as a couple in a way he had not been before.

'Well, for one thing the women have legs like you used to see on dining tables, and no tits,' Nicky said. 'God, what I'd give to see some decent legs. I want to feel I'm normal and not some kind of fucking freak.'

'But the women here are beautiful,' David began before Jack Stevens cut him off.

'I hate the pretence. I hate the way they blank out anything that doesn't fit into the agreed illusion. If you like you can take this city as one big bloody metaphor of the way I feel about Japan. Go anywhere in it, go to the glitter palaces on the Ginza, or the big tower-blocks and hotels in West Shinjuku. Wherever you go you won't be able to escape the stink of human shit just under your feet.

'This is supposed to be one of the world's great cities, but most of it is completely without pavements. There's rubbish everywhere. It must be the only capital in the developed world where you can still regularly see men pissing against walls in the street. The whole thing is a fucking con.

'It's the same with the people. You look at them in the trains and the stores and you think, Jesus, so this is what full employment can do. But follow them home. Tokyo has some of the worst housing I've ever seen. Okay, you look at this house and you probably think, well, this is pretty nice, but imagine a family of six living in it. There are families living in spaces even smaller than the one you've got. Last year an E.E.C. commission came here and pissed everybody off by saying that a lot of the Japanese had housing that was little better than rabbit-hutches, and that maybe some of the effort that went into flogging personal cassette players and all the other technological junk this country depends on for its livelihood might be put to better use in building a few decent houses. And of course *nobody* sees the poor bastards that live in cardboard boxes in the stations, and every Japanese I've ever asked has denied that there is any such district in Tokyo as the Sanya.'

David looked questioningly at Nicky. 'It's Tokyo's skid row,' she said. 'We went there just after we arrived. It's horrible. Jack used to do some work with the Simon Community in London and was given the names of people working for a similar group here. I know you can see the same thing in London probably, or any big city —'

'That isn't the point. The point is that most Japanese refuse to acknowledge problems such as homelessness and poverty exist in their society. They just refuse to fucking believe it because they all, well the ones that aren't in the Sanya anyway, subscribe to the myth of this wonderful organic society. This, remember, is the place where capitalism works! You must have had it stuffed down your throat about how the entire fucking country is middle-class and how they cannot understand class divisions in Britain. What you've actually got here is fucking feudalism, a massive majority of industrial serfs and a small plutocracy with money coming out of their arseholes. I mean, apart from all the pious shit that comes from the fact they actually lost the war, things have not changed here since the nineteen-thirties. The fucking Yanks did the same bloody restoration job here that they did in Sicily for the Mafia.'

'This also has to be the most racist country outside of South Africa,' Nicky said, pouring herself another glass of wine. 'I mean, sure, they're friendly enough to your face, but basically, if you aren't Japanese you're shit. Okay, right now, you, Jack and I are useful shit, but when push comes to shove we're still *gaijin*, still shit.'

'The money they pay to the useful foreigners acts as a kind of wall between us and them. We don't have any rights, we're not allowed to express any opinions, we don't have any feelings, the money should be enough. We're like machines that they use until they figure out how to do the job better.

'The Koreans here are discriminated against almost as badly as the Blacks in South Africa, like Nicky said. They were mostly brought over as forced labour in the thirties, the older ones, but they've got kids and grand-kids who were born here, never been outside of the fucking country, yet the kids still have to be classified as foreigners like us, still have to carry the fucking card and be fingerprinted every five years. They, get this, even have to choose whether they want North or South Korean nationality.'

'And they're discriminated against in education and jobs,' Nicky said. 'Peter Morizawa told us that when people get married here the families hire private detectives to check each other out in case there's Korean blood lurking about somewhere.'

'You seem to have this country so — so completely summed up,' David said. 'As if there is nothing to it except what you say. And you've been here for how long — just over a year? How can you know a place so well in so little time? I mean, I didn't even begin to know Fez until the last couple of years I was there, and as for this place, I have the feeling that, however long I stay, when the time comes to leave and someone asks me what it's been like I'm going to say that I didn't understand it — *wakarimasen deshita.*'

Jack Stevens looked up at the wooden boards of the ceiling, 'Oh Christ, he's speaking the fucking language now! You want to be a bit careful, mate. I met a bloke once who had a very dodgy experience because he tried going native. He was giving private lessons to this bored housewife — also a bad idea, I might add — and he had a cold, hay-fever, which he told the woman about— in Japanese. The lady says she can help him and gets the bloke to lie down on the sofa. Then she goes away saying she'll be back shortly. He thinks she's gone off to get him a couple of aspirins. Anyway, she's gone for about ten minutes and when she does reappear she's wearing a frilly black nightie, and before he can say "shit" he's being jumped on, the poor bugger.

'You see, he'd got his words arse over tit, which is not difficult in Japanese, and while he thought he was complaining about his hay-fever, he was actually saying he was impotent!'

David laughed, 'Well, perhaps he enjoyed being jumped on.'

'Not a chance, she was built like a brick shithouse, and later went on to a very successful career as a professional wrestler.'

With the laughter the tension that had been in the room eddied away. David said it was time for him to go.

As Nicky walked him to the station she took his arm. 'In a way I can understand that woman. Of course, Jack thinks all the Japanese are mad, he has this Cheshire Cat approach to the whole country. But there are days when I feel this place closing in around me and think I might go mad myself. It must be so much worse for them — the women, I mean. Girls are treated like shit the moment they are born and marriage brings no relief if there is a tyrant of a mother-in-law around — the classic revenge of the older woman. I suppose she was just looking for a way out, a means of escape. I suppose we all are. You must be careful.'

For all the loveliness of the night David shivered. He said goodbye numbly, and felt, when he was alone, that he did not want to see Jack or Nicky again for a while.

He was late for the speech contest, following the girl, who had been waiting for him at the front desk, into the hall as the other judges were being introduced to the audience. His embarrassment was not diminished by the large ribbon cluster that had been attached to his lapel in the corridor outside, as if he were in some way the trophy being competed for. He mounted the steps to the podium just in time for the editor of the *Mainichi Shimbun* to begin the lengthy outline of his career, and to catch the reproachful smiles of his fellow adjudicators. When it was over, he was escorted to his seat, gratefully turning his back on the audience.

He had not meant to be late. He had set off early for the short journey from Nakano, his heart filled with good intentions. The train stopped in the basement of the building where the *Mainichi Shimbun* had its offices, but there he lost his way. He took the wrong exit, following a long tunnel which, at last, delivered him into a wholly unfamiliar street he could not find on the map he had been given. Retracing his steps to the station he found himself misled, seduced by the confusion of ways, and it was almost twenty minutes past ten when, sweating and ill at ease, he came at last into the lobby of the building. As he did so, a grey-suited girl spoke to him and took him to the elevator.

There were twenty contestants and after the third David found it difficult to stay awake in the droning stream of tedium. The mark sheets on the desk before him were carefully divided into sections — content, quality of English, enunciation, rhythm, expression — with the maximum percentage of the total mark to be awarded in each category. The speeches might themselves have been equally sectionalized: each began with a Significant Personal Anecdote, which was followed by an Elaboration leading to the Moral. The speech was then concluded with a Summary and Imprecation relating back to the Significant Personal Anecdote with which it had begun. The subjects were equally uniform, all of them variations upon a common theme — the need for greater international awareness by the Japanese, although what this seemed to mean was a greater tolerance of Japan by the other nations of the world, usually expressed through some pious reference to the war, a war in which every speaker managed to make Japan seem the primary victim.

Each speech was given without notes, the words having been committed to memory in a toneless, sing-song fashion so that the effect was of listening to a succession of well-drilled, nervous parrots. Only once, when memory failed and a girl stood for an endless moment helplessly seeking her lost words before she collapsed into tears, was the chain of unreality broken. David gave her a high mark out of sympathy. After this, it was in an effort to fight off his drowsiness that he turned to marking the contestants' appearance rather than their speeches, for most of the speakers were young women.

It was, despite the time of year, an extremely warm day, yet each girl was dressed in a suit of heavy tweed material, with fussy blouses and small velvet bows at the collar. The hall in which the speeches were being heard was heated, and even David, the only one still wearing summer-weight material, was uncomfortably hot.

There was a break for lunch, and then the contest resumed. As the first of the afternoon's contestants began speaking David found his attention held by more than wondering how the young woman was feeling beneath the layers of heavy clothing she had on. The girl, Yumiko Ogawara, was a student at a two-year college in Tokyo. These colleges prepared girls to go into secretarial work. The speech began in much the same way as all the others, with a personal anecdote, but David was immediately struck by the sense of impassioned honesty in the voice of the speaker. She told of how her sister, a graduate of a leading private university, had met and married a man in the company in which she worked. As was the custom, after her marriage the woman stopped working. This led to a series of questions concerning the position of women in Japan and a final query as to why and for how much longer Japanese women would be forced by convention and expectation into marriage and motherhood, or else risk an isolated and suspect spinsterhood by seeking a fulfilling and continuing career. David was impressed. The girl's English was poor, lacking entirely the over-rehearsed competence of the other speakers, yet it seemed to him she was the only one who had any idea of what she was actually talking about, or who cared at all for what she had to say.

In the room to which the judges were led after the last speaker had finished there was no discussion, simply a comparison of marks. The chairman of the judges, an old Japanese professor with a head of grizzle like a badly-shaved chin, totalled the marks and announced the names of those who would progress to the finals. There was, however, a difficulty. Two girls were tied and as only four contestants could go through from this competition one of the two would have to be eliminated. One of the girls was Yumiko Ogawara.

'I can see no problem here,' the old man said, clearing a knot of phlegm from his throat as he spoke. 'This Ogawara cannot possibly be accepted as a finalist. It is inconceivable that such talk should be heard in the final competition.'

David made to protest but it was too late, the matter was settled. He traipsed back into the hall feeling himself a participant in a significantly unfunny farce.

There was a ceremony to present the four finalists with their certificates and cups gradually diminishing in size. As each girl was awarded her prize the old professor droned through an interminable paean in Japanese. For the highest placed finalist it was all too much; overcome by victory, or her proximity to so eminent a *sensei*, or, more likely, hunger and the awful heat, she made a swaying arc backwards as she reached out her hand for the proffered cup, to collapse into the folds of her skirt on the stage, like a heap of sleep-tossed blankets.

David walked disconsolately down to the train when it was all over. He had thirty thousand yen in his pocket, but there was a sourness about the money that seemed to penetrate the fibres of his clothing, stealing through to the flesh. He fed coins into the ticket machine and, as he did so, felt a touch upon his arm and heard someone speaking to him. He turned to see a girl with a curious, crocheted hat on her head of a type he had not seen since leaving Morocco.

'I am sorry,' the girl said, hesitatingly. 'I think I will bother you but I want to speak English with you. I want to ask you question.'

He smiled, 'It's okay. You're not bothering me. Were you at the speech contest?'

'Yes. I was there. It was very terrible, yes? I think so. Only one spoke as her — with her feelings. And for her there was nothing. Why? This is the question I have to ask you.'

He took his ticket. 'You mean Yumiko Ogawara, the girl who spoke of the problems facing women here who wish to work.'

The girl nodded, 'Yes. I have to ask why there is nothing for her when her speech is best one?'

'I wish I could give you an answer,' David said, 'but I can't. I agree with you, she was the only girl who said anything that made sense; however, the other judges preferred nonsense, as long as it was in good English.'

'I don't understand. You also are judge.'

'Yes,' David said, beginning to move towards the ticket barrier, 'I was a judge, but not a very good one. I'm going to Nakano, which train do you take?'

'Oh, not there. I go another way.'

They walked together towards the men who beat an endless metallic time with their ticket-punches, thoughtless human metronomes. 'I am sorry,' the girl said, 'I forget the ticket. Will you wait me?' David waited as she ran back to the wall of machines, watching her slim and pleasing figure. Like him, she was still dressed for summer, in white jeans, and a long white shirt over a white, crew-necked cotton sweater. When she came back to him she was laughing in a nervous, embarrassed way. She introduced herself as Megumi Iwase.

At the stairway where David had to cross the track for the train to Nakano the girl asked him how long he had been in Africa. He told her.

'Six years? That is long. All time you were in Morocco?' David nodded. 'Oh, I know about Morocco! Marrakesh. Casablanca. And you eat cous-cous, yes?'

David laughed. 'Have you been to Morocco? You seem to be very well informed.'

'Oh no, but I have seen *Casablanca* movie many times. It make me learn about Morocco.'

Before he left, David gave the girl his address and telephone number. 'Yes, yes. I will write you. I want to meet you again and speak English with you.'

The next day he was called down to the gate by the postman with a recorded delivery letter. It was from Megumi Iwase. She said she wanted to see him again, and asked if he would meet her at Studio Alta in Shinjuku on the following Saturday. David waited for her for an hour, watching the giant video screen that lit the crowds flooding from the station in its sickened glow, but she did not come. On the screen Humphrey Bogart put Ingrid Bergman aboard the tiny 'plane, and then walked into the mist with Claude Rains.

In November the weather grew suddenly cold and, although the sun still shone from a clear, painfully blue sky and the leaves still clung, red and gold, to the trees, a cold and bitter wind blew; the salary-men put on their imitation Burberrys, the schoolgirls wore little white gloves with their serge sailor-suits, and left the straw hats in cupboards to wait for another summer. David got back from the dry cleaners with his heavier clothes late in the afternoon to hear his telephone ringing, and ran up the iron stairway to his apartment, but whoever it was that had called grew impatient, ringing off just as he got his key into the lock.

Half an hour later the telephone rang again. David picked up the receiver expecting either Jack or Nicky Stevens, but in fact it was neither. The caller was Alison Tench, the girl he had met early in the summer, one day when he was lost.

'I know I promised to call you sooner, but I went away in August, and then, what with one thing or the other, well, you know how it is. Anyway, what about that drink?'

They went to a bar called Red Shoes, a place Alison liked because the crowd that frequented it did not include any salary-men. 'They wouldn't get past the door, love,' she told David. 'Love', she used the word easily, affectionately, without mystery. David relaxed, happy to be where he was.

She was young, graduated from Oxford and had come straight to Japan a year and a half before to teach English in a girls' school. She seemed changed since the last time David had seen her, her skin was still tanned from the month she had spent in Greece, her hair had grown longer than he remembered it, and, as she slipped her coat off in the bar, he saw that her body had shed some weight. Tall and strong, her flesh cut down to muscle, she had about her an appetite for life, an abundance of health and of hope, that David found himself hungry for.

'So,' Alison began, and he joined with her to make a chorus of the rest, 'how do you like Japan?'

Laughing with him, she said, 'I'm sorry, have people been giving you a bad time with that one?'

David, still smiling, shook his head and Alison said, 'Well then, how do you like it?'

'It's okay. Really, I think it's okay. There's a lot here that I find — what? Interesting, stimulating, a little frightening in a good way. I think I can live here. What about you? How do you like Japan?'

Alison shook her head, 'Oh no, mister. My rites of passage were done with long ago. Wait until you know me better.'

They met again a week later and ate dinner in a restaurant the severity of whose cuisine matched its decor. David watched as Alison picked at the tiny, elegant morsels on her plate. She ate like a bird. Afterwards, as they waited in the black and white tiled foyer for their coats to be brought to them, the girl reached

out to straighten his tie, her long fingers deft upon the silken knot.
David was overwhelmed by the loveliness of the gesture.

He told her that night he was married. They went from the
restaurant to a club, and sat listening to Japanese musicians
producing perfect facsimiles of American jazz. She checked,
visibly, for a moment, but then carried on as before, calling him
love, laughing at his jokes, interested in his life. At the end of the
evening, just as he was getting out of the taxi they had shared as
far as Nakano, she said, 'Thanks for telling me — most don't.'

The next day, it was a Friday, she telephoned at eight in the
morning to say she had a free day from school and would he have
lunch with her. They went to Aoyama, to a small Italian-owned
trattoria, and then walked back towards Harajuku and a tiny
jewel of a museum all but lost behind the loudness of
Harajuku-dori, with its impertinent, self-proclaimed affinity to
Paris. Wandering among the wood-block prints of the museum,
the scenes of pleasure and fine women, Alison took David's hand,
and smiled at him, 'What a lovely day.'

It was a week later, just after his classes, as David waited to cross
the road to the station opposite the main gate of the university,
that he saw Megumi Iwase again. A girl, wearing a woollen hat
and heavy coat against the cold November evening, approached
him. He thought at first she was a student, but none of the girls in
his classes dressed as this girl was dressed. She asked, in broken
English, if he remembered her and when he said that he did not,
told him her name. Megumi said she had something to ask him,
and would he go with her to a coffee shop where they might talk
for a few minutes. Reluctantly he agreed, and led her across the
road to The Mirabelle, a small restaurant where he sometimes
ate lunch with Jack Stevens.

The place was empty except for the owner and a waiter David
had not seen before. It was the odd hour when The Mirabelle
changed its identity from a restaurant to a *karoake* bar. Soon the
offices would close and the blue-suited salary-men begin drifting
towards places like this, to drink themselves senseless and bellow
sentimental songs into microphones. There was hardly any
violence among the drunks David had seen in Tokyo, or at least,

not the kind directed towards others. To walk in this city late at night was not at all like negotiating the terrifying minefield of a British city when the pubs emptied, yet the same measure of the brutal and the maudlin obtained here, in the songs the men sang, and the hurt they inflicted upon themselves.

Busy with their preparations for the coming night, the owner and his solitary staff could not be bothered for once with the elaborate ritual of greeting that a customer usually attracted upon entering a Japanese business, and the tea David ordered was somehow forgotten as well. It did not matter, he had no intention of staying very long.

As Megumi sat, almost huddled, across from him at the corner table, David found it easy to understand why he had not recognized her. In her heavy boots, and thick denim overalls and sweater, she was utterly unlike the white-clad girl of summer he had seen before. It was only the woollen hat she wore over her cropped hair that told him who she was.

She had begun to smoke as soon as they were seated, taking three or four long pulls on a cigarette before stubbing it out and lighting a fresh one. When she wasn't smoking her breathing was rapid and shallow. David had seen this panic in the Japanese, confronted with foreigners and the prospect of having to speak English, before. He tried to reassure her. 'Are you all right?' he asked, in Japanese.

She answered him in English, saying, yes, she was all right and that he must not be worried. 'Sometimes I am like this. I am very ill when I was young. Since that time I become very nervous. I am sorry.'

Meeting Megumi so unexpectedly made David late, and he was annoyed, more with himself than the Japanese girl, as he climbed the iron staircase to his room. He had promised to telephone Alison at six o'clock and it was almost half-past now. He was annoyed because he could have called from any number of public telephones, but he had never used one in Japan before and somehow he had not been able to bring himself to do so that night. In the end it did not matter, it never seemed to matter with Alison. She enfolded his apology in her laughter and gave it back to him as a gift.

He had to talk with Alison because they were to go to Kamakura together, a town by the sea some thirty miles from Tokyo. It was the home of a great statue of the Buddha, and also of an important figure representing the Buddhist personification of mercy, the Kwannon. Alison had been there only once before, and now wanted to go again with David. They arranged a time and agreed to meet on the platform at Nakano station the following Saturday.

It was while they were walking towards the Kotokuin temple, gauging their closeness to the great Buddha by the increase of souvenirs available in the small shops along the way, that David told Alison about Megumi Iwase. He said, 'I arranged to give someone English lessons yesterday, just before I telephoned you. That was the real reason I was late making the call. It's a woman I'd met once before — at a speech contest. She stopped me outside the university as I was going to the station. She was in a bit of a state really, said she had to take an exam soon so that she could go to some college in the States. I said I'd help her, now I'm not sure I did the right thing.' He paused, wondering why what he had said had been phrased in the rhetoric of the confession, as if it were some dirty little secret kept in a guilty heart.

Alison looked at him for a moment, and then took his hand. 'Don't be too kind to people, David. Sometimes you can pay a high price for it.'

As soon as he had heard what it was Megumi wanted from him, David had determined not to take her on. He disliked one-to-one teaching, and the money she offered, although generous, meant nothing to him. Yet, within minutes, he had changed his mind and agreed to accept her as a private student. When he told her she began to weep, saying the words 'thank you' again and again, until he was able to calm her.

They arranged that he would see her on Mondays in his apartment at Nakano after he had finished teaching, and then again on Friday mornings. They talked briefly about the sort of materials they would use, and what Megumi's plans were for studying in America. Then he said that he must leave. As the two of them took their separate paths into the winter darkness, David paused to watch the girl walk away, and wondered if she were not ill. On the train home he had asked himself whether he had, perhaps, acted hastily in agreeing to work with her; it was a question that would not leave him. He wondered why he had changed his mind about her and could not really find an answer to his question, unless it was that at last he had found someone he pitied more than he pitied himself.

He was astonished when he entered the courtyard of the Kotokuin Temple where the Great Buddha stood; astonished at the figure itself, but also at the tide of carnival that swept about it. He had imagined he would find himself in some holy place, a place of incense and whispered prayers. There was incense, but no whispers, only the mechanized 'clicks' of automatic cameras as noisy groups of Japanese put their backs to the statue to have their photographs taken. Those that tried to pray did so self-consciously, or spoke through the laughter of embarrassment. There were few of these, for most of the visitors this was a place of holiday, not pilgrimage, and they lined up to pay their money for a trip up inside the hollow figure to take their turn at the windows cut into its great back for yet another photograph, all the fun of the fair.

'I wonder what He thinks about all of this?' Alison said to David. 'It wasn't as bad when I was here before, it was in the rainy season and there weren't so many people.' She thought for a moment, and then said, 'But perhaps this is more real, you know, in the end.'

They turned to walk away, and David could not resist a last backward glance at the great imperturbable, impervious face so far above the tawdry nonsense that surrounded it.

It was quieter at the Hasedera Temple, where the Kwannon was housed, because the temple grounds were so much larger and the parties of school children, the groups of middle-aged women, the men's clubs, were diluted, anaesthetized by space. David and Alison wandered among the thousands of *Jiso* figures placed in the gardens.

'It's a sacred figure for children,' Alison explained. 'That's why lots have little baby hats and bibs and things attached to them. And because so many Japanese women have abortions they try to pacify the soul of the unborn child by dedicating a figure to it. They sometimes write little letters asking for forgiveness and leave them here. I feel incredibly sad when I come here, David. Can we go?'

They moved to another part of the temple gardens and bought

drinks. Alison led him to a place where they could see the town below them, the beach and the grey waters of the Pacific. It was late afternoon and the day had begun to gather itself inwards towards night. A group of elderly men and women had arrived, a society of some kind, David imagined, for they all wore identical white jackets tied with strings at the back making them look like so many enormous babies. They seemed to be in a hurry to see what they had to see, to do what they had to do. Outside the shrine closest to where David and Alison were standing was a large cabinet holding a complete collection of the Buddhist sutras. The cabinet was set about an axel and by turning it the pilgrim could gain the blessings of having read all of the holy works that it contained. The old men and women began frantically to jostle with one another for the right to push the cabinet around.

'God,' Alison said, laughing, 'they must be pretty desperate. Still, I suppose at that age —'

Before she could finish, David said, ' "Gentile or Jew/O you who turn the wheel and look to windward,/Consider Phlebas, who was once handsome and tall as you." '

Alison looked down her nose at him, suddenly transformed into a not-altogether-approving bluestocking, 'Mr Eliot, I presume?'

David turned away from the anxious pilgrims and put his face towards the sea gain. 'No,' he said, '"Phlebas the Phoenician, a fortnight dead".'

'David!' Alison said, catching his arm, 'Come on, it isn't as bad as that, surely?'

David continued staring out at the grey sea. 'No, not as bad as that.'

They walked on the beach as the sunset smeared its bloodied yolk across the horizon. Fishing boats made dim shapes in the darkness that waited close to the sand.

'It's my birthday next week,' Alison said. 'I shall be twenty-four.'

David was shocked, he had not properly understood that this girl whose hand he held was so young. They were silent for a while, watching the evening take hold of the sky. David asked if she would spend the day with him.

'Yes,' Alison said. 'Yes, I should like that very much.'

Alison's birthday was on a Sunday, and in the afternoon David walked from his apartment towards the station to meet her. He was early, but she was there waiting for him, leaning against a pillar reading a book. She looked toward him as he approached, the questioning stare of the short-sighted, and then smiled her recognition. David paused, and she moved towards him and the short journey back to where he lived. Alison was the first person he had ever asked to his room, when Nicky came it was at her own invitation.

He had some small presents for her: perfume, two gold loops for her ears, and a single white rose. She was embarrassed, said she had not expected such things, but she fixed the loops into her ears and kissed the rose. David busied himself with their meal. He had found, in the vast food-hall of a department store in Shibuya, an outlet of *Le Nôtre* and bought baguettes, and petits pots de chocolat, a fine Camembert and wine, champagne and a chateau-bottled claret. He prepared crudités and, on the gas burner, made a casserole of beef and winter vegetables. He spread a newly-purchased white cloth on the table, and set it with glassware and procelain and cutlery he had bought for the occasion. In the centre he put candles and a bowl of anemonies. It was after four o'clock when they sat down, the candles casting their uncertain light in the gathering darkness.

'Thank you for a lovely birthday,' Alison said. The meal was long ago eaten, but they still sat at the table amidst the debris, drinking coffee and the last of the wine. 'I'm very pleasantly, but quite incredibly, drunk.'

David smiled at her, 'Well, you have company.'

Alison reached across the table and took his hand, 'Who taught you to cook?'

'My Irish mammy, she wasn't very adaptable and brought me up in exactly the same way as my sisters. I can bake a cake and turn a hem with the best of them, but most of that meal was purchased.'

'I know, but you chose such nice things, did your mother teach you how to do that as well? Are you really Irish?'

'More or less, my mother and father are both from there, from the South. When I was a kid every family in the street was a Doyle or a Lynch.'

'Or a Kennedy.'

'Or a Kennedy, yes.'

'But David isn't Irish, is it? It's Welsh — or Jewish.'

'My mother had this idea that it would be better to give me a less ethnic name,' David said, with an ironic smile. 'Then she had second thoughts on the day of my baptism and gave me Brendan as a second name, which is what my parents actually call me, but to everyone else I'm David. I think of myself as David.'

'Yes,' Alison said, 'I shall always think of you as David.'

She was quiet then, staring into the flame of the dying candle. 'Could I have some more coffee, love?' she asked, but when he went into the kitchen to make it, she followed him. 'I can't imagine you married, you know. Perhaps it's because I've never known you as part of a couple, but somehow you just look too self-sufficient. It's as if you don't need anyone else.'

'Oh yes, the self-contained man,' he said waiting for the kettle to boil.

'Tell me what happened. I mean, you said you were married, but you never mention your wife. When you talk about the past you always say 'I', never 'we'. You aren't together any more, are you?'

'No, not really. I suppose we're separated, literally if not legally.'

'So what happened?'

'She just found someone else she liked better than me.'

'That simple?'

David began to pour the water onto the heaped filter, 'No, not that simple. I don't know that I can tell you really, because I don't know where I should begin. I mean, I think it started for Jean — that's my wife — a long time ago — it must have. I'm just not sure when, I don't suppose she is either.'

'Well, why don't you just try from where it began for you?'

'For me? I don't know that either — I remember in O-level history we used to do practice papers all the time, and there was this pat little formula we learned for questions that began

"Outline the causes of —" whatever it was. You always had to distinguish between immediate and fundamental. I feel a bit like that with what's happened to my marriage. Look, this is ready, shall we take it back in there?'

They went back to the table. The candle was all but out and David switched on the overhead light, but the fluorescent harshness brought out the utter drabness of the room and he turned it off again, fetching another candle. They drank the coffee in silence.

'So when did it start for you?' Alison said.

'In Morocco, I suppose. Jean couldn't stand the place, and looking back on things, we weren't really very happy — with each other I mean. I didn't like it that much either, I hadn't gone there from choice, it was the only job I could get when I finished my doctorate.'

'Why did you stay — if neither of you liked it?'

'Money. I was in the overseas aid business, more or less, and every year the funded posts were getting fewer and fewer. Anyway, the way Jean felt about being abroad, another foreign job wasn't really on. She wanted to go home, but I always said that I would never find a job. Home for Jean meant Scotland.'

'Did she work in Morocco? What did she do all day?'

'She had different jobs. There was quite a lot of work for someone like Jean, she's a languages graduate, French and Italian. She did different things. She worked for a bank, and then she had a job with Alitalia. It was mostly secretarial though, and, as she used to tell me, she hadn't got a degree to sit in front of a typewriter all day. There were two years when she didn't work at all, they were the worst. She quite literally had nothing to do. We had a steward and a cook, so Jean did the expatriate wife bit, coffee mornings, afternoons at the hotel pool, bridge. The thing was that she couldn't stand most of the other expats' wives. She used to say they either talked about kids or who was screwing who.

'Well, in the end, we agreed that she should go home, that we'd buy a house; she'd go back to university and I'd see out my contract and join her. I actually had no choice about leaving Fez in the end. The Ministry of Overseas Development was downgraded into an administration and lost a lot of its budget.

They made cuts and one of the posts to go was mine. There was no question of staying on with the local salary, so that was that.

'It was funny though, the last year in Fez was one of the happiest of my life. I missed Jean, but, to be honest, things had been so difficult between us for such a long time that in many ways I was relieved she wasn't there. Leaving was awful. I think one of the most difficult things I've ever had to do was saying goodbye to my steward and cook, telling them I'd be sure to see them again when of course I knew I wouldn't. I walked out of the apartment and I couldn't look back because I knew I'd weep.

'When I got to Britain I was completely numb. I missed it all so much. It wasn't just the money, I felt that I'd had a life and it had been left behind me in North Africa. I'd been someone there, back home I was nobody, living in a flat that wasn't in any sense mine. It was the building society's and it was Jean's, it wasn't mine. I had no friends, I had no job, nothing.

'Well, I started looking for work and it was hopeless, you know. There was nothing in the universities, and I was over-qualified, I was told, for school-teaching or further education. I tried to get a Manpower Services grant to re-train as a data analyst but the two blokes that interviewed me all but said I'd already had enough out of the government and they weren't about to give me any more. To cut a long story short we — we lost everything, the house, savings —'.

'So what did you do?'

'I moved to London, and Jean found a room in a flat with some other students — she was at Edinburgh University in the first year of a Ph.D.'

'And is that what she's doing now?'

David nodded, 'Yes. Anyway, I went to London to look for work and eventually got the job here.'

'Was it while you were away that Jean met this other guy — it is a guy she's involved with?'

David smiled again, 'Yes, it is a man and, yes, they got involved while I was away. Or at least I think they did. She's told me so many lies, I now realize, that I honestly don't know when she's telling me the truth anymore. She said she met this man the first year she was at university, he's a lecturer there, in the School of Architecture. She said she fancied him the first time she saw him, so I don't know, perhaps they were involved before I went south. I don't know.'

'And when did you find out?'

He pushed his coffee away from him, and emptied the wine bottle into his glass, 'Just before I came to Japan. I went up to Scotland the week before I was due to leave. We stayed at her mother's because Jean said the place where she was living was a bit sordid. I suppose I should have known something was going on because her behaviour was — well, she wasn't the way she usually was. One night, I think it was the second night I was there, we went out for a meal and she got incredibly drunk, I'd never seen her that way before, and she really let go at me, saying that she'd come out to Tokyo for the summer but if she didn't like it, well, that was that, she wasn't throwing any more of her life away following me round the world. You get the picture.'

He finished the wine, 'The next day, and this is where it starts to get terribly clichéd, I found "the letter". Apparently she'd been carrying the bloody thing around with her in her handbag since Easter and then she lost it when we were at her mother's. Well, I was the one who found it. I only read it because the handwriting looked like that of a friend of ours from Fez. It wasn't addressed to her, and it wasn't signed, but it was obviously from the bloke whose house we'd stayed in when I was up at Easter, and it was also obvious that they were having an affair. It was full of, you know, how much he was missing her, and he was writing it in bed and wasn't that appropriate, and it contained instructions on when to pack me off so that they could be together again. I'm sorry, I should explain that his wife is also an architect, but an extremely successful one who spends most of her time in the States, in New York. All the while I'd thought Jean was living in this student flat she was actually with her boyfriend in his wife's house. She just moved out when his wife was back, which wasn't that often, or, as at Easter, moved me in when he had to be away in New York.

'One of the things that, really, I still can't quite believe is how cunning she was. I used to write to her at the place I thought she was staying, and the people that actually lived there would bring the letters in to the university and give them to her. If I wanted to 'phone her I had to call her mother on a Thursday evening, which was when she usually visited. Once, in Morocco, I called her a liar — we were fooling around about something, I don't remember what — but anyway, I called her a liar. She went crazy. She got hold of my hair and put me on the floor and said she never lied, that I should never call her a liar again.'

'She was unhappy,' Alison said. 'People change when they are unhappy. They become selfish, and do stupid things.' She looked at him in the silence of the room and then asked if he had anything else to drink. David got a bottle of cognac he'd bought duty-free at Heathrow. He asked Alison if she wanted a clean glass, but she said she would use the one she'd drunk her wine from.

'What did you do, once you'd found the letter?' Alison said. 'Did you confront her with it? I suppose you must have.'

'Yes, my reactions were — I don't know. When I was reading it, it took a while for it to sink in. After that I just couldn't believe it was true. I wanted to hit her, I wanted to pack my bag and walk away from it all. When it came to it though, I didn't do anything; at first, when I first saw her, I couldn't even speak. There's a lot more, some of it pretty sordid, but — I don't know, I don't know what I feel any more. I feel an idiot. I trusted her completely, and that time I was with her in his house, I just didn't suspect anything. And then the last time I was up there, everyone knew except me.

'It was strange, because that last year I was in Fez there were some American students at the university on foreign study and I suppose, because I wasn't part of a couple, you know, I was around much more and I was spending time with these kids. Well, one of the girls got a bit of a crush on me, and she was attractive, a nice kid, and I was lonely and I really thought about it, but in the end nothing happened. I told Jean about this, I don't know why, maybe I was trying to say that she shouldn't feel guilty, these things happen, marriages survive. She told me I was a fool, that I should have had my fling.'

'This man that she's involved with now, is it serious, in the long term?'

'I don't know. All she said to me was that she couldn't give him up. Apparently the sex is very good, well, better than with me anyway. It was never great between us, my fault I suppose. I come too soon, or I do with Jean, I wouldn't know about with anyone else. You'll probably find this hard to believe, but she was my first, and there haven't been any others.'

'Oh David, I'm really sorry.'

'Yes, so am I. I suppose I feel betrayed in every way. I had nothing left in my life except Jean, and even she was taken from me.'

Alison looked away from him for an instant and then said, 'Don't misunderstand me, David, I really am sorry for you, but I think you're a lot more sorry for yourself. You should be angry, God knows you've got every right to be, but instead you're just bitter. It makes for dangerous waters to swim in, love.

'I don't know if this will help, but, for what it's worth — I had an affair with my tutor when I was in my first year at Oxford. I knew he was married, don't get me wrong, he never lied to me about that, he just lied about all the other women he was seeing at the time. I knew that he didn't intend to leave his wife, but I thought that he really loved me, and I loved him.

'I was at a party one night, on my own. He'd said he couldn't get away from the family that weekend, but that wasn't quite true. I got there late, and I went up to one of the bedrooms to leave my coat. He was in there fucking a girl I knew quite well. I couldn't understand why he'd done that to me. I wasn't, of course, being very logical at the time, I mean, if he'd deceive his wife, what hope could I have? The thing was, about a week after this happened my period was late and, to cut a long story short, I was pregnant. There wasn't any possibility of my having the child so I had an abortion. I thought for a while I'd come out of it all very well, but then things sort of boiled up inside me and I had a mental breakdown.

'I was ill for a long time, on and off. I actually did part of my Finals in the loony bin. I had to learn that it's quite possible to love someone and be angry with them at the same time. I had to learn not to devalue my own trust in others, just because someone I loved had betrayed it, and I had to learn that it wasn't much use wallowing in my own self-pity. I think perhaps you have to do that too.'

They cleared the table and washed the dishes. It was late, almost eleven-thirty and Alison said she would have to leave soon.

'Would you stay with me tonight, Alison?' David said. He did not look at her, his hands were still deep in the soapy water they had used to clean the plates and glasses.

She shook her head, 'I can't. Don't be hurt, I just can't. I really like you, but if I went to bed with you now it would just be because I feel sorry for you. I don't want to do that. Can you understand?'

It was time for her to go. As she took her coat, she turned to him. 'David, don't look so sad. Come on, give me a hug.'

They embraced, and Alison kissed his face. They walked through the deserted streets to the station, and a few minutes later David made his way back to his empty room, his empty bed.

The weather turned bitterly cold, and the brilliant sunlight of November was forgotten as heavy clouds, each bringing the promise of snow, filled the sky. David and Alison were walking away from the noise and people in Harajuku towards Yoyogi Park. David had not been there before.

'How's your crazy lady?' Alison asked. She was teasing him, something she seemed to enjoy. David had been giving lessons to Megumi Iwase for almost a month now, and her behaviour made him wonder if perhaps Alison was not right after all to call her crazy. There was an intensity about Megumi that frightened him a little. She seemed like a clock wound so tight it was incapable of any movement, holding only the potential to burst itself into tiny fragments of slivered metal and glass. The Friday before, David had been unexpectedly called in to college. He had put a note, telling Megumi that he would be back as soon as possible, in an evelope together with a key to his room, and taped the little package to the door. He was away longer than he had expected. He had telephoned his apartment, but getting no reply assumed Megumi had grown tired of waiting and gone home. When he got back to Nakano, it was after seven. He had found the girl rolled into a ball in front of his door, the envelope containing his note and the key untouched. All that Megumi could say to him was, 'I must see you.'

They came to the main gates of the park and stopped before a large, figurative sign showing all of the things that were forbidden inside. There were so many David wondered aloud if it was worth going in. Alison laughed, and said it was not like that inside.

As they walked along beneath the frozen plum trees David looked around him to see the Japanese doing everything that was expressly forbidden: children ran on the buff-coloured grass, kicking balls, imploring their parents to get wayward kites aloft, riding tricycles on the pathways. The sound of trumpets and saxophones echoed in the chill air, and soon they could see a group of men, each man alone with his own cacophony, pointing glistening brass horns towards bushes and trees, saluting the evergreen foliage with scales, all more or less off-key. David looked at Alison in amazement. She took his arm, saying, 'It's magic, this park. It's the only place I know of where the Japanese let go without getting smashed out of their minds. I always think that almost anything could happen here, that something wonderful could happen here.'

There were lovers in the park, young men and women swaddled in their fashionable coats, sitting on cold benches; people who shared Alison's belief came here to this open space for the privacy they could not afford or simply could not find anywhere else.

David loved being in the city with Alison. She was the agent through whom wonderful things happened for him. That first night they had been out together they had gone back by train and it had been full of the usual drunks. David had looked at the greasy, senseless faces, the dishevelled clothes, the untidy, dandruffed hair, and felt only revulsion. A space cleared rapidly around a young boy who was being sick, and he moved to shield Alison from the sight, but she only laughed and said, 'Not at their best at this time of night, are they?' Suddenly she made it all seem all right, and he loved her for it.

When it was too cold to stay out any longer they went back to Harajuku and into the steamy warmth of a café. It was there Alison told him she was leaving Japan.

'When?' David asked, unable to accept what she was saying to him.

'Soon, when school finishes for Christmas. A little bit before actually. I'm flying to London on the twenty-third.'

'But why? What's happened?'

'Oh David, you're going to think I'm a real shit when I tell you. You've been so honest with me, and I haven't been as honest with you. There's a guy in England. I knew him, sort of, in Oxford, and he was really kind when I was ill. We went out together right at the end of my time there, but it wasn't anything special, you know. Then I saw him again after I got back to London from Greece and, well, something happened between us. The thing is — the thing is that you've complicated things a bit for me. I've become much fonder of you than I wanted to. I just feel that I have to go back and see what happens with this guy. I mean, I'm either going to marry him or finish it, but we need some time together. I need some time, and a three-week vacation isn't enough.

'The British Council have fixed things with my school, so there's no problem there. I went in and talked to Richard Duckham and I have to say he was really understanding, and helpful. David, please don't look so sad. I know I should have told you, I just couldn't. I like you so much, I really do. I — well, I've said enough. "How to Spoil a Lovely Afternoon" by Alison Tench.'

David spent Alison's last evening in Japan helping her pack the few things she was having shipped back to England. He asked if he could go with her to the airport, but she was being driven there by a teacher from her school. Before he went back to Nakano, Alison gave him her parents' address and telephone number, and promised she would write.

Jack and Nicky were also going to Britain for the Christmas vacation, to be with Nicky's children and, by coincidence, they were to travel on the same flight as Alison. David thought of the three of them connected by their friendships with himself, but separated by their never having met, being carried high above the frozen ocean to the places where they had come from.

On Christmas Eve he made his way to the station through the crowds in Shibuya from the restaurant where his department had held its end-of-year party. The crush was very bad, and he had difficulty moving on the narrow pavement. Christmas was not a holiday, but the weeks before the New Year festival were the time of *O-seibo*, the giving of gifts, and corporate greed had yoked the two together into a festival of sorts. The stores were done up like whores to pull in the customers, the coloured lights and ribbons offering a good time for a price, smiles that did not cheer.

It was also the season of the *bonenkai*, the year-end office parties, like the one David had just come from. He was lost now, he had turned down a narrow lane and not emerged in the place he had thought he would. In his panic he had walked on, deeper and deeper into the dark and twisting streets, until he found himself in a lane where the doors of all the buildings were open, and women, some of them dressed like expensive tarts, others wearing kimono and the death-white make-up of the geisha, watched as inert figures were bundled into taxis. David walked along, lost, hoping to find the station so that he could get home.

The streets were like those in a city after an air-raid. Groups of swaying men surrounded figures sitting on the ground, their heads bent, spittle drooling from their mouths. Others dragged their companions along, arms held across their shoulders, useless feet trailing. In the station, when he got there, the scene was lent an even more awful aspect by the clouds of tobacco smoke that billowed from the great ashtrays set every few yards along the platform. Men lay unconscious on seats, or propped up against deserted news-stands and dustbins, their complexions like anaemic beef left cold and greasy on a plate. David saw one, his face bloody from an ugly gash across his forehead, his suit and shirt deeply stained. At Nakano a girl, hardly out of her teens, stood uncertainly against a wall, too drunk to put one foot before the other. Outside the station, the gutter by the noodle stall was choked with vomit.

The magic that Alison worked had vanished with her going, and David looked around at familiar sights grown alien and antipathetic again. He saw the city tonight as Jack did: the crowds, the flash commerciality, the filth underfoot, and what he had thought of as a place of refuge became one of exile.

A NEW YEAR

The light woke David Kennedy into his new year, the still, luminous light of snow in a city. Charged with the feeling of strange excitement snow brings to those who live among metal and concrete, he got out of bed into the freezing air of his room and went to the window. Below him was a world changed by whiteness: the empty streets made immaculate, the tiled roof across the road suddenly polar. The snow imposed its momentary, shining order upon the chaos of the hushed city. Gladdened by the weather, he lit the gas fire and then put a cassette into the tape-machine that had been his Christmas present to himself. A Corelli concerto grosso began, the waves of sound eddying into the corners of the room. David went back to the warmer spaces of his bed and enjoyed the brilliant purity of the snowlight.

The four-day holiday of the New Year stretched into the future before him, and he wondered how he would fill it. Christmas had gone almost unnoticed, marked only by the call he had made to his parents and cards from friends. Somehow the cards had drifted together onto a window ledge, all the printed frosts and robins, the mute sleigh-bells and voiceless cheer of carollers banked together, waiting only for some hand to sweep them away. The cards had almost all contained news of friends, for Christmas was now the time that most people wrote; painfully inscribing the births and partings, the trials and pains of the preceding year around the conventionalities of the season. They had come from so many places: Morocco, Los Angeles, Ireland, home. Yet the messages were familiar, the vicissitudes of humans, the awful banalities of living. Some happiness, much sorrow: desolate words in the winter season.

There was a note from Jean. She wrote:

When I got your letter I went to a solicitor. He was a nice man, not the way I'd imagined a solicitor would be. He said we could divorce on the grounds of living apart for two years, if we were not together for more than six months during that time. I told him that the separation should be dated from June last year. I know it isn't really true, but you left in October and that's less than six months together. This means that divorce proceedings could start next June and he asked me to go back to see him then.

So getting a divorce as soon as possible may only be a matter of a few months, If you were petitioning you could do it on grounds of adultery, and it would probably be a lot quicker. This way I think I just need to produce a statement from you saying we have lived apart for the required length of time and that the marriage has irretrievably broken down.

Reading through those two paragraphs again I think I sound pretty chirpy. I'm not. I'm terrified of the future and cry all the time. I'm overwhelmed by the knowledge that I've lost you. I don't know what I'm going to do, how I'm going to cope.

I'm tormented by guilt. I don't think that I'll ever truly be happy again after this. Perhaps what I mean is, I don't think I'll ever allow myself to be happy again. Please believe me, David, when I say that if I could undo all of this mess I would. I'm so sorry.

I'm sure you wonder about Cairns. His wife kicked him out of their house. She found out about us — it was inevitable, I suppose. There was a time just after that when I really thought our relationship was finished; he seemed more upset about losing the house and suddenly having no money — his wife changed their bank account, most of the money in it was hers — than he did about the hurt he'd caused her, or you. Now I don't know how I feel about him.

Sometimes I think I love him very much, but the unhappiness I feel over you and Anne-Marie is a constant confusion. My writing this has probably upset you. I'm sorry, I'm trying my best to sort this out and to be honest with you, but it seems impossible to do so without hurting you more.

I don't suppose either of us will have a particularly happy Christmas. Perhaps some day you'll feel able to forgive me for what I've done. Perhaps some day I'll be able to make it up to you for all this unhappiness.

The morning whiteness had gone by the afternoon and it was a cold, grey world that David wallked into. But at the station the drab walls were suddenly streaked with the gay figures of young girls dressed in their seasonal finery. The swathed silk gaudy of their kimono jeered the heavy clouds above the city's streets, as with dainty, white-socked feet they ignored the filthy churnings of the once-pristine snow. Enchanted, David followed the sparkling flow of girls past the ticket collectors and onto the train.

He got off at Harajuku, but turned away from the blare of music and lights to follow the crowds into the Meiji Shrine. Here the procession stopped, the finery wilted, grey vans filled with policemen ordered the throng. David took some photographs, but then walked out of the shrine and towards Yoyogi Park.

The park was empty, the snow still pure upon the grass and on the limbs of chill trees. He walked alone and thought of the day Alison had brought him here to her magic place. He wondered where she was at this moment, who she was with, whether she thought of him. He wandered off the path and through the trees, his light-coloured coat merging with the reflected light of the snow, so far from the crowds waiting to throw their pennies at the shrine of a dead emperor, so foreign to them as to be unreal, etherial, a phantom. Phantom then, he pursued the shadow of the girl he had once walked here with.

The early winter darkness began to gather as he made his way into Shibuya, scraps of snow from the park still on his shoes. Just about everywhere was closed, but he found a café, looking almost forlorn among the darkened windows and harsh shutters. He drank coffee and ate a vast slice of toast that shrivelled like candy floss in the mouth and left, unsatisfied, to wander into a cinema and sit among the families out for a New Year's treat. It was beginning to snow again when he got back to Nakano, and he waited outside his apartment in the cold wind to watch the white flakes ride the air about the street-light, like errant summer moths.

He made himself a meal of soup and cheese, and then took the bottle of cognac and a glass close to the fire. He thought he would call Alison's parents to see if she was at home and even went so far as to dial the overseas operator, but when she answered he hung up. He sat into the second day of the New Year, drinking, deciding to go to bed and then changing his mind, shunning the emptiness of the sheets, the coldness of the solitary pillow. Taking some paper from a cupboard, he started a letter to Martin Cassidy.

The life he had in Tokyo began again. Classes resumed at the university, Jack and Nicky Stevens returned from England. The holiday became a forgotten space, a hole in time into which he had somehow fallen. On the first Tuesday of the new term David met Nicky and took her to lunch at the trattoria where once he had eaten with Alison.

She seemed distant when they first met, and answered his questions about the holiday in the throw-away manner she affected, from which a sense of bitterness was never entirely absent. But in the restaurant she warmed with the wine and the food. They shared a *frito misto* and a huge, gleaming bowl of crudités with a garlic dip for the antipasto, and drank a half-bottle of Soave; afterwards, to salute the bitter weather beyond the steamy window, the frigid air that mocked the cloudless sky and the brilliant sun, they ate lasagne and drank glasses of a rich Chianti Classico.

When David asked about Jack, Nicky laughed and said she had hardly seen him since they had come back from London. He had gone into the Council the day after they had arrived in Tokyo.

'Why does he do it?' David asked. 'What does he think he gains by it?'

Nicky poured more wine into their glasses. 'Jack was pretty

well on his beam-ends when I married him. He hadn't published anything for years; he didn't even have an agent. He wasn't writing. The teaching he was doing was a joke. Then, suddenly, he found himself with a wife and two kids to look after. I think the responsibility terrified him.

'I'd been pretty comfortable really on the money Jonathan, my former husband, allowed me, and the children were away at very good schools. Jack felt he had to continue all of that. Of course, there wasn't a hope of doing so in England, but he knew some people at the Council, people from the old days when he had been very much the bright young man.

'Well, they fixed him up out here but the trouble is he was a bit of an embarrassment to those people, and I think it was made pretty clear that they wouldn't do anything else for him. Now he's scared absolutely shitless about what's going to happen next, how he's going to keep the kids at school and then put them through university. So he's trying to make sure he'll get another Council post by being, you know, a good little boy.'

As she nibbled sugared almonds and waited for a second *espresso* Nicky looked at David and said, 'Look, bugger Jack, tell me more about Martin Cassidy. I saw a piece of his work in a gallery in London, and it was odd almost knowing him through knowing you.'

David stirred the dregs of his own coffee with a tiny spoon, 'What can I tell you? He's my best friend. We were very close in London, I spent a lot of time with him and Lynne. They had this — ability to share. I was never made to feel an outsider when I was with them. They let me in, do you know what I mean? I used to eat with them a lot, two or three times a week, and Martin and I would set the art world to rights. You know the sort of thing.'

'What does he look like? I mean, I spent a long time looking at this piece in the gallery, and I couldn't imagine the man who'd made it. It was like a hunk of driftwood that had come up on a beach, except that it wasn't, you know, it was so obviously worked, but the working didn't seem to be of hands. I took Jack along there because I wanted to buy it, but you know Jack, he wouldn't let me spend the money.'

David stared at her for a moment then, but only said 'What does he look like? I suppose I would have to say that he is not a handsome man. I think his face bears a remarkable resemblance to E.M. Forster's, but when I showed him a photograph of Forster he told me I was full of shit.'

For the first time that day Nicky laughed.

'It's odd the way I feel about Martin because usually I have to be physically attracted to the people I like. The liking and the attraction seem inseperable. It isn't like that with Martin. Sometimes I don't understand it myself.

'You wouldn't think he was an artist to look at him. He's built like a brickie. He wears funny clothes too, well, not funny in themselves, he spends a lot of money on his clothes; it's just that, after a while, whatever he has starts to look odd.

'He has the most piercing eyes; I'd hate to be one of his students because I think he'd put the fear of God into me. His wrists are amazing as well, they're incredibly thick and the veins stand out from them. The only other place I've seen wrists like that was in this gym I used when I was living in London. So, that's Martin. Perhaps you'll meet him, he said just before I left that he might try to get the college to come up with some kind of a travel grant so he could visit me here. You never know.'

Outside in the cold again, they walked along towards a post-card shop David had promised to take Nicky to. As they walked, she linked her arm through his, 'You know, I think you have the nicest eyes I've ever seen. I just wish I could do something to stop making them look so unhappy all the time.'

One day, as they stood together in the crush of a late-afternoon train from the university to Shibuya, Jack Stevens asked David if he wanted to go somewhere for a drink before going home.

They went into a bar in the station, and Jack ordered beers with several small plates of food: pieces of fried chicken, sliced cheeses, nuts. He asked David how he had spent the vacation.

'Saw a lot of films. It was very quiet really, the whole town was dead on New Year's Eve. The next day was all right though, everyone was in traditional clothes.'

Jack gestured dismissively with his hand. 'It's one of the times of the year when they dress up and pretend to be Japanese. Jesus, this place makes me want to puke. Everybody's always putting on some sort of fucking front. It's like the stupid cunts where we work with the long hair and the fucking berets. 1940s fucking Left Bank exististentialists — my arse.'

'Oh, come on, they don't all look like that, and anyway, everybody poses.'

'They fucking do here, mate.'

'But how is it different from the college lecturer at home? You know, the type with the cords and polo-neck, who wanders into the class with his leather jacket draped round his shoulders, a cup of coffee in one hand, and his lighter and twenty Players in the other.'

Jack looked down at the cords and high-necked sweater he was wearing, and then at David in his grey-flecked suit.

David smiled, 'I didn't mean that personally. I was just making a point.'

'The point was taken, but the one I was trying to make is that this whole fucking country is a front, a pretence. It's like the blokes who introduce the films on television, if it's a cowboy film they've got the denim shirt and leather waistcoat on, if it's a war film they wear the blazer with the regimental badge, it's all "let's dress up and pretend". This is a nation of spoilt fucking children and it terrifies me that one day these bastards are going to rule the world.

'I know you think I'm a nutter, but what I'm saying is true, and when you've lived here a bit longer you'll find out for yourself that it's true. At the moment it's all teeth and smiles, but that's the biggest pretence of all. They hate foreigners, they fucking despise us. They just suck up what's useful, but hating it at the same time because it isn't Japanese. I went to see this film not long after I got here about some Japanese bloke who goes to Europe. He hates the place, the foreigners are either queers, nymphomaniacs, whores or thieves. Anyway, he picks up a whore in Paris, who just happens to be Japanese, and they go back to her room. But they don't fuck, they sit on the bed and talk about how great it would be to go back home to Japan.'

He drank from the mug of beer. 'This country leeches with its money on the rest of the world, not just industrially, you know buying up patents for nothing and then developing the ideas to flog back to us, but culturally as well. Nicky's always on at me to go to these art exhibitions in the department stores. Can you imagine it, the treasures of the National Gallery on display in the Japanese equivalent of John Lewis? I refuse to go, I won't enrich the bastards any more by paying the entrance fee. And I won't be on display like the fucking pictures. You know, it's as if the Goths, instead of sacking Rome, bought the fucking place.'

'You can only buy what's for sale, Jack.' David said. 'Perhaps the film you were talking about was right, perhaps Europeans are all either whores or thieves. Look at us.'

'Yeah, well I'm not here for much longer, I tell you. But if you're going to stay you'd better understand that these people are like the food they eat, they're cold fish. There's a muteness of the heart. It's all on the surface, they wear masks and the masks are changed at will. I just know that this country and this people are utterly and irredeemably corrupt. And if you want to stay here then you're going to have to come to terms with that sooner or later.'

They were silent then and sat staring at the food in front of them. At last, Jack asked about Megumi.

'I don't know,' David said. 'Perhaps I shouldn't have taken her on —'

'What is it? Losing interest, not doing the work, cancelling classes — that sort of thing? It's always the same. It's just a hobby for these bloody women, something to pass the time. Like everything else in this country, all form, no substance. They get this idea about learning English, and that's where it stops, with the idea. Try and actually get them to do some work —'

'No, it isn't like that,' David said. 'If anything she's too keen — too interested.'

Jack laughed, 'Oh yes, well just you be careful, mate. My experience has been that you can't trust any of the buggers, but the ones that speak English are absolutely guaranteed to be nutters. The better the English the loopier they turn out to be.'

David shook his head, 'I really think she might be ill. There's something — I don't know. One day she's fine, the next — I can't understand her.'

'Take my advice,' Jack said, 'and pack it in now. You don't need the money, for Christ's sake. Get on with this book you're supposed to be writing. Whatever you do, don't get involved. It's asking for trouble.'

David picked up a piece of chicken with his chopsticks and bit into it. It was cold now, and beneath the wizened skin the pale flesh gave off a faintly rancid smell.

There was a letter from Alison in his box when he got home. He tore it open as soon as he got to his room, his cold fingers fumbling the paper. 'I was wrong, I needed much less than three weeks. You can add The Great Romance to all the other short-lived affairs of the kind that seem to make up my life. Wonderful for four days, followed by doubts and recriminations and then the 'I'm-sure-we'd-both-be-better-off-without-this' bit. Now I don't know what I'm going to do. I feel I've made rather a fool of myself, but perhaps I had to. The job market looks even bleaker than a year and a half ago, so for the moment I'm sponging off my parents. As soon as the D.H.S.S. in Norwich re-opens I'll have to go in and sign on.

'I'm dreadfully tired and gloomy. Yesterday I went for a long walk, over winter fields and down to the sea. The bleakness of it all just about matched my feelings. Please write, Alison.'

David crouched on the little stool in his bathroom beneath the spray of hot water. Much of the space in the cramped little room was taken by the deep square tub. There was a small sink with a mirror where he shaved, the shower-nozzle on its short piece of rubber piping was set low in the wall. The Japanese soaped and rinsed themselves before getting into the bath, the water emptying through a drain hole set into the bathroom floor. David seldom bathed, he preferred to shower, but he never accustomed himself to the foetal posture he must adopt to do so, as he never accustomed himself to the shock of cold water seeping through his socks from the tiled floor whenever he went into the bathroom in the evening to wash after returning from work. He had tried to fix the spray higher on the wall, but the hose was not long enough, and in spite of all his efforts he could never quite dry the puddles from the floor. One of Jack Stevens' favourite stories was of the Japanese businessmen who regularly flooded the bathroom floors of some of the best hotels in Europe and North America; failing to find a drain they decided that it had been cunningly hidden by the architect and sluiced themselves down anyway. David had smiled the first time he heard the story, but he was not smiling now as the water fell upon his hunched shoulders. Beyond the panels of the folding door the gas heater slowly sent its warmth into the chilly corners of his room.

Still dripping, he stood on the kitchen linoleum and dried himself, then dressed in a suit he had bought recently; charcoal grey, with a broad-shouldered, double-breasted jacket. It was not the sort of thing he usually wore, but he had been with Nicky Stevens in the Parco building in Shibuya, seen and admired the suit and then, with Nicky's encouragement, he had tried it on, and finally decided to buy it. Now he was not so sure, but chose to wear it today because he was to meet Nicky at four o'clock that afternoon to go to an exhibition of Viennese Expressionist art. Later they were to join up with Jack for a film, and dinner afterwards.

The time was getting on and he struggled into his raincoat, swallowed the last of his coffee, and then balanced in the little tiled hallway trying to get his shoes on. It was cold outside, the road still covered with frozen slush, ridged and pitted by tyres, the cautious feet of humans. David pulled on his gloves, put his scarf about his neck. It was impossible to dress for this weather, in the overheated train, caught amid the crush of bodies, his under-shirt would be wet with sweat in minutes, and then the cold air on the walk from the station would reach through to the damp cotton and chill him again. Summer or winter, there was no comfort in the city.

Nicky was waiting for him outside the department store where the exhibition was being held. She smiled, glad to see him, taking his arm as they moved into the heat and light, the crowds of shoppers eager for bargains in the New Year sales.

The exhibition was crowded too, and it was hard to see the paintings properly. The Japanese filed dutifully past each exhibit, shuffling in line as if queuing, a momentary halt, the required glance at the work and then the momentum picked up again. Hot and increasingly impatient, David pulled Nicky to one side, 'This is impossible. We're wasting our time.'

'You want to leave?'

'No,' he said, 'I want to see the paintings, but this is ridiculous. We can't look at them like this.'

'We could come back tomorrow. You're not working, I'm free. We could get here when the store opens, take our time, perhaps have lunch together afterwards. What do you think?'

They left by the way they had come in, moving against the flow of the crowd. Glancing back over his shoulder David found himself staring at the petrified hysteria of Richard Gerstl's self-portrait.

They sat in a bar drinking Irish coffee. There was almost an hour to kill before they were to meet Jack. David, annoyed by the fiasco at the exhibition, was quiet, staring at the unhealthy-looking froth on the top of his glass. It was somehow reminiscent of the scum that formed each summer on the little brook that ran beside his parents' house. When he lifted the glass to his lips he got a sharp whiff of river-stink that caused him to put the drink down again without touching it.

'What's wrong? Isn't it good?' Nicky asked.

David lifted his hands, as if about to clap, 'No, it's — oh — I'm sorry. I'm annoyed about the exhibition. That's all.'

'Oh, come on. You don't have to apologize. We'll see it tomorrow.'

Nicky changed the subject suddenly, asking, 'Do you have many women friends, David?'

'No. Well, not here. There are women I knew at the Courtauld I'm still in touch with, and a girl who came to the department in Fez who I think of as a friend. Why?'

'Nothing, I just — You don't ever find it uncomfortable, odd somehow, to be with a woman but not be with her as a woman?'

'Do you mean do I ever want to fuck the women I'm friendly with?'

Nicky was shocked by the unaccustomed abruptness of his language, and, in truth, so was he. 'Yes,' she said.

David thought for a moment, and then said, 'I think I find, I know I find, all of my friends physically attractive, I said this before when you asked about Martin. Perhaps it applies more so to women. But there needs to be more than physical attraction, doesn't there? Well, there does for me. There are some people you go to bed with and some you don't. With friends, of either sex, I don't. Anyway, the way I thought about marriage didn't allow for other involvements.'

'That sounds so fucking smug,' Nicky said, her lip curled in displeasure.

David shrugged, ill-temper was contagious.

'I'm sorry,' Nicky said, 'I shouldn't have said that.'

'There's nothing to be sorry about. It was smug.'

'Since you came here, haven't you been involved with anyone? I mean, you spend a lot of time with Jack and me, but haven't you found a woman? It isn't as if you're really married any more. You're a good-looking bloke. I think women find you attractive. I do.'

David lied, said there had been no one.

A look of panic, of desperation, came over Nicky's face and she said, 'It's hard for me being alone with you, David. I'm in love with you and I want to go to bed with you. I want you, David. When I'm with you I want to touch you. You've never said anything, but I think you feel the same. Why don't we —?'

David said nothing for a while, 'That's quite the nicest thing anyone has said to me for a long time, but we can't. You're married. That's all there is to it.'

'There's no need for Jack ever to know. I don't want to hurt him. I don't want to lose my marriage. But I want this with you, as well. I don't see why I can't have it.'

'I suppose every man who has ever deceived his wife, every woman that has ever deceived her husband, has said what you've just said. They're always wrong. No matter how good you are at lying, in the end the lies don't work. They just poison everything. Look at me, I was so easy to deceive: the trusting husband, a long way from home, I still found out. Even with me away, Jean said the lying nearly killed her, that in the end she was glad I found out. She saw me twice in all those months, spoke to me maybe once a week on the 'phone, sent me the odd post card. You live with Jack, Nicky. I don't think you could do it. You're too decent a person.'

She sat sullenly across the table from him, the energy momentarily drained from her. At last she lifted her head. 'I'm a

woman, David, and I'm lonely. Jack does nothing but work.
When he isn't at the Council he's in his study beating his brains
out over a bunch of bloody verses that won't become poems. He
hasn't touched me in months. I'm a woman and I want a man. I
can't just be friends with you. You don't know what it's like being
here, being a woman here.'

David did not answer her. Finally she said, 'Well, Mother
always told me that if they turn you down they can at least do it
with a little grace, leave you your dignity. I suppose I should be
grateful to you for that.'

David paid the bill, and they went out into the cold street. On
the crowded sidewalk Nicky kept much farther away from him
than she usually did, and was silent until they got to the place
where Jack Stevens was waiting for them. David, walking behind
her, felt his gut turned with the knowledge that he was following
a woman who had just offered herself to him.

When they found Jack, Nicky took him in her arms, gave his
lips a long kiss that drew the disapproving glances of the
Japanese. Walking to the cinema she had her arm about her
husband's waist, in spite of the encumbering coats and gloves,
the difficulty of moving through the crowd. David wondered at
her dissimulation, found himself, adulterer anyway in his
desires, unable to meet his friend's eyes.

He went alone to the exhibition the next day and was greeted
again by Gerstl's manic face. Nicky had called him early that
morning, while Jack was in the bath, and said she could not go.
'It isn't because of yesterday. I really want to come. It's just Jack
arranged for us to have lunch with the Duckhams so I have to be
with him. I want to see you again, David. I'm sorry about what
happened. It was stupid of me.'

He wandered from painting to painting, not really looking at
them yet, scanning, getting to know the arrangement of the
room, marking this one, this one, this one, as points to come back
to. But even with such a cursory sweep he found his eye pulled to
the Schieles. They had a fascination for him. Dead from
influenza at twenty-eight, dead just days after his wife, Schiele
knew all about how the flesh deceives. He flayed his subjects,

hanging them on the canvas like meat on a butcher's hook. The flesh was given raw, as if in some savage communion, to be swallowed or spat out. You took it all, the pain, the degradation, the unpleasantness, the filth of being human, or you took nothing, left it alone.

When he got to the last piece, the portrait of Schiele's younger sister and lover, Gerti, David turned back and began to walk more slowly. He stopped before another Schiele, a painting of a man and a woman, lovers.

The tones were sinister, all browns, lit only by a spread sheet and four splashes of orange which were echoed in the man's lips, the nipples of the woman; dead carp on the surface of a poisoned stream. The perspective was strange, as if the artist were at once above and yet facing the subjects, as if he were a husband come home too soon. The lovers' sheet was rucked from their mating, which seemed to have been sudden, urgent, desperate. The man, lying back at an angle, made awkward by the odd, twisted perspective, had his arms spread, his satisfied face turned towards the viewer. He was naked but for a shirt still left half on. The woman crouched on her knees and arms, the top of her head down upon the sheet, hiding her face in the crook of her lover's arm.

David turned away, unable to look any longer. He knew that Jean had lain upon such a sheet, with such a man. He remembered questioning her when he had first found the letter, and she had tried to deny that it meant what it said, about what she did with her lover. Finally she had screamed at him, 'I let him fuck me. I let him fuck me whenever he wants to. That's what you want to know, isn't it? And if he doesn't want to fuck me I suck his cock until he does. That's what I do. That's what I do.'

After half an hour he had had enough. He went into a coffee bar and asked for coffee and straight whisky. He had swallowed the scotch before the waiter could put the bill down on the table and asked for another. The boy brought it, and David tossed it back at once as if taking a desperate cure for the illness that ate him.

In his pocket he had a letter from Martin, an answer to the one he had sent on New Year's day telling him what had happened with Jean. It was not the reply he had been expecting. He took the letter out, moving his gaze across it as swiftly as he had walked among the paintings, choosing to stop at the parts most painful to him.

I wasn't surprised to get your letter; Jean wrote in May, almost as soon as you'd left for Japan. I wasn't really surprised then either, given the situation over the past three years something of the sort was almost bound to happen.

I was in Edinburgh for a show just before Christmas and saw Jean. She's been badly messed up by all of this and wasn't particularly coherent, but from what she told me it seems as if for a long time you've been trying to hold together something that doesn't want to be held together, on either of your parts. You say you left Jean to go and look for work, another perspective might be that you weren't willing to make the sacrifices necessary to stay with her, have you thought about that? You can't make a marriage out of thoughts and ideals, David. A marriage is about being with one another, growing, compromising.

I met the man she's involved with, as well. He struck me as being a bit of a know-it-all, a smug sod, but he isn't a monster, David. You can't just categorize him as a piece of slime and dismiss him. You've always had a tendency to do that, you know, right from the beginning. He's a bloke who got involved with somebody else's wife. His own wife has kicked him out and is divorcing him, and he doesn't really know what to do. I got the feeling that the reality of the present situation terrifies both him and Jean.

What worries me most is the bitterness, the viciousness of some of the things you say. You've got to try and come to terms with this. Jean told me that you were getting a divorce so your marriage to her is over. You must try and adjust to a new life. The decision is made. I know it will be hard, and that it's easy for me to give glib advice, but try to take what you can from all that's happened. Grow, see life in a new way. Enjoy the things it has to offer, that includes women and sex when they have a meaning and a feeling that is strong for you. Fuck it, enjoy them even when they don't.

I can't say I know how to feel. What happened to me with Lynne wasn't the same as what's happened with Jean. What I can say is that, okay, Jean has hurt you terribly, but we're all human, and being human we're selfish and we're weak. What's happened to you has happened before. You are not unique in this.

David read on,

You said you didn't want me to take sides, and I won't, but I can sympathize with Jean in some ways. I haven't told anyone else this and I tell you because you're my best mate and I'm not afraid to say that I love you; the night Lynne died the people at the hospital tried to find me and couldn't. I was with some whore. I mean whore quite literally. By the time I got home and the hospital reached me, Lynne was dead. There are a lot of excuses: I can trot them out one after the other. The fact remains, though, that I let Lynne down at the very moment she needed me most. There's nothing I can do to make it up to her except get on with my life. There's probably nothing Jean can do to make things up either, although as you're still living and breathing the possibility at least exists. And for you, nothing you can do now will ever alter the facts of what's happened.

So, stop feeling so fucking sorry for yourself and get on with your life, David. Shout and cuss and do whatever you have to do, but get it over with quickly, or else you'll end up a bitter, lonely man.

David swallowed his coffee down to its dregs, paid the bill and walked out into the street. He had had enough of warnings.

The winter continued cold and treacherous, deceiving with a rash of sunlit days and then throwing another snowstorm upon the city. People shuffled along through the frozen muck, shivering, uncertain which steps to trust. David grew tired, longed for the spring. In March a week of mild weather brought the plum trees into blossom, but sudden, heavy snow broke the petals, buried them on top of the dead grass.

He worked, at the university and with Megumi Iwase. Each time she came to meet him she would bring with her a small gift, a box of candies, flowers. She liked his apartment and, as soon as she arrived, would busy herself in the kitchen making tea, or placing the flowers she had bought for him in water. David did not have a vase and so, the first time she had presented him with one of the small, beribboned and cellophaned bouquets, she had washed out a tall, all but empty honey jar she had found in one of the cupboards, filled it with water and set in it the slender green stems of a dozen yellow freesias. David stared at the flowers after she had left. The day was cold and the scented blossoms had seemed at that moment to contain all of winter. He shivered. His mother would have said someone had just stepped on his grave.

That evening, in the lamplight, he had looked again at the honey jar. The water was muddied and the white tips of the stems pressed against the glass like drowned fingers. He had a sudden sensation of the smell of a river and a woman dying, the Millais *Ophelia* in the Tate. He took the jar into the kitchen, where he threw the freesias into the trash, washed out the jar and set it on the stained drainer to dry.

Megumi Iwase was strange, her moods as unreliable as they were unpredictable. She had bad days when her whole body shook and she could not think, was only half-coherent. He wondered why she came then, and when he asked she told him it was because she needed to. Once, when her nerves were bad she stammered into tears over a reply to a question he had asked. He gave her his handkerchief, took her walking in the snow and afterwards drank steaming cups of chocolate with her in a café they passed. On her good days she was bright, intelligent, eager for the work.

In March they began meeting three times each week, at their normal times, and then on Tuesday mornings when Megumi would help David with his Japanese in return for extra teaching. Once or twice they went together to the cinema, but Megumi disliked the evening crush which left her breathless and panic-stricken, and David found it difficult to get away for afternoon shows.

When he was not working he would go to the cinema with the Stevenses. He was not often alone with Nicky now, but when he was there was little tension between them. Just once he had thought she was about to say something, but she held back whatever it was. He wrote letters, telling people where he was, what had happened between him and Jean, as if it were a death that had constantly to be reported. And as with a death, he, the bereaved one, bore himself properly in public, acted as it seemed he was expected to, as he expected to, in public. Alone he gave in to the shame and hate and despair he carried with him always, a weight that grew, slowly breaking him. His hair began to fall out, sleep was a stranger to him, or when it came would leave him in the night hours sweating with fear, certain that there was evil in the room with him, waiting for the greyness of the dawn. His skin ripened like an adolescent's and he began to take days off from his work, hiding his face in its shame.

More and more David lived for letters, quickening his pace from the station to reach his mail-box. Friends wrote, offering sympathy, advice. He replied, spreading the poison within him thick upon the paper, like a surgeon draining an abscess only for it to fill again. Alison was the one person for whom he had words other than the repetitive narration of his plight. She was in London, having moved there on money he had loaned her. She had found a job in an antiquary's shop, shared a flat with friends from Oxford, said she was happy enough.

She wrote, 'Life here relaxed and pleasant, especially Sundays. I'm usually the only one here most week-ends. I go out for the papers, croissants, and then get back and make a pig of myself. In the afternoon I stroll round to the Tate, or if I'm feeling a bit more energetic take the tube to the V&A. T.V. at night. Still, for all that, it doesn't satisfy me deep down. I want someone to share it with. More challenges.'

At the beginning of March she wrote asking if he could look out for a job for which she might apply as she thought she wanted to come back to Japan. Then, two days later, she telephoned to say she was coming back, and could she stay with him until she got settled into a place of her own again. 'To begin with, while we see how it goes, could we just share the space rather than each other?

Is that all right, love?' David said it was. And at the beginning of
March Jack Stevens announced that he and Nicky were leaving.

Jack told him one dark afternoon when he came unannounced
to David's apartment in Nakano. David was in the middle of a
lesson with Megumi. He felt startled, and for some reason he
could not explain to himself, guilty, to be thus surprised.

It seemed Jack had applied to the British Council for a post as
the director of the Council school in Lisbon, having been assured
by Richard Duckham that his appointment was a foregone
conclusion. He had been given a preliminary interview in
London during the Christmas vacation, but said nothing about
it, swearing Nicky to silence. Now he was invited to a final
selection board. The news had been telexed from London, and on
the day he had received it Jack had given notice to the university
of his resignation.

When David asked him if he thought he could really trust
Duckham's word Jack smiled, 'I don't need to. The rep talked to
me when I called in for the telex and said he intended to speak to
people on my behalf when he goes to London next week. It's the
bastards here I've never trusted. Did Ron Moody, the guy that
was here before you, tell you how he ended up back in London?'

David shook his head.

'He was walking down the corridor to his office and some
geezer comes up to him and says he's heard Ron is leaving. Now
this was news to Ron, so he was a bit surprised, right? During the
following week this happens a lot, people saying they are sorry
he's going and that. Turns out Ron had been getting a bit from
some married woman in one of his night classes; the husband
found out and reported Ron to the university. The buggers
sacked him, gave him a month's notice, without telling him why.
Never gave the poor sod a chance to defend himself. He only
found out why he'd got the push when the woman told him what
her husband had done.

'It's what I mean about living in a country full of spoilt fucking
kids. It's all right to go around screwing your students, or your
mates' wives, but you've got to do it discreetly, especially if
you're *gaijin*. I heard from one of the part-timers that the subject
of conversation in the staff-room among the men after we arrived
was the size of Nicky's tits. This is because she dresses like a
normal woman and not Mary-fucking-Poppins. They even asked

this guy if a foreign woman like Nicky would be naturally randy, and what their chances might be. He reckoned the *sensei* were practically coming in their fucking trousers thinking about it.

'I tell you, mate, the one thing I've done at that place and enjoyed is handing in my notice. You should have seen their faces, couldn't fucking believe that some poor foreigner would leave of his own free will. Couldn't fucking believe it.'

All this while Megumi sat at the table between the two men. When at last Jack Stevens had finished, she said quietly to David that she would like to make a cup of coffee.

'Be a love and make one for me while you're out there,' Jack called after her as she walked into the kitchen. Then he turned to David and asked in a quieter voice if this was the woman David had talked about. David made no reply.

She put Jack's cup in front of him on a tray, with a tiny jug of cream and a bowl of sugar. Jack said, 'The next time some bugger tells you to make a cup of coffee — or tea — you tell them to make it their fucking selves. All right?'

Megumi nodded. She drank the boiling liquid in her own cup in large sips, and then, excusing herself to David, put on her coat and ran into the night, leaving the men to their talk.

THE HOUSE BY THE RIVER

The March snows lingered on in the side-streets like soiled linen in emptied rooms. It was a time of departures. Jack and Nicky had only two weeks before their going and the house in Mitaka now wore an abandoned look as the things that had made it their home were packed away into crates, awaiting shipment to England.

Jack was happier than David had ever seen him. He raced about the city transferring money, arranging airline tickets, busy at all the tasks necessary for leaving: a terrier joyful with the long-sought rat between his teeth. Nicky's mood was harder to divine, she was quiet, and had about her an air almost of regret. One Tuesday, with Jack, as ever, busy on Council business, she had David over for a last lunch in the house before everything was taken away to the docks in Yokohama. They ate in a kitchen stripped of her pots and plants, the little tubs of herbs which still sat on the single window-sill above the sink dry and wilted from neglect, the Rothko poster from the Tate askew, peeling dusty sellotape from two corners. There was an air of finality about it all.

A part of David Kennedy's life, too, was ending. He was to leave his apartment in Nakano. On the last day of the school year, in February, David had met Asano. They had exchanged the usual pleasantries, but when asked if he was still happy in his apartment David said he was not. The next morning Asano came to David's office before classes began with a thick book, shaped like the *Manga* comics the students and businessmen read on the trains. However, instead of the violence and sexual grotesquerie that David expected, this contained lists of property available for rent in the city. Asano had already prepared a selection of possible properties for David to see, and he immediately began telephoning estate agents to arrange inspections. Within a week David had agreed to rent a house in a district along the Inokashira line called Kugayama.

The house, owned by a businessman sent overseas by his company, stood several minutes walk from a main road, at the edge of a small river. Once the inhabitants of old Tokyo had come here to picnic and view the sacred mountain of Fuji, now the Kanda was a dirty stream set between steep walls of grey concrete. Yet the pathway along it was overlapped by the gardens of the houses, and fifteen minutes brought the stroller to the quiet spaces of Inokashira Park, and the lake in which the river had its beginnings.

It was, by Japanese standards, a large house, with three rooms, a kitchen and bathroom. Two of the rooms were floored with *tatami* matting, their windows screened by *shoji*. There were huge cupboards with papered doors for storing *futon*. Facing the river-path was a garden, a straggling, winter-worn collection of vines and curled leaves dotted here and there with spoiled pots, an abandoned urn, all beneath a wide and full-spread tree.

The estate agent who showed David and Asano around had apologized for the state of decoration inside. It was a new house, and the owner had been just about to take possession when news of his transfer came through. For David, though, the whiteness of the walls, the lack of fittings, was a blessing. He took the house without hesitation.

Megumi went with him to buy the furnishings, a trestle table and chairs, carpet and sofa, a desk, shelves, coffee table. He chose everything in black, with the palest shade of oatmeal for the carpet and curtains. There was no colour, only the extremes of shade. The things were delivered and installed, and in two days the house was ready. He would stay in Nakano for another week, packing the few things he had there and arranging for them to be taken to the new house, but in his mind he already lived by the river. Before he left to return to his mean little apartment in the shadow of the black tower, he visited the florist's shop he had noticed on the corner of his new street. There he mused among the plants, choosing at last a small bowl of cacti rooted in grey, dry stones. He returned to the house and set it on a small black table by the window.

Suddenly, or so it seemed, in those last days they were to stay in Japan, Jack and Nicky Stevens again began spending time with David. Jack was always busy, finishing his work for the Council, overseeing removal men, worrying travel agents, extracting the last penny owed to him from the university, giving the last of his classes. He was happier than David had ever known him. Late one afternoon he and David walked together towards the station, their teaching finished for the day. On a winter lawn, with the sky reddening behind the buildings of the city, twenty or so girls from the university ski club were spread in a circle, each girl dressed in her uniform track suit. As the two men drew level with them, the girls bent forward, thrusting their buttocks up in unison. 'Evening ladies,' Jack said. For David he added, 'One of the few things I shall miss about this place, a ring of roses.'

He left his wife much alone at that time. David, secure in his happiness with the new house and the unshared knowledge that soon Alison would be there with him, was pleased to see Nicky. The lessons continued with Megumi, of course, but at the other times it was Nicky who was David's almost inevitable companion.

They visited the museums and galleries, the art shows in the department stores, the private galleries in the Ginza. Because his Japanese had improved so much since the lessons with Megumi, it was now David who led, Nicky who followed. With the key of language, the city opened before him and he stood aside to show his companion what treasures he had found.

On the last night he would spend in Nakano, coinciding with the last but one night Nicky would sleep in Tokyo, David took her to the *Kabuki-za*. There, in the tiers of balconies that rose before the stage, amidst the splendour of silk and brocade, the Japanese watched the passions they could not themselves show made manifest; the words they could not understand, but the gestures, the signs, they knew: love and betrayal, passion and deceit, jealousy, sacrifice, revenge. It was a world so false it was real, more real than life. Women thronged the theatre to watch the *onnagata*, actors who, in their transitions, became the unattainable ideal of a sex not their own.

During one of the intervals, David and Nicky wandered through the lobbies, watching the families arranging marriages for their sons and daughters, looking at the constant consumption of food and drink that seemed to be as much a part of the *Kabuki* as the play itself, dodging the streams of Americans hustled in to watch the one act of the drama scheduled on their Glittering Night Tour of the city. Nicky saw a table in one of the smaller restaurants, and they ordered coffee.

'So how is it?' David asked. Nicky had been quiet, saying little before they got to the theatre, and almost nothing since the play had begun.

'It's — beautiful, but somehow I don't quite think the word is right. I've never seen anything like this before. It's like a cartoon, but not Disney. It's like paintings come to life and given direction by a poet.'

'I thought perhaps you were finding it boring. Not many of the Japanese stay for the whole show, they treat it in much the same way some people do opera in the West, pop in for the good bits and then leave. It's quite unusual for this theatre to put on a whole play, in fact, mostly they do highlights.'

'Quite the expert now, eh?'

David shrugged, 'I suppose so.'

'I didn't mean that the way it sounded, David. Don't be hurt. I — you've shown me so much in the past few days. I've missed so many things in this country. I'm going to get on that plane with a bag full of regrets. Jack and me, we, it's like we kept our eyes closed for most of the time we were here, hoping that when we opened them again it would be England outside the kitchen window. Soon it will be, and I'm going to feel I spent two years holding my breath when I could have been breathing. This week I've been walking around the city unafraid for the first time, not scared about getting lost, or going into restaurants because I knew I wouldn't be able to read the menu and would have to drag the waiter outside and point at the plastic, and not worrying about money because you paid for it all. And I've been seeing it all with new eyes, your eyes. I always said you had nice eyes, David, they see lovely things. The women here, they are lovely, and it isn't all drabness and shit just under your feet the way Jack always said. We've missed so much. I swear to God when we go to Lisbon, I'm going to do it right. I'm going to learn the language, I'm not going to be trapped in my fear.'

'It's difficult the first foreign country you live in, Nicky. Second times are always better.'

She said, 'What if there wasn't a first time?'

David stared at her. A bell rang, the signal for the next act to begin.

The business of the final move from Nakano presented no difficulty. David put the last of his things into two bags and then walked to the station. He left his key in the landlady's mail-box with a note of appreciation in Japanese that Megumi Iwase had written for him. As he walked along the little street towards the station, past the kimono shop, the fruit-seller's and the florist's, he felt a certain small sense of regret, but he did not look back.

Megumi was at the house by the river for her lesson at eleven-thirty. It was one of her better days, and she seemed to share David's pleasure in his new home as she made tea in the light, airy kitchen. David had bought electric radiators and the whole house was warm. For the first time since he had known her, Megumi took off her woollen cap.

They had just begun the lesson, sitting at the kitchen table, when the door-bell rang. David lifted the entry-phone from the wall, spoke into it in Japanese.

'Hi, David, it's me. Nicky.'

He brought her into the kitchen, introduced her to Megumi as Mr Stevens's wife. Megumi shrank back before Nicky's size, her blond hair, her total otherness.

Offered tea, Nicky declined, saying, 'No, it's okay. I really don't want any. I didn't realize you were actually moving today. I went over to Nakano, but your landlady said you didn't live there anymore. The house is nice with the furniture in. I'm sorry — I'm disturbing your lesson. Look, can I wait in the other room or something. I really want to talk to you. Can I do that?'

David showed her into his sitting room, where she went to stand by the window, the fingers of her right hand all but touching the sharp thorns of the cactus garden.

'So what happened, Nicky?' David said when Megumi had gone. He had abandoned the lesson after ten minutes, Megumi, unable to speak, had simply sat and stared at him as if the victim of some terrible act of betrayal.

'Nothing, nothing happened. I mean, why should something have to happen for me to come over and see you?'

'I thought you and Jack were going to be very busy today. We're not supposed to meet up until tonight.'

'Well, Jack's busy of course, but I just wanted to see you.' She got up and moved towards him, but he lifted his hands, fending her off. 'Don't push me away, David, please. My feelings for you haven't changed.'

He said, 'I can't do anything else but push you away, I thought you understood that.'

'I don't understand anything. I just wanted to love you, David, that was all. I didn't ask you to love me back. I wanted to give you something.'

'It wasn't something that was yours to offer or mine to accept. You're married, Nicky.'

'Oh yes, I'm married to a man who, when he came here, was going to be the best bloody Council teacher Japan had ever seen, and when he found out he couldn't be, he decided to devote all that talent, all that energy, to getting out of the place. I'm not married to Jack, I'm married to whichever obsession he has on him at the time. If you and me had been having an affair Jack wouldn't even have noticed, he'd have been too busy.'

'I'm sorry,' David said.

'You're sorry. Thank you very much for the sympathy.'

There was a long silence between them, the only sounds the sighing of doorways, the whispers of sinks and closets, the secret language of an unknown house.

'If you didn't — if you weren't interested, why did you spend so much time with me? I mean, did you honestly believe Jack knew where I was all those times I was over at your room in Nakano? And always there was that bed of yours sitting there.

Why didn't you take me? Why didn't you want me? At least that?'

He said he was going to make some tea.

'I don't want any fucking tea, David! I want you. Jesus Christ, I'm leaving tomorrow, I just once — I just want once. I — just one fuck. How much is it going to cost you?'

He stared at her, 'More than I'm willing to pay.'

She left without speaking.

David Kennedy ran by the river in the early morning quiet, passing old men with dogs, paper boys, other runners stopping for breath. The sun was up, housewives, sure of a fine day, were already draping *futon* from verandah railings to air. In April spring had come, as if at a command. And, also as if at a command, the city had blossomed. Everywhere cherry trees broke into extravagant mops of white and pink, hiding the drabness of the dusty streets after the long winter. In the park where David jogged, turning the corner of his route, the light changed with the density of blossom, almost pulling the eye away from the newspapers, the sheets of cardboard, abandoned bottles and beer cans, and all the other detritus of the drunken parties the Japanese held beneath the trees to salute the sudden oncome of the season.

Wind shook the trees as he ran, scattering blossom onto the path. When David came from his house each morning, it looked as if some fantastic wedding had taken place in the night, a giant bride run from the altar, scattering confetti in her train. The pink blossoms etched with red, portents of a bloodied consummation.

He had been back at the university for two weeks now and was busy, busier than he should have been, for there was as yet no replacement for Jack Stevens and David was teaching most of his classes as well as his own. Yet the work did not tire him. He was up at six each morning, ran for thirty minutes, showered, ate breakfast, dressed and took the train to the university. Even with the extra classes he was back in the house by the river at four o'clock most afternoons. Because he duplicated his lessons he had little preparation to do and now, at night, he had begun to work on his book again. He knew he was not writing anything of worth yet, but he was writing.

Jack and Nicky were gone. The last evening had been difficult. The Stevenses seemed to have quarrelled and in the end the three Europeans did not go to dinner but, as they had so often done before, sat in a cinema in Shinjuku. Going home, David shared a train with Jack and Nicky as far as Kichijoji, and when he got off stood to wave farewell, the crowd jostling around him, Nicky's face obscured by the drunks. He thought perhaps she might telephone on the Saturday morning, but she did not. They vanished as if they had never been.

Alone now, he worked and ran, and waited for Alison. She was in London still, but working as a croupier in a casino to earn the money for her fare. David had offered to give her the money, lend it to her, but she refused, she wanted to do it alone. It would only be a few extra weeks. In May she would come, she had made her reservation. He waited.

David and Megumi prepared for her examination. The week before the test he saw her every day for long repetitious sessions, reading the nonsensical patterns of words over and over, marking her written work, timing, consoling, reassuring. The test was to be held at ten o'clock on the Saturday morning and would be over by twelve-thirty. Megumi promised to telephone.

He walked to Kichijoji to shop in the Miuraiya store for bread and cheese, and a bottle of wine. He thought to ask Megumi to come and eat lunch with him, a reward for her hard work. He had no doubt she would do well. She had left the night before, nervous but confident, aware of the arbitrariness of many of the answers to the questions, sure of her own abilities. He got back to the house at twelve, put on a kettle to boil for coffee while he unpacked the things he had bought.

The 'phone rang at a little after twelve-thirty, a wrong number. He set the receiver back in its cradle and went into the kitchen, poured another cup of coffee for himself and waited.

When he heard his doorbell at four he went to let her in, knowing that it was Megumi. She stood in the doorway, dishevelled, her face like that of some little animal dead of fright. He took her into the kitchen, sat at the table with her and waited. It was a long time before she spoke. And then it came in a torrent of disconnected sounds, English and Japanese, making no sense, yet eloquently conveying her misery. When she was quiet again, he opened the wine, making her drink. She let him lead her into the sitting-room where she fumbled in her bag for cigarettes and began to smoke.

'It isn't the end of the world, you know,' David said. 'You can take the test again. There'll still be time to register for the autumn session in the States. You made a mess of this one, well, next time you'll know better. It's good to make a mess of things sometimes, it helps us to learn.'

'You don't understand,' Megumi said.

'What don't I understand?'

'Why. About me and why.'

'You're right,' he said gently. 'When you speak English like that I don't understand.'

'I love you,' she said, beginning to cry.

'No, you don't.'

'No, I don't. I hate you.'

'Megumi, this won't help. I'm going to get you a taxi. I want you to go home, sleep. On Monday we'll start again.'

She did not come to the next lesson, or the one after that. He returned home after school on the Monday evening half-expecting to find her waiting for him, but she was not there. She did not call during the week, and there was no letter. He began to worry about her, but worry was all he could do. She had not given him an address or a telephone number. She said it would cause her parents concern if letters came to the house for her, or if a *gaijin* telephoned. They were old, she said, they would not understand.

Two weeks without a word, and then she reappeared. She looked thinner, and had cut her black hair back to a stubble beneath the wool cap. Her eyes were dark, as if she had ringed them with kohl. David asked if she had been ill and she said yes, she had been ill. Quietly, they began their lesson.

He found Alison's letter by accident. His door had a letter-box attached to the back of it, but all his mail was left in another box by the front gate. By chance his eye happened to catch the striped edge of the envelope through the grille as he closed the door behind him coming in from a run. The letter had been sent express and the postman, unable to raise anyone in the house by ringing the bell, had slipped it through the gap. He took it into the kitchen, slitting the envelope with a knife:

My dear David, at 3.10 on Thursday 29 April in Norwich Registry Office, Alison Elisabeth Tench married Peter William Davies by special licence in the presence of two lovely people . . .

After six days — I know I'm crazy — we both knew it was the right thing to do. Parents initially shell-shocked, but then so were we. Both sets of parents have now met and approved, the champagne flowed, our wedding goes on.

He's forty, with two boys of ten and fifteen from a previous marriage. He has a flat in Highgate, and a bit of a crumbling Georgian house — hard to explain — in Suffolk. He buys and sells things at enormous profits.

Well my dear — any questions??! I am absolutely happy, absolutely sure, committed with my whole being. I do hope you'll meet him, like him, or, at least, see why I like him.

Dear David, please let's go on being friends. Write. Come and see us when you're back in England. With all my love, Alison.

Megumi Iwase re-took the examination on David's thirty-seventh birthday. That afternoon she came to visit him carrying the soiled white canvas bag filled with dictionaries and grubby exercise books that was ever on her shoulder, and flowers.

'Happy birthday,' she said handing him the flowers, and then, rummaging in the canvas satchel, 'I bringed — brought you a cake. And this!' She pulled from the bag a flat, be-ribboned box and handed it to David. He carefully opened the package. Inside, shrouded in tissue paper was a darkly-stained wooden platter. David held it up to the light, examining the grain.

'It is like the sea,' Megumi said. 'The waves are in the wood, I think. I love the sea so much, David. I think it is inside me, like I am a shell. If I am in a bad time I stop and listen to the sea inside my body. Always the sound of the waves are with me. Now, you will have sea with you always. I present you with this sea.'

David sat at the table in the kitchen, while Megumi busied herself at the sink. She put the kettle on the little gas-top to boil for tea, and then began to cut away the elaborate wrapping of the cake box. The flowers sat, inelegantly, in a pitcher of water on top of the refrigerator. He held the wooden platter in his hands.

'It is a special cake for birthdays,' she said, sliding the heavily-frosted sponge onto a plate. 'Look!'

The icing was pink, and traced on the top of it in red, a Mobius strip with the names 'David' and 'Megumi' worked into it. Underneath was written, 'Happy Birthday, I like you x 1000 . . . 00.'

As they drank their tea, and David, at least, attempted to eat the impossibly sweet cake, he asked her about the test. 'I take it things went well this morning?'

She stayed on through the evening, and he was glad of her company. He cooked a simple dinner, spaghetti with a marinara sauce, salad. He opened a bottle of wine. For dessert, Megumi insisted they finish the birthday cake. Afterwards, at a sudden loss as to how he might entertain her, he took out his photograph albums.

The last time he was at his parents' house in Loxley, David had taken the family album. This book, with its paste-patterned green cover, had always been one of his life's great pleasures. It was kept in a cupboard underneath the stairs, and so had an indelibly musty smell that brought to his mind wet afternoons, and the school holidays that had seemed to be without end when he was a child. Over the years, the album had been plundered by his sisters, and the gaps left by them filled with colour prints of their own children. But there remained enough of the original, fading images for David to want to protect them. Those were his past.

He showed Megumi a photograph of his mother and father taken before their marriage in 1938.

'Your father was a soldier?'

David nodded, 'Yes, he joined the army just before war broke out. He doesn't talk about it very much, and my mother has never really forgiven him. He once told me he knew there was going to be a war and he felt he had a responsibility to help fight it. My mother wanted them to go back to Ireland, to the Free State, as she still calls it, but Daddy wouldn't go. He was sent to Singapore and was captured by the Japanese. He was a prisoner for the rest of the war.'

'I am ashamed,' Megumi said. 'We Japanese did terrible things in the war. Your father must hate me.'

'Don't be silly, my father doesn't know you, and I don't think he knows the meaning of the word "hate". Anyway, it was all a long time ago. It doesn't have anything to do with you.'

They turned the pages, filling with light the frozen images of summer, little girls in blossomy gardens, playing with their dolls, a favourite dog, or paddling in a grey, motionless sea.

'Are these your sisters?'

'Yes, they're my sisters. All three have families of their own now. Danae, the oldest, is a grandmother. I was the last born.'

In the world of the photograph album a baby appeared; fat and jolly-looking, with blond hair, always surrounded by loving women.

'It is you, David?' Megumi asked. When he said that, yes, it was him, she hid her laughter with her hand.

The baby grew into a boy, a boy in the garden where the little girls had played, a boy with the dog the little girls had been with, only old now, and feeble looking. David closed the album. 'Would you like to see the photographs I have of Morocco?'

He went to find the album with his Moroccan pictures in it, and, when he had found it, gave it to Megumi. 'Ah, that is you, David,' she said, turning the stiff, glossy pages, 'But you have very long hair and you have beard also!'

'Yes, that was just after we — ' he corrected himself, 'just after I got to Fez. That's the apartment building I lived in.' He wished he had not begun this, for he knew that soon he would have to explain about Jean.

Megumi turned another page, 'Who is this girl in the photographs?'

'It's my wife.'

She laughed, but he knew that it was from embarrassment.

'I don't talk about her very much,' he said, giving an explanation that had yet to be asked for.

'It is because she does not like Japan that she does not stay here with you?'

'No, it's me she doesn't like, not Japan. We're separated, *bekkyo*, understand?'

She nodded her head, apologized. 'And you will — how to say — *rikkon shimasuka?*'

David said that, yes, they would divorce.

'I am divorced,' Megumi said, staring at the carpet.

The loneliness that again came upon him was like the returning heat of the Japanese summer, at once familiar but yet half-forgotten. Once more it was the work that kept him sane, the necessary routine of the class-room. He had not time to question what he did, or why he did it; he did not think about the effectiveness of his teaching, he taught. He marked the assignments, prepared new material for the classes. He gave his life to the work, and the work gave a life to him. Then the term was over, and the long holidays began.

Again he made plans to impose an order on the suddenly empty days. He took out the work he had done on his book, read through the notes he had made, looked over the long sections, chapters almost, that he had written, left it all on the table ready to begin. Again the days dwindled into nothingness, aimless, hot afternoons and evenings, and then the terrible nights without sleep. On the first Wednesday of the holidays he forced himself out into the city, walking to Inokashira Park along the river in the heat of the late afternoon. He dawdled beneath the cooler trees, envying the fat carp, lazy in the waters of the lake, and then cut up a little street lined with coffee shops, meaning to reach Kichijoji, the station and a train back. As he passed along the street he saw some European girls, eighteen, nineteen perhaps, sitting in the black-tiled starkness of the Café Bois. His loneliness pushed him inside.

From his table he could see that they were even younger than he had thought. They were English, and were quarrelling in crude, northern accents. 'Shut up, you ratty cow', 'Fuck off, you!'. The motley outfits they wore marked them as 'models', a detachment of the raggle-taggle army that somehow got itself to Tokyo, earning a sort of living for a few months feeding the

Japanese advertising industry's insatiable appetite for the foreign and bizarre. After that some of them returned to wherever it was they had come from, the ones that stayed drifting into a life of cheap hostess bars, endlessly dodging Immigration, hoping one night they might take home a salary-man stupid enough and rich enough to set them up.

They had seen David come in, and soon one of the group came over to him. A tall girl, with acne pits the heavy make-up on her face could not cover and dirty, blonde-rinsed hair, she asked David if he was English. When he said he was she sat at his table, saying she was called Christine.

They were lost, she said, and almost out of money. David paid for the coffee and the cake they had eaten, told them he would take them to the station, that his train would get them to Shibuya from where they could find their way back to Roppongi. When he got off at Kugayama, the blond girl got off with him, sticking two fingers at the others as they whistled and called after her. They had been meant to be out on a photo-session, she said, but the Japanese girl who usually accompanied them had called in sick at the last moment and so they had been sent off with a hand-drawn map and their train-fare. They had ended up in the *kissaten* where he had found them.

The short July evening was darkening when they got to the house. Inside, he took the girl's things while she struggled to get out of her high-laced boots, then led her into the sitting-room. Standing apart from him she said, 'Where do you want to do it?'

Undressed, and damp from the shower she had taken, she seemed thinner than ever, the ribs and breast-bone evident beneath the skin, like an abandoned child in a Victorian illustration of poverty in the cities. David got his clothes off, asked the girl if she had any protection.

'I'm on t'pill,' she said. She lay on a white sheet on top of the *futon*, the mousy, draggled hair of her pubis covering her like a torn rag.

When he lay down with her, David asked how old she was. She said fifteen. Yet, for all her youth, she was a seasoned player in the grim rituals of copulation. David came inside her with a terrible force, her thin feet drumming his buttocks, his stubbled chin against her puny breasts, the nipples erect and wet with his slobber.

He fed her hamburgers and french fries he had fetched from the LOVE fast-food shop close to the station, not unaware of the irony of the name. He had gone alone, leaving her in the house; he could not help but wonder if she would be there when he got back and he dawdled, giving her time to leave if she wanted to, to take whatever there was that she could fit into her bag. He did not begrudge her. Yet she was still in the house, having taken nothing but his *yukata* to cover herself with. She was hungry, began stuffing one of the hamburgers he had bought into her mouth before he himself had got to the table.

He asked her about herself and her friends. They were from Lancashire — Bolton, Leigh, the surrounding towns. He wondered what their parents thought of them travelling so far from home alone.

'Us mams don't care. Glad to get rid of us for t'summer.'

He asked whether she was enjoying being a model. It was, she said, all right. 'Any road, better than t'Berni Inn. I work there as a waitress Saturday nights when I'm at school. You get good money, mind, off the drunks come in last thing. If you've got a short skirt on they're too busy sticking their hands up it to bother about the change.'

She swilled her mouth with cola, and then nodded towards the room with the *futon*. 'Do you want to go back for an hour?'

It was after midnight when the girl left. He had asked her if she wanted to stay, but she said she ought to get back to the hostel where her friends were. It was likely that they had been given work for the next day and if she did not get there until the morning she would miss the others.

Suddenly a child, she asked meekly if she could have another shower, 'See, we've only got this one big bath where we're staying and everybody has to use it together, like. Well, I find it a bit embarrassing.'

While she was washing he put some money into her purse.

He walked her to the station, buying a ticket himself and going with her onto the platform to make sure she got a through-train. Saying goodbye she thanked him for the hamburgers.

David Kennedy got back to the house and sat for a long time at the table in the kitchen. There was an emptiness within him that could not be explained by the silence of the empty house, he knew that he should feel something for what had just happened, excitement, shame, something. In fact he felt nothing, except for the slight, yet nagging, fear that the girl had been diseased and might perhaps have infected him.

When he woke the next morning, he knew he had to get away for the rest of the summer. He began telephoning travel agents and by the afternoon had made reservations for the following Monday on a flight to Boston, where his second sister, Sinead, lived. He would spend two weeks with Danae in California on his way back to Tokyo. The next day he went to the American Embassy for an entry visa, paid for his ticket and called his sisters to say that he was coming. He had not seen them for six years.

The only thing he regretted about leaving for the summer was Megumi. She had passed the examination with a good enough grade to take the place she had been offered at a college in Vermont, but she said she wanted to go on with her lessons until it was time for her to leave in late August. As the date of her departure drew close, David sensed that she had lost much of her enthusiasm. He knew it would be difficult to tell her of his plans when she came on the Friday.

Megumi seemed to bloom with the summer. Her hair had grown out from the cropping it had been given, and now was thick and heavy again on her head. She had put on a little weight, and her eyes had lost the look of fear that was so often in them. It was true that she still smoked constantly, although she tried to curb herself, David knew, when she was in his house, and always there were the tremors that shook her body. He hated himself for what he was going to say to her.

She knew he had left the kitchen door unlocked and so she came in unannounced, calling his name. She had flowers for him, and there was a melon in the basket she had taken to using for her work-books and dictionaries.

He told her as they sat over glasses of *mugicha*, the cold barley tea which is the drink of summer in Japan. She seemed to shrink from him as she understood what he was saying, and at the end of all his excuses could only say that she was sorry.

'Why are you apologizing, Megumi?' David said. 'I have to apologize to you because I'm letting you down. I'm really sorry, please believe that. The reasons I've just given you for going away are all true, but there's another, more important one that I haven't told you about. I have some problems in my life that I'm finding very difficult to deal with at the moment. I'm unhappy and I need to be with my family for a time.'

There was no lesson that day. Megumi's tears came violently, despite her obvious efforts to control them. She said she could not stay, and then ran from the house, knocking over the half-drunk glass of barley tea as she went.

The next morning he found a note from her in his mail-box, 'David, I wonder what I can began with? If there are several necessary rules to write a letter. I don't know.

'I really care about you, but you are in so bad a mood and going away. What did I do to deserve it? Now I will never see you again. I know this.

'I don't ask very much about you. I think I shouldn't ask you without you telling me. But remember, I always care for you. Sorry for my bad English and handwriting, Megumi Iwase.'

THE FIELD OF
AUTUMN LEAVES

He came back from America sickened by the excesses of an obese and diseased republic, a nation polluted with its own abundance. In Seattle, trapped for three days by a fog that had poured inland from the ocean's throat, he sat in an hotel coffee shop watching immense women devour wax-paper pitchers of ice cream and hot fudge, before ordering diet-colas. Eyes sunk in fat, polyester-wrapped thighs and arses that, in motion, rippled like congealed seas. He longed for the containment of Japan, the obedience to limitation. America made him foreign. He reached the house in Kugayama feeling that he had come home, and at once put on his running shoes, going out into the hot September night to sleek his body through movement. An act of purgation.

Whatever he had gone to look for in the United States he had not found. His sisters' sympathy, when he told them of the coming divorce, was for his parents, and neither of them would believe the little he said about Jean's infidelity. He had sat in their houses through long days of half-dressed children, the endless squalling of the television. Sometimes in Boston he would walk the unsafe streets, repulsed from any human contact by an antagonistic indifference. He was set apart, aside, like the food his sisters' children craved and then would not eat. America made him foreign.

The new term began. David was introduced to Jack Stevens'

replacement, a young man newly graduated from Cambridge, and ostentatiously homosexual. David gave the new teacher his telephone number, told him to call if he needed anything. The young man made a small and supercilious moue of his lips, and then turned back to pouring his refined contempt upon the Japanese who, oblivious, sat around him, rejoicing that at last they had an English gentleman and scholar among them.

It was two weeks later that he heard from Megumi Iwase. She telephoned; David, confused, asked where she was calling from. She said she was at Shibuya Station, that she needed to talk to him.

Megumi wore her summer clothes still. She had cut her hair again, and the little crochetted cap was back in place. He asked why she was not in America.

'I could not go. There are many things you do not understand of my life. It was impossible for me to leave.'

He asked her then what she intended to do. She did not know. 'Perhaps next year I will go. But I need to continue with our lessons. Since you went away I have not spoken English. My English is very bad.'

She got up to make some tea, and he followed her into the kitchen. As she turned her back to him, her shoulders heaved and she hung her head, she could not even bring the kettle to the sink for water. David moved quickly across to her, took her arm, asked her what was wrong.

'David, I miss you so much when you go to America,' she stood, half-turned from him, his hand still upon her arm.

'I know you are so strong person, and I want your strongness near to me. I know you have a lot of bad things in your life now, but you are strong for them. When I am near you I feel my foolishness pass away, and I am strong too, but when you go away my strongness goes with you.

'I think when something happens to you you don't lose control like me. You think calmly and always give a good judgement to yourself, and I know it that you always try to love me so I thought we don't have to discuss each other to know our way of thinking. I've thought always there can be an unspoken agreement between us. But then you go away to America and I think I can never see you again.'

He tried to comfort her, telling her it had not been in his mind that they would never see one another again when he left for Boston. He asked if this was why she had given up her place at Bennington College.

'No, no, there were other reasons, but really I think, I thought, you left Japan because you did not want to see me. I have to say a difference between us. You usually seem passive to your destiny. You try to do utmost in the destiny you are given. Even though I am weak I fight against my destiny. I try to live my life actively. I try to live like every day is my last day. When you go away I thought you would break our friendship, so now I want to tell you these things but my English is bad and you cannot understand me.'

She turned from his grip and moved away towards the door. David watched her. 'You don't have to go, you know. Not unless you want to.'

'I am ashamed.'

'There isn't anything for you to be ashamed of. You said you think I'm strong, I wish I had your strength, I wish I had your courage. You can stay if you want to, and if you want to, then I'd like you to stay.'

She remained by the door as David filled the abandoned kettle, and put it on to boil. When the tea was ready he carried it into the sitting-room not knowing whether she would follow or go off into the night. After what seemed like a long time she came in after him, sat down on the carpet by the coffee table and poured the tea.

David knelt beside her, took the white cap from her head. 'Why do you do this to your hair?' he asked, running his hand over the shorn stubble.

She answered him that it was her foolishness, but was silent as, later, he took the clothes from her, her body shivering as if she were a child come from the sea, afraid to cross the shingle to her parents and the proffered towels, the tray of sweet tea, cheese rolls. When he left her momentarily to fetch a cover for them to lie on she did not move. It was only after he too was naked that she became fluid, fitting her skin against his.

Megumi would not sleep at David's house after that first night; it was not possible, she said. There were things that David did not understand. Nor would she see him other than on the days when they had their lessons. He began to wonder if she had, perhaps, lied to him about being divorced and was still married. He grew concerned that his involvement with her might destroy him in the same way that Jack Stevens had said a similar involvement destroyed David's predecessor.

It was an odd affair. Megumi would come to the house on the days she had always come there, they would have their lesson and she would hand David the envelope containing the ten thousand yen. Almost at once she would leave the table and go to the room where he slept, pull the *futon* from the cupboard in which it was kept during the day, and, when the bed was made ready, undress and wait for him. Once, the first time, David watched, but she had sent him away saying that his eyes made her nervous. Afterwards, she would go to the bathroom to wash herself and put her clothes back on. She would not let him walk with her to the station, she would not let him embrace her before she left.

More and more it seemed that their coitus had become an extension of the sequence of movements that began with Megumi making tea. There was little spontaneity, less passion; it was as if the body into which he emptied his seed was vacant, a form without spirit, a house bereft even of its ghosts. She denied him nothing, but never herself made response, never spoke, allowed no sound past her lips, no sign upon her face.

Yet he was grateful to her, and felt she sensed that at least. He enjoyed her body, enjoyed its pale slimness, the sheen of her skin, the budded form of her tiny breasts with their dark, raised nipples. When she lay on top of him he would cup her sleek buttocks in his palms, or reach under to touch the smooth skin of her groin. When he wrapped himself about her he felt that she was like some fantastic sea-creature caught by a fisherman, a mermaid who would, if he did not hold on to her, slip from his grasp and back into the water that was her true element.

That first night, with Megumi sleeping beside him, David had dreamed of dolphins. He was visiting Jean in a city that was familiar, but where he knew he had never been before. She was surrounded by people, friends, men he knew were her lovers. They decided to go swimming, and soon, to his surprise he found himself in the baths that had stood at the back of his parents' house in Loxley. They were as he remembered them from his childhood: the pool, the tiered wooden seats, the drab, cream-painted lockers scarred with grotesque depictions of the human form, the physiology of ignorance. What was different was that there were sea-creatures in the pool, seals and dolphins, pale grey torpedoes that streaked below the surface tempting the human swimmers to follow them.

Jean and her friends were quickly in the water, but David lingered on the side, unsure of whether he could swim. He walked along towards the deep end, where the diving boards were and it was there, lying on the side, its poor tail in the guttering with the slops of the pool, that he saw the dolphin. It seemed dead as he approached, and only when he knelt by it, caressing the muted head, the closed eyes, did he know the creature was not dead, only dying. He called to Jean, who ignored him, intent on the games she was playing. Then, realizing he must act alone, he cupped his hands and began to splash water onto the dolphin, until slowly it started to revive, turning its eyes on him, rubbing him with its snout. He lifted it in his arms and put it into the pool and it was gone, leaving only a clear, viscous substance on his body where it had touched him.

He had awoken then into the half-light of the room, putting his hand onto Megumi's body, running it over the smoothness of her limbs as, in his dream, he had the smoothness of the dolphin. She had moved then and, half-awake, still wet between her legs, taken him into her again.

The days of September and October drifted by, each day breaking from the week like leaves from the twig, falling away to the litter of the past. In November, in David's garden, along the path by the river, the ground cleared itself for the harsh measures of the coming cold.

The ringing of the telephone woke him on a Saturday morning. He thought for a moment that he had overslept, but when he looked at his watch he saw that it was still only half-past six. The house was chilly this morning, and he did not feel like getting up into the cold for a wrong number, which it inevitably was. He turned over, closing his eyes. Whoever it was would get tired in a few moments, ring off.

The telephone continued to ring, insisting that it be answered. Panic suddenly emptied itself into the pit of his stomach. Perhaps it was a call from home, something had happened to his parents, or to Jean. He got up quickly and went into the kitchen. Lifting the receiver, he expected the shrill tone that announced an incoming overseas call, but there was nothing. He spoke in Japanese, still there was nothing, and he was about to hang up when he heard Megumi's voice calling his name.

She had not come the day before, but it was not that unusual for her to miss one of their days. She seemed to be sick a lot, complaining of headaches and fevers, skin rashes that erupted in the night and kept her confined to her house. David had missed her, but, because she still would not give him an address or telephone number, there was little he could do. Now, though, it was evident that she was distraught, and, from the few coherent pieces of language she was able to force from her throat, in some sort of trouble. She needed to see him at once, and so he told her to come over, but then she said he did not understand, she was in a hotel in Shibuya and had no money to pay for it. David got her to give him the name of the hotel and the address, and then, putting on the first clothes that came to hand, he ran out of the house for the station.

She was waiting for him in the lobby of a small, but quite decent-looking, business hotel in one of the small streets behind the Tokyu department store. She sat in her coat and hat, with a small suitcase and a couple of carrier-bags at her feet. A tired-looking clerk, a man in his forties perhaps, was behind the check-in desk, and, playing on the floor with a toy train, was a little child. When Megumi saw David come through the door she closed her eyes and her face broke as she began to sob. It was as if her body were suddenly collapsing, the flesh falling inwards with each expulsion of air from her lungs. David looked from her to the man behind the desk and then back to Megumi. Whatever the desk-clerk felt his face showed nothing to David, and the child on the floor continued to play with equal unconcern.

He knelt by Megumi for a moment, held her to let her know that he really was there, before going across to the desk. He said he wanted to pay the lady's bill and, when he had done so, returned to her. He spoke to her in Japanese, saying that he was going out to find a taxi, that he would be back as soon as he could. She said nothing, but gripped his hand so tightly she broke the surface of his skin with her nails.

He had to walk back to the Tokyu store to find a cab and the first one he hailed would not stop, so it took him longer than he had thought to get back to the hotel. Megumi was where he had left her, she had not moved, she looked completely incapable of any independent action. He helped her up from the chair, and then, half-carrying her, got her as far as the door. The child had begun to whimper as David was helping Megumi to her feet, now it screamed and ran towards them, clutching at Megumi's legs. Megumi opened her eyes, stared at the child and then at David. 'She is my daughter.'

He paid off the taxi and hustled Megumi and her little girl into his house. Megumi was weeping, incoherent; the little girl, terrified by all that had happened and, David knew, by his presence, stayed close by her mother, hanging on to her coat. He had some sedatives left over from the supply his doctor had given him the summer before, and he took two of them for Megumi to swallow with a little water. Then he got her into the room he used for sleeping, where the *futon* was still spread on the floor and, helping her from her clothes, made her lie down. All the time the child, whimpering in her fear, stayed by her mother. David covered them both with the quilt.

'The tablets I gave you will make you sleep,' he said. 'Afterwards, when you feel better, you can tell me about whatever it is that's happened.'

His eyes fell upon the child's face. She had her eyes screwed up tight, and her little cheeks were apple-red with crying. She lay, gripping her mother's arm as if it were the last thing in the world she could be sure of. 'What's your little girl's name?' he asked.

Megumi said that it was Kayoko. She began to cry again, but there was less terror, less pain, than before. 'David,' she said, 'you are so kind man.'

He left the room, sliding the door shut behind him. Then moving quietly about the kitchen, he made coffee. When it was ready he poured some of the thick, black liquid into a mug, stirred in a spoonful of honey and, just before he drank it, added a large measure of whisky.

Megumi slept on through the morning but David, sitting and staring at his empty coffee-mug, found his thoughts disturbed by a small voice which called '*Gaijin-san, gaijin-san*' behind him. He turned to see Megumi's little girl standing uncertainly in the doorway of the room where she had been with her mother.

'*O-shikko*,' the child said, but he did not understand. '*O-shikko datte-ba!*'

The comic urgency with which she spoke made clear what was the matter, and he led her across the kitchen and down the hall to the lavatory. When she came out to him again she was still trying to buckle the straps of her overalls, and David helped her. For the first time she smiled, the fear of him she had shown in the morning gone with her dreams. He asked if she was hungry; she said she was.

There was nothing in the house to eat and so he decided to take the child to the hamburger bar near the station. He asked her if she liked hamburgers. She nodded her head enthusiastically. Before going out he washed her face and combed and re-plaited her hair, then, when he had written a note for Megumi explaining where he had gone, the two of them set off.

Kayoko became very talkative as they walked along towards the station and David found it hard to follow everything that she was saying, but the little girl seemed not to notice or not to mind, and chattered on as if he understood every word. When they came to the main road she reached up and took his hand.

The hamburger bar was crowded with teenagers, but David found a place at a table close to the window and lifted Kayoko up onto the high stool. When he returned with his tray the child's eyes were wide with excitement. He handed her the burger and french fries she had asked for, and she began to eat.

The women who worked in the LOVE hamburger bar knew him by sight. Now, sitting with Kayoko, he was aware that they were staring at him. One of them came across to clear away the mess of paper and half-eaten food at an adjacent table. When she had finished she turned to David, asking if Kayoko was his daughter. He answered that she was the daughter of a friend. The woman fussed over Kayoko and then went into the back of the shop, returning a few moments later with some candies for the child. Kayoko, her face still serious with the business of eating, took the sweets and put them in her pocket.

They walked across the railway tracks to the supermarket when they left the hamburger shop. David bought some groceries and fruit and then took Kayoko upstairs into the section selling clothing and hardware. The things the child was wearing were filthy and he did not know what Megumi had brought with her. He held a pair of gingham dungarees against Kayoko to check for the size, asked her if she liked them. He also bought a sweater and blouse for her, and some underwear and socks. When he had finished getting her clothes, he allowed himself to be led over to the toy section. Kayoko asked if she could have a colouring book and a packet of felt-tipped pens. He put them into his basket with the clothes.

Megumi was still asleep when they got back to the house with their shopping. David took the little girl into the bathroom, ran water into the deep tub, and then helped the child out of her clothes. He took his own socks off, rolled up his trousers and his shirt-sleeves, and gently washed her tiny body. When she had been soaped and rinsed, he lifted her into the tub and stood watching her for a moment as she splashed and played in the water, before going out into the kitchen to take off the wrappings and tickets that festooned the clothes he had bought.

Late in the afternoon, when Megumi called from the bedroom, Kayoko, who had been colouring at the kitchen table with David, rushed in to show her mother her new things. Megumi smoothed the child's hair, but then pushed her gently away. She looked ill and frightened, and David was concerned for her.

He asked if she felt like eating something and when she said that she would like some soup, he went back into the kitchen to get it ready. He could hear Kayoko's excited chatter as she told her mother where the *gaijin-san* had taken her and the things they had done together.

Megumi ate the soup, but then said she must sleep again. David took the tray back into the kitchen, sliding the door to the bedroom shut behind him. He did not know what to give Kayoko to eat and so, when she said she was hungry, he took her to the hamburger bar by the station again.

They spent the evening together in the sitting-room. The colouring book was now completely covered with a garish assortment of tones and shades, and David amused the child by filling sheet after sheet of typing paper with the cartoons he used in his language classes.

It was almost midnight before Kayoko fell asleep. He went to fetch a blanket and a pillow, and then, gently easing off the dungarees and sweater he had dressed her in earlier, he laid the child on the sofa, covering her tiny body with the soft folds of the blanket.

Exhausted himself, he wondered where he should sleep. He did not want to sleep with Megumi. It was partly so as not to disturb her but, more than this, he did not want the child to find them together in the morning. He put some cushions on the carpet by the sofa and made his bed there. He was soon asleep.

It took a long time to find out exactly what had happened to Megumi. Like a small animal hibernating from the terror of winter she slept on and on, waking only when her body's needs urged her to the surface of consciousness. It was the Sunday evening before she came to sit with him and Kayoko in the kitchen, and then she asked for more of the tablets she had been given the day before.

David shook his head, 'No, I can't do that. I think you should take a bath while I make us something to eat, and then I want to know what this is all about. I want to know what has happened.'

She took Kayoko into the bathroom with her. When they came back there was food on the table. Kayoko constantly chattered to her mother, but Megumi ate in silence. It was late when the meal was finished and while David cleared away the things Megumi made up a bed for Kayoko in the sitting-room. When the child was settled she came back into the kitchen and sat at the table. David turned from the sink to face her. 'So, what happened?'

Megumi had often told him that he did not understand about her life, and when she had finished telling him her story he knew that what she had said to him then was the truth.

'Before I can tell you what happen now, I have to tell you my story. My English is so poor and the things I must say are difficult, I think. Please do not grow angry with me. I want to tell you, I want you to understand.'

'When have I ever been angry with you, Megumi?' David said. 'I just want to know what has happened so that we can decide what is the best thing to do.'

She began to cry. 'I know, you are the most kind man I have met. Really I want to tell you what happened but I must tell you about myself before, or you will not understand the thing that happened yesterday.

'My parents are very old now, and I am all their children, but once I had a brother. He was so clever a boy, David. He was my father's great pride in his life. He was a student at Todai, the great university of all Japan. He was so clever, the best boy in his class, the most popular. Then he died. He lived in a small apartment close to the campus and came back to us at the weekend. Except that one weekend he did not come. My father went to his room and found him there. He had been dead for a long time. The doctors said it was heart attack, but I don't think that is the truth. I think he takes his own life. I think my father believes this also.

'When I am eighteen years age I go to university. I want to be dancer and I win place at the University of the Performing Arts in Kyoto. A very great professor there is my father's friend and I am to live with his family while I am student.

'In the beginning everything was very fine. I am happy, my work is very good. But soon this *sensei* begins to talk to me that he is very unhappy, that his wife is not a kind wife to him. He come to my room in the night and then he — I don't know what to say — it was not rape, he did not hit me, but he slept with me against my will. How can I explain this? I was so young, and he was my father's friend, he was a great *sensei*. I let him sleep with me because I was frightened to say no.

'When I graduate I think all that happened to me will be finished, but this *sensei* tells my father he has found place as graduate student for me and that I should stay in Kyoto. I beg my father, please, please, I want to come home, but he will not hear me. He tells me I can become teacher at a university one day with this great man's help, that I can bring to my family the honour that my brother would bring if he lived. I could say nothing more. I had to stay at Kyoto.

'I cannot explain you my unhappiness, David. I hate this man. When he touches me I want to be sick. His fingers are like cockroach on my skin. I ask him let me go. He says he will never allow this.

'Then something happen, I don't know. He brings another teacher to the house. A young man, handsome and kind. He tells me that if I like this young man I should marry him. He says it would be good thing for me now. This young man became my husband, David. Again, how can I explain you what I did, why I did such a thing? I am not in love with this man, I tell you this, but he is kind to me and said he wants to take care of me. I marry — married — him because I think now, now that I have husband, I can be free.'

She was smoking all the while she talked, the peculiar habit she had of lighting a cigarette, drawing on it three or four times and then stubbing it out only to take a fresh one from her pack and light it. The pack was quickly emptied and she was close to panic as she rummaged in one of the carrier bags she had had with her in the hotel to find more. David, drinking whisky, waited for her to begin again.

'And were you free then, when you married?' he asked her.

'I am never free. We Japanese are never free. Don't you understand this of our lives? Now I think this man, this *sensei*, he found my husband not to free me but to keep me to him, close to him. My husband is also teacher at the university so when I am married I cannot leave Kyoto. It was just as before, everything.

'I am married for a short time when I find I am to have a baby. I was so frightened, David. Can you understand? I did not know what I can do. I did not know to who belongs this baby inside of me? Can you understand me? Can you feel what I feel then?

'I think I will become mad until, at last, I tell my husband — everything. I trust him. He is always so good and kind for me. But when I tell him — when I told him — he pushed me away from him. He tells me I must kill the baby. I cannot do this. My husband divorced me then. He tells me I am his shame.'

'And then?' David asked. 'When you were divorced?'

Megumi looked at him, 'Do you know how easy a thing is divorce in Japan? No, I will tell you. It is easy. When I marry my husband it was four hours, when we get a divorce it was five minutes. But for the women afterwards comes the not easy thing. I go back to my parents. They take me into their house again.

'My mother is so kind, David. Always I know she loves me. My father, though, was very angry. He did not understand. How could he? How can I tell him the truth? How can I tell him what his friend has done to me? In his ignorance my father tells me I am his shame. He tells me that if my brother lived he would have kill me for what I have done. He knew only that I am having a baby and that my husband divorced me, David. What would he think except that I had done something very bad? He could not know.

'And then that little Kayoko is born and I am very ill. When the doctor gives her to me I turned my face from her. For a year I was not a mother to my baby. I was ill. My father put me into a hospital and that was very bad. One day I ta — took the glass from the light in my room and cut at myself but I cannot die, somebody finds me. My mother helped me then, and when I am strong again she take me home.'

She sat for a moment, looking down at her unquiet hands, 'Because of my illness and what I want to do with myself I am so nervous person, David. Can you understand?'

He poured more of the whisky into his glass, 'Why were you in that hotel yesterday?'

'My father discovers us, David. That we are lovers. When I left you on Friday my father comes to me in the station with another man, a detective. My father tells me he has seen me, he has seen me lying with you. I could say nothing to him. What can I say?

'He takes me to my house and tells me that it is finished for me now. He tells me that I am dirt, that I bring nothing to his house but shame. It is not enough that I betray my husband and born another's child, now I go with a foreigner. I try to tell him that you are a kind man, David, that I know you will never hurt me. He said he will not hear, that now I am dead to him. He said it would be better for him if I were dead. He said if I were dead with my brother he would know only sorrow, but with each breath I take he feels upon him the weight of my shame. And all the time my poor mother is there with that little Kayoko. I truly wanted to die then.

'It was so terrible the things my father said to me. He told me he will destroy you, but I beg him not to harm you. At last I say to him that I will go away, that I will take Kayoko and he will never see us again. I will take my name from our family's register so that it will be as if I am dead for him. He will have a daughter to bring him shame no longer. I do this thing, David. I know it is finished now. I am dead. And you should not look so sad or fearful, he will not harm you now. He has no reason. Only, I wonder what I will do now. How will I live? How will my daughter live?'

They say — these Japanese men say that in Japan it is women who keep the power. Do I mean this word "keep"?'

David suggested 'have'.

'Yes, "have", it is the women who have the power. And they speak all this foolishness of how because the women do not have *chii* — in English what is *chii*? Do you know what is *chii*?'

He did know. It was a word he heard often here. *Chii to meiyo*, status and honour.

'Yes,' Megumi said, '*chii*, because we have not *chii* in our history we must work with brain, silently, with cleverness, and now women have power — in the family, in the spending of money. But it is not a true thing that is said. Here, without *chii* there is no power. There is only nothing. I am a woman. Have I this power? And in my father's house, has my mother this power? No, she has nothing and I have nothing. Now, very much I have nothing and I do not know what is now for me in my life and in the life of my daughter.'

Looking at her, David knew there was only one answer he could give, 'You must stay here with me. You and Kayoko must stay here with me.'

She seemed then to fall from the chair, and crouched at his feet, kept her head close to the floor, repeating again and again, '*Arigato gozaimashita, arigato gozaimashita*, thank you, thank you', her voice choking. David knelt by her, raised her up. She laid her head upon his chest and let her grief flow from her.

So it was that David Kennedy found himself with a new wife and child. When Megumi was stronger in her mind he explained to her about his situation with Jean, that their divorce had still to be granted, and that even when it was there would be a lapse of time before it became absolute and he would be free to marry again. He explained his situation as a teacher in Japan, how necessary it was for him to be above any suspicion and why, because of this, they must be very careful until the time came when they could marry and he was able to present her to his colleagues as his wife. He explained all of this, and she accepted it. What he did not explain were his feelings. He knew he had taken Megumi and her child into his house, he knew that he would marry Megumi when he could, because he felt sorry for her, because of his responsibility for her. He did not love her. He had loved Jean and all of that had come to nothing. He could not love again, he distrusted the emotion.

The days of winter advanced, although the weather remained autumnal, altogether lacking the bitter coldness of the previous year. Slowly, David grew used to his new circumstances. There were changes in the house. Megumi asked him to make a bedroom for Kayoko in the small *tatami* room, a bedroom like a little English girl would have. He bought a carpet to cover the fragile straw-matting, and replaced the *shoji* with curtains. The child's bed had a Mickey Mouse cover spread over it, and on the sliding doors of the cupboard where the *futon* were stored Megumi stencilled other Disney characters. In the rest of the house the pristine neatness that had formerly been its leading characteristic crumpled in the presence of Megumi and her daughter. He watched it go.

Megumi could not care for a house, she did not know how. Always before she had lived in another woman's home, even when she had been married she and her husband had lived with his mother. Megumi could not shop, or cook or clean. He tried to get her to help him. He would ask her to dust when he cleaned or washed the floors, or leave a list of the things they needed from the supermarket when he went to work each morning, but Megumi broke things or grew bored when she cleaned, and said that the other women in the supermarket stared at her. In the end he gave up and did everything himself. He also found himself looking after Kayoko. Before, Megumi's mother had taken care of the child, now it was David who woke her and got her ready each day. She began attending a local kindergarten, and it was David who took her there. The class finished just after lunch, and sometimes Megumi would manage to get out to meet the child, but more often than not Kayoko found her way home alone.

Each day she lived was difficult for Megumi, all that altered was the degree of difficulty. She would often wake up weeping, even on her good days, and lie on her bed, her despair folded about her with the quilts. It took her a long time to get up and make herself ready to face the empty house. More and more she took to staying in, venturing into the streets only when David made her. On Sundays he would take Kayoko along the river path to Inokashira Park, the child pedalling furiously on the tricycle he had bought for her. Megumi never wanted to come with them, but, more often than not, David was insistent and so she would trail along, her head sunk into her jacket.

The bad days were very bad. Then she would stay in bed all day, unable to talk or eat. On those days David would not leave her, if he had classes he would call the university saying he had a cold. He feared for her then. She went so deep it was impossible to reach her; he could only sit in the kitchen, watching over the child, waiting for Megumi to win her struggle with whatever it was that possessed her. When it was over, at night, or the next day or the next, she would stroke his hair as if he were her child, and tell him how much she loved him for his kindness to her and her daughter, how she hated herself when her illness took her so far away, how she never wanted to leave him.

She would not speak Japanese in the house. Even when she spoke to Kayoko she used English. 'She must learn,' she said when David protested that the child could not understand, that it frightened her when her mother spoke in a foreign tongue all the time. Megumi would not listen to him, 'She must learn because one day we will live in England. I know this. She must not be Japanese.'

'She is Japanese, Megumi,' David said. 'So are you, and nothing anyone can do will ever change that. And we won't be going to Britain. There's nothing there for me. I have work here. I've told you this before.'

Kayoko no longer called him the foreigner, now he was David to her. One day, a Friday when he was not at the university, he met her from the kindergarten and she asked if he was her father, her 'papa'. He told her he was not, but that he loved her very much and if she wanted to call him her papa then it would make him happy. She called him papa for the rest of the day, but by the next she had forgotten and he was David again.

Sometimes he lied to Megumi, but he always told the truth to Kayoko. He did love the child, and he found his love for her growing daily. He spent most of the time he was not working with her. He bought her clothes and toys. He took her to the park on her tricycle, or to play with a ball or kite. On Saturday afternoons he tried to go somewhere special with her, to the amusement park at Korakuen, the Tama zoo. Twice that winter they made the long journey to the new Disneyland, built on top of millions of tons of trash dumped in Tokyo Bay. They stayed all day and in the evening, on the trek home, he sat with Kayoko in his arms, her limp body given entirely to sleep, her trust given entirely to him.

The train ran through its stations on the way to Mitaka, ran through Takodanobaba where, so long ago it seemed to David, he had waited bewildered for Jack Stevens.

In the winter vacation a weekend conference was organized for British teachers at Japanese universities. David did not want to attend the conference, but he had not visited Kyoto and, as his travel expenses were being paid by the university, he decided to go. At the last moment Megumi asked if she and Kayoko could accompany him. He was pleased that they were coming but, at the same time, surprised, for Kyoto had been the place of Megumi's great unhappiness. When he said this she answered that it would be different to be there with him, that she would not be afraid.

They stayed at a hotel on the slopes of Mount Hieizan, surrounded by temples. It was far from the centre of the city and the hall where the lecturers' conference was being held, but David did not care. He registered, and sat through the morning session, but never went back.

They had reservations for three nights, and the first day was so successful he thought perhaps they might extend their stay. They had eaten lunch at the hotel, in spite of Kayoko's pleas to be taken to a McDonald's, and then gone by taxi to the Golden Pavilion. There was snow in Kyoto, a light dusting upon the ground, and occasional flurries in the air. They followed all the other sightseers, the families, the tour groups and the hordes of uniformed schoolchildren, but lingered where the others hurried by once they had taken their photographs.

The building was new, the original having been destroyed by arson in 1950. The house that now stood by the lake was a replica, exact in every detail, the reflection it cast upon the water the same that had shimmered there in all the days since the fourteenth century. David read aloud from the guide book he had with him, when he had finished Megumi said, 'We can never escape from the past here. When it is destroyed we make it again with our own hands.'

Their room at the hotel contained two large beds. Kayoko, tired from walking in the afternoon and filled with the hamburgers and french fries she had finally prevailed upon David and her mother to buy, was asleep early in one of them. David and Megumi left her and went down to the bar for a drink.

'Are you feeling all right, Megumi?' he asked, as they sat at the long counter.

She smiled and took his hand, 'I know you are always afraid for me. Don't worry, I am very all right, always all right when I am with you.'

Later, as they lay together in the darkness of the room Megumi pressed herself against him, silencing his fears that the child would wake with a finger laid across his lips.

They took a late train back to Tokyo on the Monday. The compartment was almost empty, one or two businessmen going up to the capital, a group of foreign tourists, Australians by their accents, and a Japanese family with three little girls. The train had hardly pulled away from the station before Kayoko ran to show the other children the teddy bear David had bought for her from a shop in the station.

'More and more she becomes like a foreign child, so brave!' Megumi said approvingly. 'When we go to England she will truly free and have the courage to rejoice in her freedom.'

She smiled and took David's hand. He remained silent, looking at the darkness beyond the window.

They were about an hour out from Kyoto, the great train speeding through the night. David kept waking from sleep to see what Kayoko was doing, for she and the three little girls had taken a section of seats for themselves and were playing house or some such game. Suddenly he felt his hand being gripped urgently by Megumi and turned to see her always pale face utterly white, her eyes pinpricks of fear.

'David, I am very ill,' she spoke in Japanese.

'What? What's the matter?' he asked, her fear infecting him.

'I think I am dying.'

He took her pulse, felt it beat wildly beneath his finger. Her skin, when he touched his hand to her forehead, was cold, covered with a thick, chilled layer of perspiration. He did not know what to do. He would have to find a guard, but the bullet trains were almost a half-mile in length end to end, and he had no idea where to look, or even what he could say in Japanese once he found the man other than that his wife was ill.

'Do you think you could walk with me to the restaurant car, Megumi?' he said. 'We can get one of the waiters there to fetch a guard. I don't know what else to do. There may be a doctor on the train, I don't know.'

They got up and moved towards the door leading from their compartment. As David passed Kayoko and her new friends he asked their parents to watch her while he was away. 'My wife is ill. I'm sorry.'

In the restaurant car Megumi said she felt a little better, 'The air is cooler in here. I want to stay here for a little time.'

He ordered brandy and made her slowly sip from the glass. Some colour began to seep back into the whiteness of her face. She kept apologizing, again and again.

David felt a huge surge of relief as the train pulled into Tokyo Station. He got Megumi and Kayoko onto the platform, and then went back for his bags, but the father of the three little girls was already bringing them out for him. David thanked him profusely, and turned to the long walk to the station exit.

Megumi still looked dreadfully ill, and she was walking uncertainly as David lagged behind, their bags held in one hand, Kayoko hanging on to this other. In the street again he hailed a taxi.

She would not see a doctor, even though he said he would take her to the clinic in Shiba where there were British and American physicians. Instead she stayed in bed, eating almost nothing, sleeping, hiding in unconsciousness from whatever it was that assailed her. David took care of Kayoko, shopped, worked, waited for Megumi to come back into the world.

It took a week. He was sitting at the table in the kitchen, writing another paragraph for his book on Schiele. He was alone. Kayoko was in her room, bathed, changed into her pyjamas. She would call him to kiss her goodnight when she was ready for sleep.

He had taken up the work again just after Christmas, without really knowing why. Now, in the holidays, he tried to give it two hours every day. Kayoko knew that she should be quiet around him when he spread the file cards and notes on the table, but she often stayed close to him, sometimes making her odd little drawings, or mutilating another colouring book with her felt pens. David liked to see her there across the table from him. He would sometimes look up and stare at her, if she caught him she would put a finger across her lips, a gesture she, like her mother, had learned from him, and say, 'I am busy. I'll talk to you later, okay?'

He heard Megumi come into the kitchen, and as he turned in his chair she knelt before him, laying her head on his knee. He asked her if she was feeling better, and she began to cry.

'I don't understand why you are so kind to me. I give you nothing. Every time you leave the house I think you will not come back, and every time you come back I wonder why. You are so good to me.'

He stroked her hair, knowing that the answer to her question was neither kindness nor goodness, but an acceptance of his fate. That, and the presence of the child. Megumi was wrong when she said she gave him nothing, for he considered that she had brought with her into his house the greatest gift he had ever received, the child, Kayoko.

Megumi wanted him that night, and for the first time in all the time they had been together, she seemed to utterly abandon herself. He could not satisfy her, and at last, as the wintry light of the dawn began to light the room, they turned from one another to sleep.

He was wakened by Kayoko jumping on him. She usually came into their room in the mornings, she was used to their sleeping together now, unconcerned by the fact that often they were naked. He took the child by her arms, lifting her up into the air. Then, as the sleep cleared from his brain, he realized that he and Kayoko were alone.

'Where is your Mama, Kayoko?' he asked. It was unusual for Megumi to be up before him, but he thought perhaps she had gone early to bath herself.

Kayoko said she did not know. He asked if Megumi was in the bathroom, but the little girl said no, she had been to the bathroom a few moments before and there was no one there. Concerned, David got up to see for himself. The house was empty.

She came back at four o'clock that afternoon. She had David's parka on over an old pair of jeans and a tee-shirt. She had been wearing track-shoes but no socks, and her ankles were blue with cold. He asked her where she had been. She said she had walked, sat in coffee houses. He asked her why.

'I don't know,' she said, covering her face as the tears started from her eyes.

For the first time he was angry with her, the concern that had ravaged his gut all that day emptying itself through his suddenly violent mouth. In the sitting-room Kayoko hid, terrified of the noise in the kitchen, the rage and the sorrow.

It was the beginning of a bad time for them. Day after day Megumi would lie in bed, eating nothing, saying nothing. She would not wash or comb her hair. She would not open the windows to air the room. The days she did get up she sat by the window smoking cigarette after cigarette until the house stank. When term began in April David was glad, and he spent longer and longer in his office, paying the price for his absence in the sad eyes of the child who waited by the door for him to come home, as if she were his little wife.

One evening he came in and Kayoko was not there. Her room was to the right, just off the hall, and he looked for her there. She was curled up on the bed, her teddy bear held tight against her. She had been crying, and seemed frightened. When David asked her what was wrong she said her Mama had scared her. He comforted the child, lifting her up, and carried her into the sitting-room.

Megumi was there, sitting amongst the debris of the destruction she had wrought. The cactus garden was smashed, the coffee table overturned. On the sofa were shards of glass from the frames that had contained Martin Cassidy's drawings. The drawings themselves had been shredded. She had used a piece of the broken glass to score deep lines across the surface of the wooden plate she had given him for his birthday. It lay now, bloodily smeared, on the carpet.

Kayoko was crying again, and David spoke gently to her, his free hand soothing her head. His voice was still gentle when he asked Megumi why she had done all of this.

'Because I hate you. And I hate sitting every night under these pictures of your girlfriend.'

'You know they are not drawings of my girlfriend. I told you a long time ago that they were pictures of a friend who had died, that they were made by my best friend and were very precious to me.'

'She was Korean!' Megumi shouted at him. 'I know you like those Korean women. That is why you stay so late from this house now. You go with those *sensei* to bars filled with Korean women.'

David stared at her. 'I'm going to take Kayoko out and get her something to eat. I don't suppose you gave her anything today. I don't know when we'll be back.'

Megumi had shut herself in the bedroom when he got home. He bathed Kayoko and put her to bed, then set about cleaning up the mess in the sitting-room. That night he pulled one of the spare *futon* from the cupboard in the child's room and spread it on the carpet for himself to sleep on.

She apologized for what she had done. It was the next morning and David was tending to her hurt hands. She said, 'I don't know why I do these things. It is a little because I know you do not love me and I fear that you will leave me. Then I grow angry and want to hurt you, but by hurting you I know that I will drive you away, that you will leave me.'

He put down the bottle of antiseptic he had used to clean the cuts on her palms. 'The more I'm with you the less I understand you. I won't leave you, try to believe me, I won't leave you. Just tell me what will make you happy and I'll try to do it.'

'Take me to England.'

'I can't do that.'

Summer came. Kayoko had been asking if they could have a

television and so David and Megumi took her to Akihabera to buy one.

It was the centre of the electrical retail business in Tokyo, a dense quarter of the city where every shop sold the products of the Japanese electronics industry. Megumi told him the name of the district meant 'the field of autumn leaves'. There were no leaves here now though, no field either. Nothing grew, it was an acre of concrete and noise, nothing blossomed but the banks of televisions in the stores, each tuned to the same channel, image after image repeating itself, searing the eye.

They moved through the confusion of men shouting, calling people from the streets to enter their shops, touting for trade as if they worked for the clip-joints in Shinjuku. Inside the Laox store David became separated from Megumi and Kayoko, and soon found himself agreeing to buy a television and video recorder, at a bargain price the salesman assured him. He told the man he must consult with his wife before finally deciding and went to look for Megumi. He found her crouched on the floor in one of the aisles, bent double, her hands clasped over her ears. Kayoko stood by her, frightened, unsure what to do. When she saw David she ran to him, shouting that her mother was ill.

He got Megumi up and took her out of the store. They found a seedy café in a side-street. The tables were dirty, littered with empty cups and plates, the table tops stained by coffee slops. There the now familiar ritual repeated itself. Megumi apologized, begged him to forgive her, not to leave her. He asked her what was wrong, what more he could do to make her happy.

'Take me to England.'

HOME

The First Class compartment of the train to Loxley smelt of coffee and hot, sour milk. David Kennedy, sitting opposite Megumi and Kayoko, looked about him with distaste, his eyes flicking from the filthy, torn carpet, the worn seats and finger-smeared windows, to the business men in shiny suits, shirt-collars like yesterday's bread.

It was late April, a cold spring. The Kennedys, for David and Megumi were married now, had been in London for three days. On the first afternoon they had gone down the Thames to Greenwich. It had snowed, as it seemed it would do again today. The train pulled out of the long tunnel into the daylight, and at once the windows were splashed with harsh drops of half-congealed rain. The sky above the high terrace-backs was a forbidding palette of black and grey, and slate blues.

They had married by presenting a clerk at the Suginami ward office with documentary evidence that they were neither of them legally bound to anyone else, and signing a marriage contract. It took only a few minutes and no vows were exchanged. They married because it was the only way David could take Megumi and Kayoko to England and keep them there with him.

He had written to Martin Cassidy asking for copies of the vacancy columns from the educational supplements. It had been a difficult thing for David to do because he still held a grievance against Martin for the letter about Jean. But Martin did help, finding jobs for David and for Megumi in Belfast. The Language Services Unit of the Polytechnic where he taught were, subject to interview, giving David a one-year contract teaching English as a foreign language to incoming overseas students, and Megumi was to teach Japanese to scientists and technicians in the genetic engineering section of the biology department at Queen's University. Two years before, when the Minister of State for Northern Ireland had agreed to cut all funding to the section, the Mitsu Corporation of Japan offered finance for five years. There was to be an exchange of staff between Belfast and the corporation's Kobe research facility. Megumi had no formal contract; before leaving Japan she had been hired by Mitsu, not the university, and was regarded by them as one more member of their immense family.

The train stopped at Luton, the last stop it would make before Loxley. David looked at the grim terraces, the brick-faced office block which leered over at them like some old man watching girls at play. A cold wind gusted the rain against a faded board announcing 'British Rail Luton'. At the bottom of the sign someone had sprayed the word 'wankers'.

He glanced across at Megumi and Kayoko. The child was sleeping, exhausted by the long flight from Tokyo and the subsequent days tramping about in a strange and barbarous city peopled by giants. On the first bus they had ridden she had become hysterical when the Sikh conductor approached them for their fares. Megumi was awake, and her eyes were wide. When she saw him looking at her she took his hand and thanked him again for bringing her to this place. In Anchorage she had emptied her purse of Japanese currency and would have tossed her passport away had she been able to. 'I feel I am to be born again,' she said. 'I take nothing from the old life.'

The train moved on through a landscape of flooded clay-pits, chimneys that rose from an earth still violated by tracked cranes and diggers. A stench of sulphur penetrated the carriage. Abandoned factories seemed cut into the land. Allotments, untidy gardens; a copse, half-submerged in greasy water, the trees hacked raw.

Megumi saw none of this. Before her eyes unrolled a green and gentle land of fields flecked with woods. 'This country is like your eyes, David. Now I know why they are so beautiful. They hold forever the first things they see.'

She woke Kayoko to look at the marvels that flew by: the little bridges that spanned a twisting river, lichened and forgotten, a house like a slice of cheese, animals. Megumi and Kayoko had never seen cows and sheep before. The child looked across at David as if to ask him to confirm that this was not all some English Disneyland.

When the train slowed as it passed the Kiddysox plant, David reached up to get Kayoko's coat from the rack. The fields ran to scrap yards, filled with abandoned cars; the houses thickened on either side of the railway lines. A road bristling with arched street-lamps followed along by the side of the track, a school playing field, the clock on the fire station tower, and then the tangled banks of the cutting, a tunnel and the voice of the guard uncertainly announcing, 'Loxley, Loxley Station. This is Loxley. Change here for Birmingham New Street.'

They were to spend a month in England before crossing to Belfast where they would stay with Martin Cassidy while they looked for a house of their own. It was all but five years since David had seen his parents, and only six weeks before that he had told them about Megumi and Kayoko. They had learned of the divorce from Jean, who had written from Edinburgh just after finishing her doctorate. David's mother had sent the letter on to him with one of her own, a short, bitter note blaming him for all that had happened. When she learned of Megumi her bitterness increased as she saw what was obviously the reason for the marriage's collapse.

Coming back here he was always surprised how much everything had changed. Once, when he was a boy at school, Loxley had been a complacent, comfortable market town, grown rich spinning yarn and making shoes. In the 1960s it was said to be the richest city in Europe, and the city fathers had called for a plan of civic redevelopment. The centre, 'the town' as everyone called it, was torn to pieces, and grey concrete thrown up — a shopping complex, a new theatre. To keep pace the older stores followed suit, gutting and re-designing their premises; those that could not, closed. Now the clock tower, scrubbed clean to match the new surroundings, stood in the middle of a nightmare. The wind swept through empty halls that stank of piss, and trash littered the urban walkways. The High Street was abandoned, its dereliction covered with a papier-maché of indifference, advertisements and fly-sheets plastered one on top of the other over the windows of once prosperous emporia. In the shopping centre that had replaced it, old women shuffled nervously past the gangs of unemployed teenagers, and policemen walked in pairs. At night the town became a no-go zone for all but those of violent intent, a place loud with the synthethized roar of game centres, the screams from fun-pubs where no one smiled.

The taxi David hired at the station took them through streets of decrepit houses, where abandoned cars straddled the broken pavements. On deserted corners the wind had found a home for old newspapers, empty crisp packets. There was dog shit everywhere.

They drew near to Beeby Street, where his parents lived. The lumber yard that had once scented the air with the smell of sawdust and resin had become a Sikh temple, festooned with orange banners. There were second-hand shops in the little houses where his schoolfriends had lived. On the corner of Eastlake Road two women waited, young and hard-faced. A car with a man driving stopped by the women and one of them got in.

His father opened the door to them, and they were immediately in the front room, struggling to find space to embrace between the crowded furniture and the suitcases. Mr Kennedy took Megumi's proffered hand, but pulled her gently towards him, kissing her cheek, welcoming her, before he stooped, slowly in his old man's way, to greet the child. He offered his arms to her, Kayoko, unsure of what was expected, what she should do, looked towards David. He spoke to her in Japanese, saying her grandfather wanted to kiss her. Kayoko smiled, let herself be lifted and carried into the middle room.

'Where's Mammy?' David asked, the word sounding odd upon his tongue. Megumi looked anxiously at him.

'She's in the town, son. You know your mother and her little routines. It wouldn't matter if the Queen of England was coming to visit; if it was a Thursday your mother would still be out for the shopping. Will you have a cup of tea?'

Megumi went into the kitchen with Mr Kennedy, and David

could see how pleased his father was. He smiled at Kayoko who sat with her teddy bear on the rug in front of the gas fire.

'That's a fine child you have, Megumi,' Mr Kennedy said. 'And her name now, does it have a meaning in English?'

'No, it has no meaning. My mother named her because I was ill when she was born. If we use certain way of writing the name it could have meaning, but how I write it there is no meaning.'

'And what of your own name?'

'Megumi? How it is written means nothing, perhaps, in one way of writing it, the name, could have a meaning — blessing. My mother and father did not think of me as a blessing.'

Mr Kennedy turned to look at her. 'I'm sure that isn't so. All your children are blessings, even when the trials and troubles they bring home seem never ending. I know we've had our share, especially with the girls, but I wouldn't change a thing that's happened, and I wouldn't change one of my children for a king's ransom.'

Megumi said, 'You are so kind man, Mr Kennedy. Like David. You love your children and it is why David is filled with love also. My father did not love me. My mother told me that when my brother is born my father is awake all for two nights searching in books for his name. He has to have so special a name. With me my father does not even ask my mother for one week what I am called.'

Mr Kennedy poured the boiling water into a big brown teapot. 'The Mammy and I don't truly know all that's been going on in my son's life these past years, but the moment I saw you and your little girl I thought you'd be a blessing to him, no matter how they spell your name in your own country.'

It was almost three o'clock when David's mother came home. She was a big woman, reluctantly bowing to age. She made a fuss of setting down the bags she was carrying before greeting her son and his wife. She made them welcome, asking the usual questions, but there was a perceptible coldness to her manner. She did not ask about Kayoko, who was upstairs sleeping; and later, when the child was awake and handed her the present David had bought for his parents, his mother seemed embarrassed. Throughout the whole of that first afternoon and evening she did not once speak directly to Megumi.

Martin Cassidy had suggested that David buy a car in England rather than wait until he got to Belfast, and so the next day he and Megumi took Kayoko with them as they made the rounds of the used-car lots that had bloomed in the dying city like so many sad flowers. He had thought to buy something large, a Ford estate car, but Megumi saw and fell in love with a bright green Renault 4. The car was less than a year old, still under warranty, and the price was good. He paid by cheque, and the salesman, anxious for space, let him drive it away as soon as it had been serviced and cleaned.

Having the car was important because it freed them from the house where, increasingly, David's mother was showing her dislike of Megumi. The first Sunday they were in Loxley his third sister and her family came to visit. The small house was suddenly full of noise and it was hard for David to talk to Deidrie, but after tea, as they washed the dishes, he asked what had been said about his new marriage.

'Mammy was very bitter when she heard. You know how she is, how much she thought of Jean. Then there's all the business of Daddy being a prisoner out there during the war.'

'But it was Jean that let me down, Deidrie. She even said so in the letter she wrote. I saw it. And as for all that stuff about the war, Megumi wasn't even born.'

'I know, I know. I think she's lovely, and the little girl is beautiful, but they're still Japanese. Mammy can't get over the fact that you married one of them.'

'You know it was Megumi who wanted to come here, don't you? She hates Japan, she hates being Japanese. I don't expect you to understand, but that's how it is.'

'Give Mammy time. She'll come round, especially for you. You were always the favourite.'

In the evening they played cards, Deidrie, her husband Michael, Mr Kennedy and David. It was what they always had done on Sunday evenings. David's mother sat in the big chair by the fire, looking through the newspapers, watching the television that flickered in the corner of the room before the enraptured eyes of Deidrie's children. Megumi busied herself putting Kayoko to bed. The child was exhausted by the sudden excitement of the day and when David set down his hand to carry her up to bed she was already asleep. Megumi followed behind on the stairs, and, for the first time in their life together, they both kissed the sleeping child.

'She is so happy,' Megumi said. 'I am so happy. We are so happy.'

The evening moved through its quiet hours. At nine o'clock Megumi asked David's father if she could make herself a cup of coffee. Mr Kennedy said that of course she could, 'You've no cause to ask for permission to do things in this house, child.' He called her child now, the word came about Megumi like an embrace.

She had been sitting by David since she had come down from the bedroom with him, watching as he lifted cards from the table or set down tricks. Now she stood up to go into the kitchen. David looked at her, aware also of his mother's eyes.

'Would you make me a cup while you're out there, Megumi?' Deidrie asked, dealing a new hand.

Megumi stopped by the door which led into the kitchen, and turning to face the card-players at the table, said, 'Make it your own fucking self, please.' She smiled then.

There was a silence which was only broken by the sniggering of Deidrie's children. David felt his face turn to rubber, he wanted to speak, to explain and excuse what Megumi had said, but he could not, his mouth would not work. Once Martin Cassidy had told him of being caught by the blast of a bomb in a Belfast street. How it was like a great wind that eddied about the face, pushing and pulling at the flesh. How the sensation had seemed to last for a time beyond time. It was this way now for David.

And then his mother was up from her chair and shouting that she would wash Megumi's mouth out with soap for such talk, and Deidrie was shouting that it was a mistake, that Megumi had not understood what it was she had said, and, not understanding, had meant nothing by it, except, perhaps, to please. Megumi, afraid, trembled against the wall, a terrible, uncomprehending fearfulness upon her, as if she was waiting for a blow to fall.

David sat mute through it all. It was his father who ended things by going to Megumi and taking her by the arm. He quietened his wife and daughter, and said he would help Megumi in the kitchen. 'It was a mistake,' he said in his quiet way. 'The child did not know what she said. Deidrie is not offended and I see no cause for you to be either, Doreen.'

When he came back it was as if nothing had happened. The card game was resumed, Michael told his awful jokes, the television blared in the corner. At half-past ten Deidrie and her family made ready to leave, and when they were gone Mr Kennedy said he would go to bed. David and Megumi followed him up the stairs, going quietly into their room so as not to wake Kayoko. Only David's mother sat on in her chair by the fire. As David had stooped to kiss her goodnight he felt the violence of her anger in her stiffened cheek.

He tried to keep Megumi and Kayoko away from the house for as much of the day as he could. He took them into the quiet lanes of the county, to visit country houses and the smaller market towns. Often they would go farther, up into the Derbyshire peaks or into Lincolnshire. They spent the second weekend in the Cotswolds, staying in an hotel near Moreton-in-the-Marsh.

He was glad to leave the town behind. Everything was falling to pieces, the roads pot-holed or awash from broken water-pipes. Even the new buildings were covered with the signs of blight. The tall towers of the university leaked a brown ooze through their cracked facings, and the red brickwork of the science block was streaked with a white mould like pidgeon droppings. In the town he felt that people stared as he went by with Megumi and the child, and he hated them with their soft bodies fed on flour and fat and sugar, their faces crusted like the piles of dog shit on the pavements.

In spite of the tension in the house Megumi said she was happy. She was trying to stop smoking and by the end of the first week was using only a pack a day. When they were out together she seemed less nervous. The night they spent in the Cotswolds she told him how grateful she was that he had taken her away from Japan, 'I was so unhappy, David. Every day I felt I could not breathe. I know it was very hard for you to be with me. Here it will be different. I am free. I will be easier for you, I promise.'

At lunch-time on the last Sunday they were to stay in Loxley the house was heavy with the smell of basted meat and steamy vegetables, loud with the screaming of Deidrie's children as they raced around the large, starchily spread table with Kayoko. David had been with his father and brother-in-law to drink at The Rifle Butts, a few streets away. When he came back he saw Megumi sitting unhappily in one of the armchairs by the fire, pretending to read the Sunday paper. Deidrie was in the kitchen with Mrs Kennedy, sometimes the sound of their voices could be heard above the noise of the children. They were arguing.

'Are you all right?' he asked Megumi.

'Yes. It's just the noise. It gives me headache.'

'You should have come to the pub with us. Kayoko would have been all right on her own here.'

Megumi shrugged, took his hand.

Megumi seldom ate meat, and the sight of the joint of beef sitting in its pool of watery blood the day before had sickened her. Now that the food was cooked and on the table she took only a little of the stiff, creamy potatoes, the sodden sprouts and beans.

'Are you not hungry again?' Mrs Kennedy asked abruptly, looking at what Megumi had taken.

'Yes, thank you. This is very nice.'

'So what did you think of The Butts then?' Deidrie said to her brother. 'Of course, people round here, well all the old ones, were livid when they found out an Indian had got the license.'

'And why should they have been anything else?' Mrs Kennedy said. 'This used to be a respectable neighbourhood, clean and tidy. Now it's nothing but a dump, and all the fault of the blackies and their dirty ways. The whole country's run for the benefit of foreigners today. If you ask me the whole lot of them should be sent back to where they came from.'

'Mammy darling, you're a foreigner and so is Daddy,' Deidrie said.

'Oh, and how is that now? Didn't your Daddy give the best years of his life defending this country against just the likes of those that they let come in and treat like kings and queens?'

Deidrie, unable to interrupt her mother's invective, looked across at David.

'They come here with not a word of English, and get taxis from the railway station straight round to the Social Security. Yet God help the likes of us if we try to get anything. Televisions, cars, anything they have a mind to ask for they're given.'

'Can we not have a little peace to eat the Sunday dinner?' Mr Kennedy said quietly. His wife gave her displeasure to the food on her plate, angrily cutting at her meat.

No one spoke. The emptied plates were passed to Deidrie, who scraped and stacked them ready for the kitchen. Megumi had eaten almost nothing.

'Is the food I cook not good enough for you, young lady?'

Megumi looked up at David's mother, 'I'm sorry. I don't understand.'

'Oh yes, I'm sure. You're all alike, deaf, dumb, blind and witless when it suits you so to be, but smart enough to steal a young girl's husband so you can get over here, you and your brat from God knows where.'

'Mammy, will you hold your tongue,' Deidrie shouted.

'I will not. It's time this madam knew exactly what I think of her. She doesn't fool me with her simperings and smarmy ways.'

David pushed his chair back suddenly. 'I didn't even know Megumi when my marriage fell apart. If you want the truth, it's that your precious Jean would open her legs to anything in trousers. All the time I was alone in Morocco, all the time I was alone in London, she was fucking herself stupid with other men, that's what she was doing!'

'How dare you, how dare you speak such words to me in my house?' his mother asked with her tone of injured indignation.

'I'm telling you the exact truth. And, just for the record, I do know where my daughter comes from, which is more—'

'David!' Deidrie cautioned him.

In all the noise a vacuum of silence had fallen over the others at the table: Deidrie's husband and children, Kayoko. David looked at Megumi, rigid with fear in her chair. He picked up the child, 'Megumi, come upstairs with me while I get our things together. We're not staying here.'

When they came back down Deidrie was waiting, alone. Her father and mother were in the front room.

'Mammy's having one of her, you know, "attacks". I've sent for the doctor. Michael's taken the kids home. I'll stay until the doctor's been, I don't want to leave Daddy on his own with her.'

She turned to Megumi: 'I'm so sorry. I can't explain or excuse my mother's behaviour towards you. Brendan, I mean David and the other sisters don't know how difficult it is, the things I put up with because I'm the one who stayed close to home. She's never liked Michael, my husband. I've never understood why he's taken the things he's taken from her. What can I say but that I'm sorry? You're my brother's wife, and you and your daughter will always be welcome in my house.'

She kissed Megumi, and then Kayoko, before embracing David. 'You'd best be off. I'll settle things here, it'll smooth over, it always does. Do you want to stay with us tonight? We can find the room, you know?'

'No, it's all right,' David said. 'We're going north. There's a couple of places in Derbyshire I know. It's Sunday, there's bound to be a room free in one of them. Say goodbye to Mike and the kids, eh? And Daddy. Tell him I'll write.'

Deidrie went with them down the path of the ruined garden to the street. She held Kayoko while David put the bags into the back of the Renault.

They drove north towards Edinburgh. He had not wanted to go, he feared meeting Jean somewhere on the streets. It was his Kyoto. But Megumi said she needed to see where he had lived before knowing her. 'I must to know everything about you, everything.'

Their route took them across a barren, fog-bound moor where once, with the car slowed because David could not see, two horses ran out of the mist at them, their eyes wild in the glare of the headlamps. From Edinburgh they made their way to Stranraer, and the boat to Larne.

The car was searched on the dock at Stranraer. When Megumi wondered at the number of policemen checking the passengers, David told her that in Larne the policemen would be wearing flak-vests, and carrying pistols and self-loading rifles. That there would be soldiers with them.

'Are you still glad we left Japan?' he asked her.

'Yes,' she said, taking hold of Kayoko as they climbed the steps up to the passenger deck, 'I am still glad we left Japan.'

The ferry was crowded, and they found themselves sharing a window seat and table with two couples. The men were fat and loud, with moustaches and expensive clothes. The women had

Rolex watches on their wrists and too much make-up on their faces. Their skirts were pulled high above their knees, showing off the tanned, leathery skin of their legs. All of them were drinking spirits and smoking long, gold-tipped cigarettes, talking loudly in their harsh Ulster accents. David looked for somewhere else to sit, but all the other seats were taken.

'It's not handy to Belfast, so it isn't, it's not handy to Belfast at all,' one of the men in blazers said.

'Oh no, it's not handy to Belfast at all,' his friend replied.

One of the two women leant over towards Megumi and said, 'Excuse me, love, but your little girl's a wee darling so she is, a wee darling.'

Megumi could not understand her, and the woman repeated what she had said, 'Your little girl — a right wee darling so she is.'

They drove into Belfast along the Shore Road, the cranes of Harland and Wolff's shipyard high and dark against the skyline. The air smelt of the coal and peat smoke that gusted down into the streets from the rows of terraced council houses that lined the hills along the road. An army patrol passed them, the young soldier sitting in the open doorway of the armoured personnel carrier carrying his rifle in the crook of his arm. A hoarding proclaimed 'Murder, Explosives, Threats', as if it were a concise history of the city. Megumi asked David if they were safe, driving in the darkness.

Martin Cassidy lived in one of the large old houses in Eglantine Avenue, close to Queen's University. As the Renault pulled up he came to the door, a young girl with him.

'You must be Megumi,' he said, embracing her. 'Welcome to Ireland.' He bent to lift up the child who had followed her mother from the car. 'And this has to be Kayoko.'

He introduced the girl as Stephanie, and said she was staying with him. 'She's homeless, thrown out onto the streets by a cruel and vindictive landlady.'

Megumi worried that he did not have room for so many

visitors, and apologized saying that Kayoko could sleep with her and David.

'There's no need. It's a big house, and anyway Stephanie sleeps in my bed.'

'Oh,' Megumi said, not understanding such openness in company. 'But where will you sleep?'

'Och, I'll sleep in my bed as well. Only don't let on, it's a secret.'

He led them inside to a bright room warmed by an open fire. A Moroccan blanket, a present from David and Jean, was thrown across an old settee, and a thick rug covered the bare floor in front of the black-tiled hearth. Megumi and Kayoko had never been in a house where a fire burned in a grate, and they were at once entranced, unable to resist the flames that beckoned them to approach.

'Watch little Kayoko there, David. I don't have a guard for that fire and I don't want her burning herself.'

Martin served supper at a large table he moved in front of the fire: huge plates of sausages and bacon, with eggs and mushrooms and tomatoes. There was fried soda and potato bread, and deep ironstone cups filled with thick tea.

'Ulster's national dish,' Martin proclaimed. 'The fry. You know, I've often thought that if people ate this every day of the week instead of just on Saturday nights they wouldn't have the time or the inclination to go around killing one another.'

Megumi looked up at him. She had hardly touched her food. 'I feel afraid,' she said. 'We saw soldiers. I think it must be a very dangerous city. Perhaps I was wrong to ask David to come.'

Martin Cassidy smiled, 'Probably the greatest danger you'll face all the time you're here is my cooking, which you're quite rightly avoiding.' He turned serious.

'Things are very quiet at the moment. The security forces and the English politicians talk about "containment" and "acceptable levels of violence". I hate to say it, but it's true. You would be very unlucky to run into trouble here. There are certain areas in this city you wouldn't really want to go to, but mostly the bad things that happen are up on the border. You'll hardly see a British soldier in Belfast these days, the lads in khaki on the road would have been U.D.R., local boys.'

'Aye, things in Belfast are really looking up,' Stephanie said. 'Ever since the security barriers came down in the city centre things have really got back to normal. There's new restaurants opening up, clubs, discos.'

'People suddenly seem to have a lot of money, at least the ones in work do, and they're looking to spend it in Belfast again and not out in the country. The only things you need to be afraid of, Megumi, apart from my fry there, are the two big Ps — Parochialism and Provincialism.' Martin began to laugh.

Megumi, not understanding, turned to David, who smiled at her and said he would explain it later.

If Megumi did not like the food Martin and Stephanie had prepared, Kayoko did. She kept emptying her plate and then pointing to the things she wanted more of. She rewarded those who served her with her bright eyes and '*Domo arigato.*'

'*Eigo de hanashite kudesai,*' Megumi said sharply.

'She's telling Kayoko to speak English,' David explained. 'Her English isn't very good, but she can speak a little. She's shy with new people, and perhaps a bit lazy.'

'She'll be better tomorrow. It's lovely to hear her speak though,' Martin said. 'What was that? "*Domo arigato*"? Is that "thank you"? I like that. '*Domo arigato*", Kayoko. "*Domo Arrigada*", "*Dummy Alligator*". It's great, a great language so it is. I'll have the hang of it in no time, and be sharing the crack with the wee girl there.'

Kayoko was laughing. '*Anoshto omoshiroi-ne?*'

'Yes,' David said, 'he's a funny man.'

When they had finished eating, and the dishes were soaking in the kitchen sink, Martin asked David if he would like to go for a drink, 'Just down the road to Lavery's.'

David asked what they would do with Kayoko, thinking that Martin meant for all of them to go, but Martin said, 'No, just me and you, for a chat, you know. Steph will keep Megumi and the wee girl amused. Come on, a pint and a dram'll do you no harm.'

David looked at Megumi, but she smiled her approval. She liked Martin Cassidy, he could tell, and she trusted her husband with him.

Lavery's was crowded with young people, stiff-haired boys in leather jackets, and tarty-looking girls. A girl with spikey hair lifted her hand in recognition as Martin led David through the crowd to the bar. Martin ordered Guinness, with chasers of Black Bush.

The girl who had waved to Martin as he had come in wandered across to talk to him. She was one of his students, wanting advice about a project she was working on. Martin introduced her to David. As they talked David found himself looking at the girl; she was thin, dressed in carefully chosen rags. Beneath the brittle points of hair her face was ashen except for two sudden bursts of red blushed onto the cheekbones by her ears, like the marks of some disease.

'So how is it?' Martin Cassidy asked, turning back to face David.

David lifted the squat tumbler of whisky that had been served to him with the pint of creamy Guinness, 'Fine.'

'I wasn't talking about the drink. I was surprised when you wrote about jobs over here, you know. I got the feeling you liked Japan. I couldn't understand you leaving.'

'I did like Japan. I came here for Megumi. She had a lot of problems, health problems, her family. Living in Tokyo was making her ill.'

'And this place is going to be better?'

David said Megumi thought it would be.

'What about you? Is it going to be better for you?'

David did not answer him.

As the time moved towards eleven o'clock a rush of people came in and Martin suggested they make a move homewards. It was wet outside in the dark streets. David felt chilled, uncomfortable, his bladder full. He asked about Jean.

'I haven't heard in a while. The last time I saw her she was talking about moving to London. There was the possibility of a job there.'

'Was she still with the same bloke?'

Martin stopped to light a cigarette. 'No, no that didn't last much past your divorce.'

They found a house they liked very quickly. It was a large, detached property in a newish development off the Lisburn

Road. Megumi knew that she wanted it as soon as she stepped inside. She was drawn to the sense of space and light in the rooms, the pale colours of its wooden floors and unpapered walls. The young woman who owned the house had been widowed and was anxious to move as quickly as possible. David told her he could pay cash, and they agreed the sale at once. He spent what was left of the money he had brought back from Tokyo on furniture.

They moved in at the end of the Easter vacation with Martin and Stephanie to help them. Through the long hours of placing furniture and unwrapping crockery and glassware, Kayoko raced up and down the stairs, in and out of rooms bigger than any she had ever seen before. The next Tuesday Megumi began her new job as a teacher of Japanese, and in that same week David drove out to the Polytechnic's Jordanstown campus to be interviewed. Afterwards he was invited to the Staff Club for a drink to celebrate his being given a one-year contract with the Language Services Unit, to start from September.

Spring came and with it the lengthening evenings. Megumi was happier than she had ever been before. Alone with David she would tell him, again and again, how happy she was, how free she felt. She was suddenly easy to be with. She was a wife to him.

She taught for twenty-five hours each week, the only native Japanese speaker. She cycled to the university, the same canvas satchel she had lugged around Tokyo slung over her shoulders, only now it contained the lighter load of her lesson materials. David helped her with the preparation work in the beginning, but as time went on she found she needed his help less and less.

She seemed to have endless energy. She would shop each day after finishing her classes, mistrustful, like any Japanese housewife, of food not freshly bought for the evening meal. She liked the gaggle of stores that clustered in Botanic Avenue: small shops selling faintly unusual vegetables and fruit, a French bakery, enterprises tinged with bohemia. The panniers on her bicycle filled with crusty bread, some carefully chosen vegetables and fruits, perhaps a paper screw of fresh-roasted Colombian coffee for David after dinner, she would cycle home, bathe and then begin to cook, usually one of the dishes she had learned in the cookery class she went to with Stephanie, but increasingly things she read of in magazines, or the recipe books that had begun to filter into the kitchen.

Kayoko was attending school. That had been one of the few problems they had faced in the new life. The head teachers of the schools David had approached in the beginning were wary of taking the child. Her English was still poor, and none of the local schools had a special language unit for children like Kayoko. In the end one of Martin's colleagues suggested the Rudolf Steiner School. It was a long way to travel, but after a week of David driving Kayoko to and fro each day he was recognized by a near neighbour whose children also attended the school. The woman said she would be delighted to take Kayoko and bring her home if David would take over in emergencies. Each day when the little girl got back to the house, after she had her milk and biscuit, he would use his skills as a teacher to work with her to improve her English. Kayoko would laugh as they went up together to the room he and Megumi used as a study, saying she was going to her *juku*, her private school, just as if she were still in Japan.

David filled the days with work around the house: re-painting the woodwork on the outside, fixing shelves and lights, learning to understand the increasingly temperamental central heating. He worked, too, in the garden. The house had lawns and flowerbeds at the front and at the back, as well as a thin border that ran along the side of the gravelled driveway. The garden had not been cared for and he soon cleared it of every haphazard planting, turning and lightly dressing the beds. He bought rose trees and, when the nights grew less cold, ready-hardened annuals. He sowed seed. He cut the lawns and tined them clear of moss, scattered coarse lawn-sand, picked out the weeds.

As the evenings became lighter it was his pleasure to stroll in the garden he had made so full of coming flowers. He especially liked to do this at the end of a day when the grass was freshly cut and the lawn still wet from watering. Then he would carry Kayoko with him, wrapped in her dressing gown, socks and slippers on her feet. At those times they would speak together in Japanese; far from the ears of Megumi they could neither of them be scolded.

Yet for the most part he disliked Ulster. He found Belfast a bleak, cold place, its harshness reflected in the faces of its people, and echoed in their mouths. He was apart, an expatriate in what was supposedly his own country, although he never felt, was never allowed to feel, that the North was ever his country. He disliked the Ulster types, the cocky, swaggering men and hard-faced, hard-mouthed women. Hearing his accent they at once classed him as one of the English, citizen of the degenerate, controlling land across the water. For all their Union Jacks, the ostentatiously proclaimed loyalty to the Queen, these Ulster Protestants despised the English, their own felt inferiority fuelling a powerful, self-righteous contempt. With the few Catholics he met the hypocrisy was less complex, he was simply a Brit.

He did his best to hide his feelings from Megumi. He had never known her so happy and his dissembling was an act of charity towards her. As he slowly righted the house, the pleasure he saw her have in it, in him, in the child, entered his own sensibility, a benign infection. He began to work again on his book.

Martin Cassidy owned a small house in Castlerock, a seaside town on the North-West coast of the Province, not far from Londonderry and the border. For most of the year it was let to students at the New University of Ulster, but in the summer Martin moved up there. It was where he did most of his work. In July he asked the Kennedys to come and stay with him.

They took the coast road, leaving the city behind. The day was clear and hot, the first of a period of real summer the radio had said that morning. Across a placid sea the coast of Scotland was clear to the eye.

The heat spread itself across the days, turning the grey Atlantic into the Mediterranean. Martin worked in the morning, after joining Megumi and David for breakfast. He began a series of drawings of Megumi and so David and Kayoko would go out to leave them in peace. They walked the long, silver strand to where the River Bann met the sea, threading their way amongst holiday makers drunk with sun and their own good fortune at coming to this place in such weather. David would carry a basket filled with Kayoko's sand toys, soft drinks and fruit. He soon learned to ignore the wondering eyes that passed from the oriental face of the child to that of the man who walked behind her.

One afternoon David took Megumi and the child along to what was left of a house gone to ruin, the empty folly set upon the very edge of the high cliffs, like a toy by a petulant child. Across the distant mouth of the Foyle stood the Bloody Foreland and the cloud-shadowed hills of Donegal.

Later, they sat in the lea of a sand-dune, sheltered from a wind that had begun to come in off the ocean. Kayoko constantly toiled up its sheer, foot-treacherous face for the pleasure of rolling back down. It was hot out of the wind, and the child wore her bathing suit, a blue polka-dot bikini, the superfluous upper band askew from her thin chest. David watched her, his heart swollen with love for her sun-darkened skin, the perfection of her little arms and legs, her sand-peppered hair tossed in a careless braid that fell down her back. She was so complete for him, at once his universe and ruling planet.

Megumi lay close to him, her hand in his lap. She was looking at an old hardbacked edition of Yeats' poems she had found in Martin's house, its cover eaten with mould.

'Read me something,' he said.

She looked up, uncertainty in her face. 'You will laugh at me. Anyway, it is very difficult for me. I have only thoughts of understanding, as if I am sitting with this man in a room and neither of us speak each other but still we know our feelings.'

'That sounds very Japanese to me — or Irish.'

'You see, you are laughing at me.'

David smiled, shook his head. 'No, I'm not laughing at you. Read me something you do understand.'

She turned the pages, 'This one, this one is about me.'

Quietly, hesitantly, as if read by a child, the words of the verse fell from her mouth:

> 'That crazed girl improvising her music,
> Her poetry, dancing upon the shore,
> Her soul in division from itself
> Climbing, falling she knew not where. . .'

She went on, her lips carefully shaping each syllable of this foreign tongue she had taken for her own, until she came to the end.

'I think once he was kind to a woman like me, as you are, David.'

He took the book from her then, setting it down on the sand, and caught her head with his hand. She moved towards him, willingly into the kiss.

Kayoko paused in her climb, watched her mother and David. Sometimes when she saw them like this she was jealous, but today there were things more important to her. She continued on her way to the top of the sand dune. When she stood on its thin summit she could look right out over the beach.

BELFAST

'What are you doing?' Megumi asked.

'Applying for jobs.' He was in the room they had made their study, sitting at the big table they both used as a desk.

Megumi put down the tray and gave him a cup of the tea she had made. 'Why do you have to do this? I don't understand. We are happy here, why should you think about taking us away?'

'You know why. I have a one-year contract with no guarantee of renewal. With this college merger coming up a lot of people are going to lose their jobs. It's obvious that I'm likely to be one of them. We need to be thinking about the future.'

'I think we cannot do anything about the future. Something will happen. We can only do what we have to do and try to be faithful to our own lives.'

He drank from his cup, relishing the sweetness of the honey she had spooned into the tea. 'You told me once I was too passive to my destiny, that I ought to fight against it. I'm taking your advice.'

It was Sunday evening, the last Sunday of September. The summer heat that had so surprised in August lingered on, gentler in its warmth, comforting and familiar, like an old lover. In the afternoon streets the school children still went about in shirt-sleeves, their blazers slung carelessly from crooked fingers, as if at the end of their year, not the beginning. Office girls, laughing in the short hour of freedom at lunchtime, picnicked in the City Hall gardens, blessing passers-by with smiles and skin still brown from holidays weeks away, unspoken promises that no one would grow old, or ill or unhappy. Yet the signs of autumn were there to see: the leaves turned, fell in spirals to the earth, and mornings were chill, the evenings heavy with the smoke of fires.

There was a fire burning in the downstairs room now, and David followed Megumi down to sit by it. Megumi loved the fire, she tended it as if the flames were some deity she had been appointed to serve. She kept the hearth immaculate, cleaning out the ashes each morning, washing the tiles.

She sat on the rug, apart from David, close to the flames. He watched her from his chair, asked what she was thinking about.

'About this room and how much I like it. How it gives me happiness. I am thinking about the fire, the pictures the flames make. I am thinking about the scent of the flowers in the vase on the table. The fruit on that white plate. I am thinking about how sharing these things with you makes me happy.'

He reached out his hand to touch her hair. Even after so much time the first sensation of it against his fingers always surprised, with its wire-like strength and tension. He asked if she was really happy.

'Yes, I am. Don't you think I'm so different a person here? Remember, we used to talk about my bad days? Here there are no bad days for me, only good ones. Look.' She held her hands out in front of her. They were perfectly steady in the lamplight, and the stains upon the fingers were fading since she had stopped smoking.

'But are you happy because you're here or because you're with me?'

'I am happy because I am here with you.'

It was late, but she turned on the television for the news. There had been more trouble on the border. Two days before, police in an unmarked car had chased and shot to death three prominent members of the Provisional I.R.A. just after they had crossed into Northern Ireland from the South. The Provisional Sinn Fein representative interviewed after the shooting talked of R.U.C. death squads operating in the Province.

Now it seemed the I.R.A. had responded. That morning gunmen had entered a Protestant church in a village near Newry and fired on the congregation. Six were dead, eighteen wounded. Two off-duty police reservists who were thought to have been the targets of the attack escaped unharmed. The faces David remembered from visits to Ulster going back fifteen years appeared again, condemning, justifying, appealing for calm, for vengeance; the faces were the same, yet subtly changed, wizened, rotting, so many apples garnered in the attic of despair.

They turned the television off, yet still sat on, somehow reluctant to leave the room while the fire burned.

'Do you ever think of Tokyo, of Japan?' David asked, breaking the near-silence of the room, the soft music of the coals shifting in the grate.

Megumi turned her brown eyes away from the flames. 'I try not to, very hard. The things that happened to me there have to be forgotten or I cannot hope to escape them. I am very calm here. There I was never calm. So much happened to me, so much sadness. I have to forget.'

'It might be better to remember and try to understand what happened.'

She moved, a tension manifest in her body. 'Please David, I don't want that. I don't want to understand, because I know I cannot, you cannot, especially you cannot. Maybe I endured too much something — I don't know what it is. Perhaps a sort of poison Japan itself holds. We Ja — the Japanese sometimes eat poison. Do you remember? Did you eat *fugu*?'

David had not eaten it, but he knew what she was talking about: the blowfish with its bladder of poison. Only licensed restaurants could serve it. There, those that wanted this delicacy would go, to be served courses taken from every part of the fish. At the very end of the meal a morsel of the bladder itself would be taken into the mouth, that the numbing effects of the bile might be felt upon the tongue. Every year there were deaths from eating *fugu*, yet still the Japanese went, the anticipation of imminent extinction adding to the thrill of each mouthful that was swallowed.

'It is as if they feed upon this thing, this corruption and cruelty. Since I come here with you I have seen many things that I do not like. In London there were a lot of strange people, people wandering about, people mumbling some meaningless thing over and over to themselves. There were many tramps in the street, and so many frightening young people. And here there is so much sadness. All of this hatred that I cannot understand and that no one will talk to me about. All of this is a poison as well, I know it. But everyone here thinks it is a poison. They want to get rid of it. No one wants to eat it. In Japan you must swallow it, perhaps you die. But if you refuse to swallow, if you just hold it in your mouth, then absolutely certainly you will die. That was me. I was dying there, every day a little bit more. I'm sorry. You can't understand me, I know. I am tired and my English becomes poor when I am tired.'

As they went up to their bedroom Megumi said there was something from her old life she remembered. 'Often I think of my mother.'

He told her she should write, or telephone, but she shook her head. 'It is the past.'

Most of the students in David's class were Iranians, condemned to fifteen weeks with the Language Services Unit before they could go on to their courses in engineering or bio-chemistry. He tried to speak Arabic with them outside the class-room, but his Moroccan dialect was incomprehensible to them, they knew only the classical Arabic of the Koran. There was one Japanese, Mr Matsuzaki, a professor at a private university in Tokyo. He had come to Northern Ireland to study community relations in the Province, but spoke little English, and so he too had found his way out to Jordanstown.

At the beginning of the first session David asked some of the students how they had spent the last weekend of the holiday. He put the structure he wanted them to use on the board — 'Last weekend + past tense + activity' — and gave them some examples. One of the boys volunteered 'Last weekend I go barty.' David corrected him, and asked for someone else to speak. He could see Matsuzaki leafing through his Kodansha dictionary, and pointed to him, 'Yes, Mr Matsuzaki.'

Mr Matsuzaki cleared his throat, and then, with considered enunciation said, 'Last weekend I am in London with harlot.'

There was total silence in the class-room and David asked someone else to answer his question. It was only when the others succeeded in finding the one word in the sentence they had not understood that the laughter began. David kept it down, but he felt Matsuzaki's bewildered discomfort and afterwards had coffee with him in the refectory, talking about the research he hoped to do. He thought to tell Megumi of the incident that night when he got home, but in the end decided not to.

The community relations Mr Matsuzaki had travelled so far to study continued through the days of warmth and falling leaves. Two young men shot by soldiers in Londonderry, a police Land Rover blown up by a bomb left in a culvert on a lonely Fermanagh road. In Belfast a judge and his daughter, Catholics, were shot down as they came out of mass one Sunday. The judge survived, the daughter did not. The Provisional I.R.A. admitting responsibility for the attack, expressed profound regret for the death of the girl, 'an innocent victim of British terrorism'.

The shooting took place at a church not far from where David and Megumi lived. They heard the volley of shots and later in the afternoon, as they sat with Kayoko watching television, Megumi got up to answer the door. She came back into the room, her face pale and frightened, behind her a police officer, absurdly young, his broad cap in his hand, a black flak-vest over his tunic, a holstered pistol on his hip. He asked them if they had been out during the morning, whether they had noticed anything unusual around the neighbourhood over the weekend, strangers about, unfamiliar cars parked anywhere. He left a telephone number for them to call should anything come to mind.

When he had gone Megumi shivered, in spite of the warm afternoon. David asked if the policeman's visit had upset her. 'Yes,' she said. 'When I opened the door and saw him there, and the others in the street, I thought it was — I don't know this word in English — *yocho*.'

David found the word in the dictionary later; it meant bad omen.

He worked in the garden, with Kayoko to help him. Megumi was out, playing squash with one of the researchers she was teaching Japanese. The woman was Scottish, and with her height and pretty, narrow face, reminded David of Jean. He did not like her. She had been over to the house once for dinner and he had felt uncomfortable. It was as if Megumi had selected this woman especially. She had seen his photographs of Jean, had even commented on the resemblance.

Megumi had a lot of friends, most of them women. They called her Meg, telephoned in the evenings to invite her to their houses, to their gyms, to take her to their favourite hairdresser or to go shopping. It seemed every time he picked up the telephone one or other of them would be there asking to speak to 'Meg'. Then he would call out to her, '*Megumi-san, o-denwa desus,*' and afterwards she would ask him why he spoke to her in Japanese.

He was speaking Japanese now to Kayoko. She was struggling to clear the lawn of leaves with the tining-rake, while he pruned the rose-bushes. The garden was getting ready to sleep through the winter, only the chrysanthemums were left in flower and, by some freak of the season, a small hydrangea, the one thing that remained in the garden from the previous owners, had thrown out heads of tight, almost blue petals at the end of September that still refused to lose their colour.

He had promised to take Kayoko to the zoo at Bellevue, but the weather forecast for the weekend had said the fine weather would come to an end. Heavy rain and high winds were predicted. David explained to the little girl that he must mow the lawns one last time. She did not seem to mind and asked if they could make a fire of the leaves they would gather. He said yes, and the zoo was forgotten. Kayoko loved fire as much as her mother.

David worried about Kayoko. Now that he was working he saw so little of her. Yet it was more than her mother did. The child's English was not improving as quickly as he had hoped, and she never mentioned that she had any friends at school. In the mornings, when she went off with Susan Adamson, she set her features into the same mask-like pattern he had seen on the faces in Tokyo. Here, even when they were together, when he knew she was happy, Kayoko seemed set apart, removed from him and everyone else, everything else. She was like a fish he had taken from the sea, mutely intact in the alien element, yet dying slowly and with a rigid dignity. Only once had she broken the shell that she carried about her. He had been with her in the garden when a cat, a tigerish tom from two houses down, had jumped over the back fence. Then Kayoko had run at it, shouting, 'Get out of here, youse,' in a broad Belfast accent. She had turned to him and smiled afterwards, uncertain whether to be proud or embarrassed because of what she had said.

The next weekend when the Kennedys drove up to Castlerock with Martin, the threatened rain still had not come, although the sky was heavy with dark clouds, and the wind gusting from the sea buffetted Martin's car. The talk was about the weather.

Megumi, sitting in the back with Kayoko, laughed, 'Why are you always talking so much about the weather. If it is raining, if it is not raining, if it is hot or dry, or windy or not windy. It is so funny.'

'It isn't funny at all,' Martin said. 'We talk about the weather a lot because we never know what it's going to do from one bloody minute to another. Ask your husband about it, he's the linguistics fella.'

'Applied linguistics,' David added.

'Aye, well that'n'all. Anyway, you know what I mean, it's like the Eskimos having all those different words for snow, well, we have a lot to say about the weather.'

Megumi was still laughing and Kayoko, infected with the general mood, began to point at Martin saying, '*Omoshiroi-ne? Omoshiroi!*'

'I didn't mean to — to what?' Megumi wondered.

'Take the piss?' Martin Cassidy suggested.

'No!' Megumi exclaimed, laughing again, 'I don't want to use such words. David, say what I want.'

David suggested 'make fun of'.

'Yes, I didn't mean to make fun of you. Really, I like your weather. I like it because I never know what will happen each day.'

'Well, for Christ's sake, what's the weather in Japan like? It can't be that different? I mean, weather's weather.'

'There speaks a man who has spent his entire life in a collection of small, wet and fogbound islands somewhere off the coast of Europe,' David said.

'In Japan, everything is different,' Megumi said, the laughter fading from her voice. 'There is a certain, can I say "type", yes, type of Japanese writer — called *Nihonjin ronsha* in Japanese — who spends all the time saying what are the differences between Japan and some other country. It is something that fascinates the Japanese, how special they are. They think they are unique people. There is a phrase the writers use a lot, when they have been talking about a foreign country and then want to say how it

is in Japan, "*chotto chigaimasus*"; in English you could say it means
". . . but here it is different".

'Everything is organized, everything is the same. The
Japanese are afraid of anything that does not conform. To
organize means to control. In the schools the little children,
children smaller than Kayoko, are taught not to stand out. They
are given a terror of being individual. Even our non-conformists
belong to groups of other non-conformists. Or it is a hobby, like
golf.

'On Sundays a lot of young people go to a special place in
Tokyo and dance in the street. They look very tough, the boys,
like American singers, you know, with those leather coats and
greasy hairs. But they are pretending. They all dance in groups,
very carefully organized, and at the end they go back home and
wash away the grease and take off the leather coats.

'With the weather it is the same. Of course, no one can control
the weather, but the Japanese pretend that even this is different
in Japan. So, summer begins on this day, so, autumn on this day,
winter, spring. Today it stops being cold, tomorrow it rains, the
next day it snows, the next the sun shines. Like soldiers.

'They fear what cannot be controlled, and the greatest fear is
jishin, earthquake. But even that they try to organize. Each
autumn, in September, the department stores sell things to help
you survive earthquakes. Because the big earthquake came in a
September they expect all the other big ones to come in the same
month.'

'Well, why do you think the Japanese are like that?' Martin
asked.

'Because they are a people of extremes. They cannot walk a
middle way. With them it is one thing or another. And everyone
has to agree on the one thing. If you cannot agree they must
destroy you. When Kayoko was born I was very sick, perhaps
David has told you. One of the doctors said I had a picture of
myself in my head that did not fit with reality. I asked him what
was reality, and he said it was what everyone else agreed was
real.'

A gale was blowing by the time they reached Castlerock.
Martin's house was one of four in a little terrace facing the

strand. He had decided not to let it out this year, but was working to renovate it each weekend, knocking down walls, putting in a bathroom.

'Sorry, it's a bit rough just now,' Martin said as they stood in the hallway, shaking off the rain that had pelted them when they ran from the car.

'Are you planning to sell the place?' David asked, looking around.

'Not at all. I'll probably be living up here full-time from next year, what with the merger. There's a lot of talk in the art college that we'll be coming up here.'

'You really think the merger's on then?' David said.

'Oh aye, no doubt about it. The Coleraine people are only fighting for the best deal they can get now. It's just a matter of months before the Secretary of State signs the papers. No new tenured posts, no contracts beyond next September.'

'I know,' David said.

From his first day at the Polytechnic the chief topic of most people's conversation had been the proposed merger with the New University of Ulster. The University was no longer viable, it was said. It had been built at the end of the 1960s to attract students from across the water, to bring a certain width into the narrow educational life of the Province. But the most recent round of 'the troubles' had begun the very month it opened, when police and 'B' Specials charged a civil rights march in Londonderry, and the looked-for British students never came. With the opening of the Polytechnic those students who could not find places at Queen's went there rather than make the journey to the north-west. After the merger many of the Polytechnic's departments would be transferred to Coleraine, bringing their students with them. But there was a price for all this. Staff were to be cut. All recent appointees, like David, had been given one-year contracts with no options for renewal.

The house was cold, and filled with that peculiar builder's smell of concrete and putty, and stale tobacco smoke. Megumi heated some soup in the kitchen, while David and Martin, unsuccessfully, tried to light a fire. The wind was striking the house directly from the sea, and the chimney would not draw. Kayoko, still wearing her duffle-coat, complained of the cold.

'Bugger this,' Martin said, as they drank the soup from cups, 'why don't we go over to the Bann Bar for a drink and a sandwich, and then head on back to Belfast. We'll bloody freeze if we stay here the night.'

But in the end they did stay. The bar was warm, and Megumi and Kayoko, remembered from visits during the summer, were pampered by the landlord and the few other customers that had braved the storm. They got back to Martin's house a little after ten o'clock, and spent the time before they went to bed wedging towels, and wads of newspaper against the windows to soak up the water coming through the casements.

Kayoko still complained of the cold, and so David took her into bed with him and Megumi. She lay between them, her face towards David, sleeping in the warm darkness, while outside the storm threw itself upon the little town.

'You always seem happy when Martin's around,' David said.

Megumi, her head on her pillow, opened her eyes, 'I am always happy now, since you brought me here.'

'What I meant was you seem to like to be with him, you laugh a lot.'

'Yes, he's funny. *Omoshiroi-ne?*'

'He tells me he's asked you to model for him again — he's got some sort of big project in mind. Are you going to do it?'

'Don't you want me to, David? Yes, I want to. I like him, and we should be kind to him. I think he is lonely because Stephanie went to England. You told me he was your best friend, but I feel you have a coldness to him. In Tokyo you were never cold. I remember you as loving and kind.'

'That was a long way from Belfast. But you're right, there is a distance between Martin and me. We had a sort of quarrel soon after I went to Japan. It hasn't been the same since then.'

'And this is why you don't want me to help him? I have never known him only as your friend.'

David eased his arm from under Kayoko's head. She stirred in her sleep when he moved, and he gently stroked the hair from her forehead. 'No, you can do what you want to do, but I worry for Kayoko. You're out so much as it is, she hardly sees you. If you start something else she won't see you at all. She needs her mother, Megumi. She needs you. She's been pushed and shoved around so much these past three years, you're the one thread in her life that links her with anything. She needs you to tell her who she is, where she comes from.'

'I have never been a mother to that little Kayoko. First my own mother was her mother, now I think it is you. I don't know how she thinks of me. Maybe as some kind of sister.'

She smiled in the darkness, 'Tonight, when you and Martin played with the others at darts, she told me I am like a seabird, free to fly in the air or swim on the water, but very ugly when I try to walk on the land. She is so funny, and so old in her thoughts.'

'Have you ever thought that it might be good for her to have a real sister, or a brother?'

'You mean for me to have baby?'

There had been a long silence before Megumi spoke that last time, and, for all the battering of the wind outside, David heard her heart stop and start again before she answered him with another question. He said yes, he meant for her to have a baby. 'It might be good for us as well.'

'I — no, not — I think I am too tired to talk about this. Please, I want to sleep.'

David began to work at weekends with Martin on the house in Castlerock. Mending the house they mended their friendship. David would drive up with Kayoko each Friday evening, leaving Megumi, who had begun playing squash with her women friends on Fridays, to take the train the next morning. David enjoyed getting away from the city where a dark, oily rain seemed always to be falling, and Kayoko loved the ride along the coast, the freedom she had in the half-finished rooms, the wind and sand and sea.

'Are you beginning to get settled here in Northern Ireland?' Martin asked David one Saturday afternoon as they were re-plastering the ceiling in the largest of the house's bedrooms. Megumi had taken Kayoko for a walk along the beach, and the two men were alone with their work.

'I'm afraid to feel settled,' David said. He was mixing the plaster for Martin, and his back and wrists ached from the effort.

'What you mean because of the uncertainty about next year, with the merger and all?'

'That and other things. It's hard to explain. I almost feel I don't want things to work out with the Polytechnic, I don't know why. Like I said, it's hard to explain.'

Martin stopped to light a cigarette, and then asked David for the next bucket of plaster. 'Are you missing being in Japan, or what?'

'Yes. But again, I don't know why, I mean, I wasn't particularly happy there. I was lonely for a lot of the time, and then, well, things weren't that easy with Megumi and me.'

'Do you think you'd go back?'

'I would, but it's out of the question. Megumi was so unhappy there. She — she's not very strong, emotionally, you know? This place is so much easier for her. If you'd known her in Tokyo you wouldn't believe she was the same person. But I do miss it: I miss the little streets, and I miss the people, the shape they are, their hair. The first week I was there I was given a free ticket to a concert. I sat right at the back of the theatre and it was just amazing, this whole uninterrupted sea of black heads, row after row. And people, colleagues, were very kind.'

'Still, you must be glad to have the wee girl out of the place. Megumi was telling me about the school system, how the kids all go to regular school and then these cramming schools — what are they called?'

'*Juku,*' David said.

'Aye, that's it, *juku*, in the afternoons and evenings. And you have to get your kid into the right junior school, so it can get into the right senior school, so it can get into the right university, and all by entrance exams. When do the poor little buggers have time to be children?'

'She was telling me, too, about how if a kid is a little bit different it's persecuted by the others and by the teachers. She said that was how it had been for her. You surely couldn't have been happy letting Kayoko go through all of that now, could you?'

Before David could answer Megumi called up the stairs to let them know she was back.

Just before Christmas Eric Smith, the head of the Language

Services Unit at the Polytechnic, asked David out for a drink. It was evident that he had something to say, and he was not long in saying it. A group of private universities in Japan had decided to finance a centre in a British institution where Japanese academics on sabbatical in the United Kingdom could receive intensive English language instruction before beginning their research. A working party from the group would be in Britain during late March, visiting various universities and colleges. Eric Smith wanted them to come to Ulster. He wanted to convince them that whatever came out of the merger between the Polytechnic and the university at Coleraine was the place for their centre. He wanted David's help.

'I don't need to tell you how important this is, David. At the moment our department has no future. If the merger does go through — and it looks more and more likely that it will — then the Language Services Unit will be scrapped. I'll be all right, more or less, and so will Dave Rodham. We've already been told that we will be taken into the Department of English proper. But for people like you, people on one-year contracts, well —'

David said, 'So you're telling me that my job depends upon us getting the money from the Japanese?'

Smith nodded, 'I didn't want to put it as bluntly as that but, yes, if we don't get this proposed centre then your contract will not be renewed.'

David asked how he could help. Smith said, 'If, and it is only if, I can get the Japanese party to come over, I want to give them as good a time as possible. I want to make them feel at home here, because if they feel at home then it follows that other Japanese will feel at home. I was talking to Matsuzaki the other day and he told me you speak Japanese very well. I want you to be the contact man with the group. Meet them at Aldergrove, go around with them, smooth over the problems.'

He hesitated then said, 'I was hoping that we might be able to get your wife involved in this as well.'

'Megumi works,' David said.

'Yes, I know. What I wanted was to let these people see that it is perfectly possible for a Japanese to function quite happily in this community, in spite of the political situation. I thought perhaps that you and your wife, Megumi, might entertain the group at home, dinner perhaps. I thought Megumi might cook for them, something Japanese, and, if she could, wear the national costume. Just to make them feel at home.'

David said, 'I'll ask Megumi, but I don't think she'll do it. She — she isn't particularly at ease with other Japanese, especially men. I know that must sound odd to you, but she isn't. We came here so that she could get away from Japan. She won't even speak to our little girl in Japanese. And I don't think she has worn a kimono in her life. She certainly doesn't own one.'

The conversation moved to another topic, and ended. David went home knowing that he could not ask Megumi to help him, and knowing that he must.

The Kennedys spent the Christmas holidays in Castlerock. Martin had gone to London to see Stephanie and so they had the house to themselves. Christmas was damp, a light, drizzling rain wet the air, and it was almost warm. A soft day, Ulstermen called it. After lunch they walked along the river, to the sea, brown and slow, and went home collecting driftwood. In the evening, far from the squealing television, they played a card game with Kayoko and fed the wood into the hissing fire. When the child had gone to bed, exhausted from the excitement of the day, David and Megumi drank toddies of lemon and honey, and Bushmills Whiskey.

Kayoko had been given a kitten for Christmas, something David had been unhappy about but reluctantly acquiesced to in the face of Megumi's promises that she would make sure the child looked after the animal. Now the kitten was sleeping in his lap, dreaming its little cat's dreams.

'I think it loves you more than Kayoko,' Megumi said.

'That might be because I don't keep picking it up by the tail.'

'Oh David, you sound so angry but I know you really like the kitten. It knows you like it too, it has no fear of you.'

'Yes, well, kittens change,' David said. 'This one is going to grow into a real cat that we'll have to look after for the next ten or twelve years. I hope you, at least, understand that.'

'You are angry. But perhaps it is me that makes you angry, not the little cat, perhaps the cat makes you think of me.'

David said he did not know what she was talking about, but he was lying. He had spoken with Megumi on the beach that afternoon about the thing Eric Smith had asked him to do. She had become uneasy as soon as he had mentioned the fact that the Japanese were coming, when he told her they should entertain them she had run from him into the mist of rain. She had come back to David and the child, and nothing more was said until they reached the house. Then Megumi caught at David's sleeve, 'Please, please do not make me do this thing.'

She was calmer now. Now it was David whose anger hissed within him, like the wet wood upon the fire. Megumi knew it. She said, 'With me you were as Kayoko today with her kitten. When we were lovers you did not know of my life, you did not know of Kayoko, you did not know that you would have to take us into your house and care for us, bring us here to Ireland. None of these things you knew. Like the child you were carefree.'

'None of that is true, and you know it. I just want you and Kayoko to understand that you have to be responsible for the cat, that's all. There was no hidden message.'

'In Japan did you hear stories about *bake nekko*? They are stories of men travelling lonely roads far in the country. At night a man stops at an inn and a beautiful girl shows him to his room. She smiles for him and later in the night returns to his room to make love with him. Afterwards the man sleeps, but is awoken by a strange noise coming from behind the screen, where the lamp is. The girl is not by his side and he becomes a little afraid. He goes to see what is making the noise behind the screen and finds the girl there, but changed in her shape to a big cat with long, long claws, licking the oil from the lamp. If the man does not run from the room at once she will scratch him to death with those long claws. Perhaps it is how you think about me since I came to live with you, *bake nekko*, something that will destroy you unless you run away.'

David scooped the kitten from his lap and went to her. She was crying, the first time she had wept since they had come from Japan. 'I'm sorry,' he said, gently. 'I was in a bad mood. I was annoyed about the kitten, and I was annoyed with Eric Smith and his stupid plans. It was the way he made my job conditional upon winning favour with the Japanese — and involving you. It had nothing to do with you. You were just an easy target for my temper. Don't cry any more, I really am sorry.'

Her hair fell down past her shoulders these days and David ran his hand over it. 'Please don't cry. In Japan you used to have your bad days, remember? Here I sometimes have bad days. It's just a mood, it comes and it goes. It doesn't mean anything.

'I didn't know about *bake nekko*, but Christmas is a good time to tell ghost stories. That's all it is, you know, a story to frighten yourself with. The cats I remember from Japan are the *maneki nekko*. Perhaps you and Kayoko can teach this little cat to beckon some good fortune into our house.'

There was a bomb scare at the Polytechnic on the first day back after the holidays, and David spent most of the afternoon in Carrickfergus, sitting in a bar with some of his students. By the time the buildings were declared safe it was five o'clock and he had to go to a departmental meeting. He was annoyed, hungry and feeling drunk, although he had taken only a pint of Guinness during the afternoon.

Kayoko was standing in the garage when he drove up to the house that night. In the light of the headlamps her face looked pinched with cold and fear. He got out of the car and picked the child up, asking what was wrong. She said the cat had made a mess in the house and she could not go in.

'And have you been out in the garage all afternoon? Where's Mummy? Why didn't you stay with the Adamsons?'

Kayoko's kitten seemed to have begun a systematic campaign to destroy the house in the two weeks since Christmas. It shredded curtains and upholstery, upset plants, chewed books; it gorged itself when it was fed then inevitably vomited, and was proving resistant to David's efforts to house-train it. Megumi seemed not to notice, or not to care, and it was David who cleaned up each mess the kitten made. Now the stench of cat-shit hit him in the face as soon as he opened the door.

There was a puddle of watery faeces on the kitchen floor and a thin trail of the stuff leading through the hall into the sitting-room as if the cat had bled shit. The carpet was badly soiled, and there was more mess on the sofa. David opened the windows to try and disperse the smell, and sent Kayoko back outside again while he continued to search for the kitten. He expected to find it dead, and did not want the child to see.

Eventually he came upon it in Kayoko's bedroom. It had dragged itself under her bed and he would not have found it except for the trail of diarrhoea it had left behind. He picked the kitten up, it was alive, but weak. As he took it down the stairs the little body was seized by a series of spasms and a thin, foul liquid ran over his fingers.

He wrapped the kitten in a towel, and then lined a small cardboard box he found in the pantry with newspaper. He put the kitten in the box, washed his hands and went outside to Kayoko. He told her the kitten was very sick and they must take it to a doctor. Kayoko's face seemed to turn grey with worry.

David had to ask Susan Adamson where he could find the nearest vet and the subsequent drive through the rain along the Stranmillis Road was not made easier by Kayoko's constant questioning of why the kitten was ill. When, at last, he found the address he had been given, he left Kayoko alone in the empty waiting room while he took the box with its pathetic contents into the surgery.

The vet, a young woman with startlingly blue eyes, lifted the kitten from the box, discarding the soiled towel, and put it on the table. It was obvious that the little creature was dead.

'I'm sorry,' the girl said. 'How old was it? Six weeks, a couple of months? The shops have no business selling them so young.'

'It was a Christmas present for my daughter,' David said.

'Aye, it's the same every year.'

When he asked what had killed the kitten, the veterinarian said it was probably feline enteritis.

'I don't know what to say to my little girl.'

'Tell her you had to leave the kitten here with me, then in a week or so, go on round to The Cats' Protection League and pick out a nice healthy tabby. Your daughter won't know the difference.'

She showed David to the door. 'All right now?'

He drove with Kayoko into the city centre. The child was hungry and David did not want to take her back to the stinking house to get her something to eat. They left the car and walked to Ann Street where there was a restaurant Kayoko liked. When he had got her some food he went to telephone Megumi. He knew she would be worried, the house covered in the kitten's filth and no one at home. The telephone rang for a long time, but there was no answer.

The house was as they had left it. If Megumi had been back at all there was no sign of her, no note, her bag of books was not in the hall. David began the job of cleaning up. He put the sitting-room in order first, and got Kayoko settled in front of the television, then he set about the rest of the house.

He was on his hands and knees scrubbing the carpet on the stairs when Megumi came in. It was almost nine o'clock.

'David, what happened? Why have you opened the doors and windows?'

He dropped the nail-brush he had been using to clean the carpet into the bucket of water and came down the stairs towards her. 'Stay there,' he said.

He went into the sitting-room and turned the volume up on the television. When he got back into the hall he asked Megumi where she had been.

'I went for coffee with Carol and Rosslyn.'

'You were drinking coffee until nine o'clock at night?'

Megumi edged away from him. 'I went to Martin's house. I came from there now.'

David glared at her. 'I am sick of you and your friends. I am sick of answering the telephone to Debbie and Rosslyn and Carol and the rest of them. I'm sick of hearing about Martin and what a wonderful person he is. You have a husband and a daughter. Your daughter — Kayoko was in the garage when I got back tonight. She'd been out there the whole afternoon because the kitten was sick and had shat all over the house. Jesus Christ, Megumi, she's only seven years old and she was outside in the rain and the cold and darkness! You were supposed to be back here at four today because you knew I would be late getting home. I told you last night.'

'I forgot,' Megumi said, frightened. She could see how angry he was.

'You forgot? Okay, I'm going to help you remember in future, I'm going to take away some of the things that are distracting you from your family. You're not to see those friends of yours any more, do you understand? And you can tell Martin that you're not posing for him from now on. No, I'll tell Martin. And something else, I spoke to Smith again today. He asked about our plans for when the Japanese arrive. I told him everything would be all right, and it will be.'

He had got hold of her by the arms, and was pinning her against the wall. 'You're going to be a mother to that little girl in there, and you're going to be a wife to me, or I swear before God I'll break your neck! I've had enough, Megumi. Do you understand me?'

'Please David, I will do all these things, but please do not bring those *sensei* here, please do not bring them here. I hate them, those men, and I am afraid of them. Please, I will be good. I will not see anyone ever again. I will live only for you and Kayoko. Only please do not make me see those Japanese. Please do not make me. Please do not make me. Please do not make me.'

He turned his head to see Kayoko standing by the door watching them. He let Megumi go. She was crying. She stayed close against the wall for a moment where he had left her, but then pushed past him and ran up the stairs, upsetting the bucket of water as she went. He heard the bathroom door close, and the sound of the lock being turned.

Kayoko asked him what was wrong with her mother and he said that Megumi was not feeling well.

'Like the kitten?' Kayoko asked.

'Yes,' he said, 'like the kitten.'

It was April when the research group from the Federation of Private Japanese Universities arrived in Ulster. They flew into Aldergrove from Newcastle, the plane descending from skies which promised snow. It was bitterly cold on the ground and, as David drove the large Mercedes saloon the Language Services Unit had hired for the visit out into the stream of traffic moving away from the terminal building, the first flurries beat softly upon the windscreen.

He chose to drive down the mountain into Belfast instead of taking the motorway, and the snow was falling heavily as he followed the curves of the road, all but obliterating the views of the city and the lough he had hoped to show his passengers. The

Japanese did not seem to mind, or if they did, hid their feelings behind a screen of polite banter, the formulated courtesies that David had not heard for so long.

There were five of them, all men, senior professors from some of the most important private universities in Japan. The leader of the group was Professor Morisawa. David had met him once, fleetingly, at a conference he had attended, and Morisawa remembered him. David was surprised and flattered. The Japanese seemed relieved. Of course, nothing specific was said, but David sensed that perhaps their visit to the mainland had not been all they had hoped for. Morisawa explained that a decision had been made in Tokyo to site the new centre away from the usual British haunts of the Japanese academic community, and so they had visited places like Leicester and Newcastle, rather than Oxford, Cambridge or London. This posed the problem that most of the business the Japanese had been required to do was transacted in English and, although three of the five men were professors of English literature, they spoke very little of the language itself. The sense of a great strain being eased was palpable in the car and when, after he had delivered the men's suitcases to the new Europa hotel, David took his leave of the Japanese in the office of the Rector, handing them over to Eric Smith, the concern was evident on their faces. David said he would meet them again after lunch and Morisawa nodded, reassured.

Eric Smith was with David when Megumi got home from her classes at Queen's. They were in the kitchen, sitting at the large, scrubbed table where the Kennedys ate most of their meals. Kayoko was there as well, working at a picture of a wintry landscape. Kayoko was developing her skills in art very quickly. Her teachers at the Rudolph Steiner school were very pleased and Martin Cassidy, who had become her patron, often took her work home with him, paying for his purchase with whatever the child could find that interested her in his briefcase. When Martin came back from London after Christmas, he had given her a complete set of Caran d'Ache pencils. She was using them now. David watched her, his pride and love making him all but deaf to what his head of department was saying.

Megumi made tea for the men, uncertain in her actions as if the kitchen were an unfamiliar place.

'I thought I'd call in and see if there was anything I could do to help with the arrangements for tomorrow,' Eric Smith said as she brought the filled tea-pot over to the table.

'I think everything is under control,' David said, answering for his wife. 'We've to collect the fish first thing in the morning. Everything else is ready.'

Megumi said she had some work to correct for her classes and left the kitchen to the two men and her daughter. She had capitulated in the face of David's anger, afraid of him, afraid of the emotions she had roused in him. Since that night when the kitten had died, she had been contrite and dutiful. Although she still sat for Martin Cassidy, she saw much less of her women friends. She had agreed to help her husband in his effort to keep his job, and had even written to her mother, sending the letter to a close friend of her mother's so that her father should not see it. In the letter she asked for one of the kimonos her mother had bought and despaired of her daughter ever wearing. It had arrived in a beautiful light wooden box made of *kiri*, paulownia wood, and was wrapped in a yellow *furoshiki*, dyed with turmeric, with *tatooshi* folded about the silk. David had seen such boxes before and knew their value. He said to Megumi that it showed how much her mother cared for her. 'Yes, when I die she will put me in a coffin with such care,' Megumi answered him.

Megumi came back down to the kitchen just after seven to begin making the evening meal. Eric Smith was still there and, after telling Kayoko that she must clear her things from the table soon, she asked him if he would stay for supper. It was a listless invitation, accepted with more enthusiasm than it had been given with.

She made ratatouille, served with hot French bread and garlic butter. David opened a bottle of claret in honour of the cold snow that lay just beyond the door. They had fruit and a piece of creamy Brie for dessert, and David poured tots of Bushmills into the coffee when they had finished eating.

Eric Smith told a story of a disastrous dinner party he had once been to, and the tale stirred a memory in David, something Jack Stevens had once related to him. David said, 'A bloke I used to know in Japan told me about being invited to one of the professor's houses. I never knew which one this was as this bloke had funny little names for all the Japanese staff — "Greased

Lightning", "the Empress of India", "Big George" — the one he got the invitation from was called "Sid".

'Anyway, they got out to the town where he lived, a terrible place called Toride, about two hours from Tokyo, and waited in the station for the other guests, a Japanese teacher and his wife. Now you have to understand about this town, it's a terrible place, the last frontier sort-of-thing, you know, pigs running through the streets, people with straw in their hair. The next train pulled in and there in the crowd were the Japanese couple. I should tell you that my friend called these two "Fred and Ginger" partly because their hobby was ballroom dancing, but also because the woman dyed her hair red. Well, apparently they were dressed as if they were about to take part in "Come Dancing". Fred had a tuxedo on and Ginger was wearing this off-the-shoulder, split-to-the-thigh combination of sequins and feathers, with six-inch heels. When they met with my mate and his wife the woman, Ginger, said, "Am I overdressed?"

'Sid, when he finally arrived, was wearing a long undershirt with a pinstripe, double breasted jacket on top, a pair of luminous green trousers and wellingtons. His house was this very typical, incredibly cluttered, Japanese house with the straw-matting on the floor. Usually you have to take your shoes off to go into a Japanese house, and you don't even wear slippers on the *tatami* because it's so delicate, but Sid insisted that, because he had foreign guests, everybody had to be very international and keep their shoes on, so immediately there were holes in his floor because of Ginger's heels.

'There were these incredibly thick clouds of black smoke gushing through the door from the kitchen, and once some distraught little woman put her head into the room where everyone was and screamed when she saw the two foreigners, or it might have been Fred and Ginger. Sid said it was his wife.

'The food, when it came was inedible. They each had a whole fish of some sort put on a plate in front of them which, according to Sid, was Dover Sole, but when my friend stuck his knife in the one he'd been given, its guts came out, the bloody thing hadn't been cleaned. Amazing!'

Later that night, when he was alone with Megumi, she asked him why he had told the story. 'You always say how much you love Japan and Japanese people, you make me do this thing that

I do not want to do, be this person I am not, wearing a kimono that I do not know how to wear, pretending to be a good Japanese wife for these *sensei*, and yet in your heart you laugh at this other man in his simplicity. Yes, you laugh at the stupid orientals who try to be like you. You are hypocrite, David. *Gizensha*.'

She prepared herself for the dinner the next evening like one condemned to death, enacting each step in the ritual resignedly, all thought of innocence or guilt forgotten in the necessary actions of imminent execution. Most of the food was prepared in the afternoon. Her mother had suggested she make *tara-chiri*, a stew of cod and vegetables cooked at the table. Megumi had cancelled her classes for the day and Kayoko was with Susan Adamson. At five o'clock she put on the kimono, fumbling the folds of the garment with her unaccustomed hands. Her mother had sent a ready-folded bow for the back of the *obi*, but still it was an hour and a half before she was dressed. She brushed her hair, adjusted her make-up and came downstairs just as the door-bell rang. She ran to open the door, the constriction of the kimono binding her legs to tiny steps, and then, as David introduced her, she stepped back, greeting Eric Smith and the five Japanese men with a deep bow. '*Irashaimase. Saa dozo ohairi kudesai*.'

The meal went well. The five men were impressed with the food, for it complemented the snow that lay upon the streets of Belfast and the bitter night air. David knew they approved from the grunts of satisfaction they made. His eyes caught those of Eric Smith, and the look the two men exchanged was one which confirmed that everything was going well.

Martin Cassidy was one of the guests. Megumi sat next to him, and when she spoke, which was not often, she spoke to Martin. Then, at ten o'clock, Martin said he must leave, 'We've a life class all tomorrow morning and I can't face the model the college uses without a good night's sleep. She's seventy if she's a day and has a mouth on her that would curdle the milk.'

He made his goodbyes, and then David and Megumi saw him to the door. The two men shook hands, 'Thanks for coming, Martin. It meant a lot.' Megumi offered her cheek to be kissed and Martin joked with her, saying she was his favourite *geisha*, before he went out into the snow.

The dining-room was thick with cigarette smoke and the smell of food and drink, and seemed unbearable after the freshness of the air outside. David went to the bathroom, and Megumi said she would start to clear away the glasses from the table before preparing *hojicha*, something else her mother had sent, suggesting it might make a fitting end to the evening. But when she offered the tea none of the men wanted it. They had been drinking heavily for most of the night, wine with the meal, vodka and whisky before it. The Japanese were drinking now, the *mizzu-warri* they had asked for as soon as the food had been eaten, in spite of Martin Cassidy's protests that they were drowning the world's finest whisky in so much ice and water.

Megumi began clearing the choked ashtrays from the table and David watched the look of utter contempt that swept across her face, like a cloud passing across the moon. She had been impassive all night, compliant, but she was tiring now, David could see it, and her control over her emotions was diminishing with her fatigue.

She moved around the table to where Martin Cassidy had been, intent on removing the glass he had left there. The men were talking drunkenly together still, almost oblivious of her presence. David wished they would go. He had hoped that Martin's leaving might have initiated the mass exodus so common at parties and dinners in Japan, but it had not.

One of the crystal ice-buckets the Japanese had used through the evening was empty again, and as Megumi stooped to lift Martin's glass, Morisawa, without turning from his conversation to look at her, snapped his fingers and pointed at the bucket.

At once, Megumi threw the tray she was carrying down, spilling ash and stubbed cigarettes across the table, and cried, '*Iikagen-ni shite-yo!*' It was as if she had received a shock from an electric cable. David watched in horror as she began to scream the bitterness that was in her, her hurt life spreading from her as inevitably as the wine from the glass she had knocked over was spreading its stain across the white linen tablecloth.

'*Ittai jibun-o nanisama dato omotte irunoyo! Watashi-wa anata-no meshitsukai janai-wa! Anata-wa jibun-no koto-o rippana erai sensei dato omotte iru kamoshirenai keredo honto-wa ningen-no kuzu yo!*'

She staggered then, and seemed to fall, but gathered herself and ran from the room, ran from the house into the night, calling the name of Martin Cassidy as if he were her saviour. David followed her into the driveway but he could not catch her. Scattered on the soot-pitted surface of the corrupted snow were the ornaments from her hair, the elaborate *obi* bow she had torn from her as she fled, the cast-away chains of servitude.

When he went back into the house he began to apologise, saying that Megumi was ill, that she had not known what she was saying. The Japanese remained silent. They had one more drink together, as if nothing had happened, and then Kamachi, one of the younger members of the party, said that it was time for them to leave. Half an hour after David had closed the door upon his guests, Eric Smith telephoned him. He was angry. He asked what exactly Megumi had said, why she had said it. David tried to explain that she had objected to the way the men had treated her, that she had told them she was not a servant, yet translated, the words seemed so innocent that the Englishman could not understand how their force lay in the fact of her having uttered them. And all the while he heard Megumi's pleas not to bring into her home the very people she had run so far to get away from. He put the telephone down then and set off through the cold streets to Martin's house and the tears and recriminations he knew he must find there, the expected forgiveness he no longer felt he could give.

RAIN

He walked with Kayoko through the November rain towards the Arts Council gallery in Bedford Street. Tonight was the opening of Martin Cassidy's show and Megumi was already there; she had gone earlier to help Martin and the two girls who worked in the gallery finish their preparations.

He could see the crowd through the plate glass: there were teachers from the Polytechnic, other artists, pretty people, a currently fashionable Ulster poet. Kayoko asked if her mother was inside. He pointed to the huge poster in the entrance which showed a reproduction of one of the exhibits: a plaster relief of Megumi's face over which lines of Japanese script had been superimposed, part of the translation Martin had asked her to make from the libretto of *Madame Butterfly*. The exhibition was called 'After Puccini'.

Martin saw David and Kayoko come in and greeted them, saying, 'Ah, there y'are now. Come on while I get you a drink.'

The gallery was very crowded and David lifted Kayoko as he followed Martin to the table set with glasses and bottles of wine. He could see Stephanie, talking to the Arts Council's Exhibitions Officer, a man David had met once before and disliked.

'Stephanie came over then,' he said. He knew from Megumi that things between her and Martin had become difficult recently. She was seeing someone else in London.

'She did,' Martin said, handing David a glass of wine. 'What

about this wee girl? We've no coke, but there's tonic or orange
juice.'

'Mix her some tonic and orange. Where's Megumi?'

'Oh, she's there in the thick of things. Star of the show, so she
is. In fact, the way things are going tonight you'd think it was her
show, not mine.' He gave Kayoko the orange juice, 'Still, I
wouldn't have had a show but for her. She was a great model,
David. I know it took her away from the house a lot, and you and
the wee girl, but thanks for being so understanding.'

Martin went off to greet more latecomers and David wandered
over to talk to Stephanie, trailing Kayoko by the hand. Stephanie
was alone now, looking unhappy.

'How are things?' David asked.

She seemed surprised, then happy, 'Och David, how's about
ye?' She hugged Kayoko, spilling some of the child's drink.
David took the glass from Kayoko's hand.

'So, is life in London treating you well?' he said.

Stephanie made a face, 'A bit complicated at the minute, to tell
you the truth. What about yourself?'

'Not great. I've been out of work since the autumn.'

'Aye, Martin was telling me, the merger and that?'

They stood together for most of the evening, the crowd slowly
thinning around them. Kayoko was tired and restless, she kept
asking when they could go home. David said they must wait for
Megumi.

'God, I hate these things,' Stephanie said. 'What a collection
of utter pricks. I don't know why I came over.'

Kayoko saw Megumi and wanted to go to her. David let her
go, telling her to be careful. 'Are you staying with Martin?' he
asked, his eyes following Kayoko across the gallery floor.

'No, I'm not. I'm at my sister's house over in Orangefield. I'm
just here for the one night, taking the shuttle back first thing
tomorrow morning.

'Ach, I shouldn't have come really, you know, David. It's all
over between Martin and me, but he just won't accept it. I'm
living with this other guy over there, and it isn't just me, Martin's
been seeing somebody else while I've been away. Like I say, it's
complicated, you know what I mean? I don't love him, I love

somebody else, he loves me, he doesn't love somebody else, she loves him —'

David said yes, he knew what she meant.

Kayoko came back, crying. David picked her up, asked her what was wrong. She said Megumi had sent her away.

'Look David, I'd better go,' Stephanie said. 'It's great seeing you again. I just want to have a quick word with Martin before I leave, you know.' She kissed him, and then the child, and walked over to where Martin was, talking with another lecturer from the art college. David watched as Martin excused himself to follow Stephanie outside into the dark and the rain.

Megumi was standing, deep in conversation with her friends Rosslyn Lowden and Carol Meagher, by a large painting which showed her seated, cross-legged, on the blanket David and Jean had given Martin, a present from their first year in Morocco. The painting was representational, except for the face where Martin had taken her features and stylized them into a mask-like fixity; with her hands positioned under her chin, it seemed she held her face before her like a visor which, perhaps, she was about to remove for the artist.

David approached her. 'Are you ready to go? Kayoko's tired.'

Megumi was smiling at something Carol Meagher had said and she turned to David with a certain distraction evident in her eyes. 'There's a party soon at Martin's. I thought we could go.'

'You go. I'm taking Kayoko home. She has school tomorrow.'

'I won't be late. I promise.' She smiled and turned back to her friends.

Out in the street again, he looked back through the gallery window. That afternoon he had watched Megumi dress for the opening. She had put on a white blouse with pearl buttons, and a full skirt of black, taffeta-like material. The stockings she wore had small bows worked into them at the heel, visible over the black patent pumps she had on her feet. She seldom wore jewellery, but had slipped two silver bangles Martin Cassidy had given her onto her left wrist. Her black, heavy hair was cut to shoulder length, with a fringe that almost hid her eyes. The pale powder on her face was stark against the black hair and vivid carmine of her lips.

He thought how she had changed from the nervous girl who used to come to his house in Tokyo, in her white jeans and tee-shirt, the little crocheted hat she wore on her cropped head. In the winter she had changed to heavy-weight trousers with thick, check-patterned shirts and a down-filled jacket, the crocheted hat of summer giving way to a woollen ski-cap, or a Tokyo Giants baseball cap in black serge. She had left most of her old clothes behind her in Japan, and thrown out the few she brought with her to Britain as soon as she could, discarding them as it seemed she had discarded her old self, a butterfly shaking off the skin of its former life.

A white-haired, full-bearded man, a writer friend of Martin's, went up to Megumi and kissed her. David turned his face into the rain, holding Kayoko close to him, and walked to the car park where he had left the Renault.

He was in the kitchen, reading and eating biscuits, when Megumi came in. It was early in the morning. He had heard a car stop out in the road, a door close quietly and then the sound of her key.

She paused when she saw him, as if expecting some rebuke. None came. He asked how she had enjoyed the party.

Later, as they lay together in bed, she was loving towards him, lying close, her hand tracing the features of his face in the darkness. She told him she was undeserving of the kindness he showed her, the freedom he gave.

He had heard that his contract would not be renewed in May. It was not a surprise to him, but the news left him with a sickness in his gut that took days to fade. When he told Megumi she said it did not matter; they would be poorer, but the house was theirs, they would be able to manage on her salary.

'I think I could make extra money giving private lessons. There is a lot of interest in Japan now. People telephone the university asking about Japanese teachers.'

He asked what he was meant to be doing while she was out earning money.

'You can finish your book, David. It is such an opportunity, and there will be a job for you soon, I know it. While you are looking perhaps there might be some part-time work you could do, or perhaps you could re-train. Last year Carol's husband took a course in data processing and has a good job —'

'I do not want to be a data processor!' he had shouted, making her cower before him.

His responsibilities to the Polytechnic ended with the summer vacation. He went to Greece with Megumi and Kayoko for three weeks, using money from the summer bonus Megumi was given by Mitsu. When they returned he spent much of his time in the garden, cutting the grass, weeding, caring for the roses. He kept the house clean, shopped, cooked and looked after Kayoko. In the afternoons he would take the child to the cinema or the zoo. It was a wet summer, but on fine days he drove with her to Helens Bay, or the forest park at Tullymore. Once they set off in the morning with a picnic and went to Strangford. It was in September, when Kayoko was back at school, that the hollow life he had known once before returned. In October a cold rain pelted the leaf-choked gutters in the streets, the days grew short and winter closed about the Province again.

Megumi bloomed in the autumn weather. She seemed to David one with the chrysanthemums in the night-frosted gardens he passed every morning on his way to the little shop where he bought milk and the newspapers, slowly stretching their glistening petals in the meagre sunlight, sleeping princesses woken too late for the summer ball. It was as if, in bringing her away from Japan, she had passed beyond his control. Each day she grew stronger, as, each day, he grew weaker. He felt like some idle jack, who had planted the beans he had brought home from the market, and now gazed terrified at the leafy monster that towered in the sky above his head.

David drove through the darkness of the late January afternoon, following the motorway back to Belfast. He had been to Coleraine for an interview. There was a post vacant at the technical college, Liberal Studies. He had known as soon as he had seen the interview panel that he would not even be considered for the job. The row of well-fed Protestant faces, the tweed that reeked as much of self-satisfaction as it did of naptha. They had made the usual comments — he seemed over-qualified for the post, he had moved about the world a lot, he must find Ulster small and provincial — and then thanked him in that tone in which dismissal is always apparent.

He listened to the radio. On the B.B.C. Ulster news a plumb-choked voice told of a man in Carrick whose left hand had been hacksawed off by Protestant paramilitaries. David changed stations to where Ella Fitzgerald sang, 'And when the day is through/Each night I hurry to/A home where love waits I know/I guess I'm a lucky so and so'.

His home was dark as he drove past to collect Kayoko from the Adamsons'. Megumi was out, busy with one of her private students. She had found three people wanting to learn Japanese, two businessmen and a woman potter. They paid her well for the teaching. On the days she had private classes she did not get back until almost ten o'clock at night. Yet she seemed to grow stronger the more she worked. She was never ill, never depressed. Her skin was clear, her hair thick and glossy. She found a beauty in those months she had never known before, moving in a world of work and friendships where neither David nor Kayoko had a part.

He watched from an accepting distance, defeated. He was strong for Kayoko because he was her father, but for nothing else. Not for himself. He measured the empty hours of the mornings and afternoons in cups of coffee, drank one after another for nothing more than the action of watching the pan of milk heat, the brown granules dissolve in the mug. He listened to the radio, feeding as much on the endless succession of horrors it brought into his consciousness as the biscuits and sandwiches he swallowed. He began to put on weight. In the mornings he had to drag himself from sleep to get Kayoko up and ready for school even though he dozed through most afternoons and was in bed again before eleven at night. It seemed to him his life was a nightmare he slept to wake from.

The times he did not sleep were when Megumi was out at a party. There seemed to be many parties that winter and Megumi was wanted at all of them. At first she asked David to go with her, but after a while she stopped, presuming his refusal. She would not get back to the house until two, sometimes three in the morning. He went to bed at his usual time but never slept, for his heart and head roared with anger and suspicion. At those times, waiting in the darkness for the sound of her key, he felt he hated her.

He was convinced now that she was having an affair with Martin Cassidy. Even though the art college had moved to Coleraine, Martin had kept on the house in Eglantine Avenue and was there from Friday to Monday each week. David knew he was usually at the parties Megumi went to, he knew that she was often at his house. She hid nothing except the fact of her adultery.

When this thought first came to him David considered confronting the pair of them, but in the end kept quiet. Megumi had all the power. It was not her money, it was Kayoko who gave her the strength he dared not test. If she chose to take Kayoko away from him he would have nothing at all.

And so he accepted what, even if he could prove, he could not change. It was, he knew, his fate to be deceived, as it was hers to deceive him. Perhaps, he thought, what men call fate is actually traced in the blood, a genetic destiny patterned at the moment of conception.

He had read of convicted murderers and rapists being shown photographs and asked to select victims from the faces shown. Almost all of those chosen had already been the subject of some form of violent attack. There was no element of the accidental, the criminals knew upon whom they could prey, almost as if the one chosen were in some way an accomplice in his own assault.

It was the same for him. It was not that he accepted his fate, as Megumi had once said. He was marked, the stain waiting in him as a seed waits, until the required circumstances accrue. It was the same for them all. Martin had been between some whore's legs at the moment Lynne was dying, why should he have scruples at taking his friend's wife. David looked at the probabilities, the things said and not said, and knew they were not probabilities at all. It was, and the word came back to him again, their destiny, just as much as it was the destiny of this dreadful corner of a country where the rain seemed never to cease from falling to give itself over to the shedding of blood — murder, explosives, threats.

He walked with the crowds in Oxford Street. He had just come from the first of the three interviews for which he was in London, a post as director of studies at a small language school in Madrid. He wanted a drink, but the pubs were closed. In the end he settled for coffee.

It was late when he got into the street again, and the winter darkness closed around the figures on the pavement. It was his second winter without work. It felt strange to be in England. He had not been back at all in the time he and Megumi had lived in Belfast. He had almost no contact with his family, a card from Deidrie at Christmas, but that was all. Now he felt more foreign than he had coming home from Fez or Tokyo. Something of Ulster's willed isolation had seeped into him.

His sense of loneliness made him look into the faces of the crowd, thinking they belonged to friends. The day before, coming out of the tube station at South Kensington, he had called after someone he thought he knew, a woman who had taught with him in Fez. The face that had turned to him was that of a stranger and, muttering an embarrassed apology, he had hastily backed away.

He decided to walk to the West End and see a film. He was staying at the Central Y.M.C.A., paying for a week what one night would cost in an hotel. His room was pleasant enough, but he did not want to be on his own. He preferred the crowded, anonymous darkness of the cinema.

He had been walking for five minutes or so and was passing the John Lewis store when a blond woman walked by him. At first glance he thought it was Nicky Stevens, and he almost paused to look back at her. Then he heard his name being called and turned to see the woman looking at him in disbelief, 'David? It's me, Nicky.'

They went back to the café he had just left and found a table by the window. Nicky looked at him, shaking her head, saying she could not believe he was real. 'It's been such a long time.'

She wanted to know if he was in London on holiday from Tokyo. He told her, as quickly as he could, all that had happened to him in the years since they had last met, his marriage, the job in Belfast.

'That was the woman you were giving lessons to?'

'Yes, you saw her once, the time you came over to the house in Kugayama.'

'And you have a little girl?'

David nodded, 'What about you and Jack? Are you still in Lisbon?'

'We never got to Lisbon. Jack's in Saudi Arabia.'

'With the Council?'

'No,' Nicky said, moving her purse from the table to make room for the coffee that had just been brought to them. 'He didn't get the job with the Council, or at least, not the one he thought he was getting. I mean, you remember how he was when we left Japan. He was just so sure. What they actually offered him, in the end, was a post as a language teacher at the school, on a salary a kid couldn't have lived on. He couldn't believe it. He called Tokyo two or three times to try and talk to Duckham, but he was always either busy or out. Finally Jack got the message.

'He was unemployed for six months and then got the thing he's doing now, teaching English in the middle of the fucking desert. It's an unaccompanied post, I never know when I'm going to see him. He sometimes gets back here for a week or so on a charter. He earns a lot of money, and he could get back more often but, well, you know Jack. He's still saving up for that rainy day.'

'So what do you do?'

Nicky stirred her coffee. 'I live — alone — in the flat he bought. It's very nice, except I hate being in the place, especially at night. I'm scared all the time. I do a lot of shopping. Sometimes one of the children comes to town for the weekend. They're both at university now. Lives of their own.'

'You didn't ever go back to art school? Your work was good, you know. You just needed a little more time with the right people.'

'I thought about it, but Jack said what was the point when there was always the possibility he might get moved up to the coast. I could be with him then, you see.'

David looked at his watch, and Nicky said she was sorry to keep him. 'Are you meeting your wife?'

'No, she's in Belfast. I don't know why I looked at the time just then, there isn't anyone I have to meet, or anywhere I have to be.'

Nicky asked if he would like to go back home with her and have something to eat, 'or, you know, if you don't want to do that, we could eat out. I'd just like to spend some time with you.'

Nicky's flat was in Islington, on the second floor of a converted Victorian family house. The rooms were large, with windows at the front that looked out over a small park where willows dipped wintery tendrils into a tiny lake. David sat in the kitchen while she cooked their food: veal in a tomato sauce rich with peppers and zucchini. She had taken a bottle of muscadet from the refrigerator as soon as they had got in, and by the time the meal was ready they had finished it.

He ate what was set before him, but with little appetite. For dessert Nicky produced fruit and a very good piece of cheese with which they drank the last half of a bottle of Bordeaux. She said she would make coffee and bring it through into the sitting-room.

The room had an empty feeling to it. It had been sparsely, but very carefully, furnished by someone with a great deal of money to spend. It lacked what could not be bought, people. On the wall facing him were two paintings by Martin Cassidy.

'I'm hardly ever in here,' Nicky said. 'I go to the cinema a lot, sometimes the theatre. When I'm in the flat I stay in the kitchen. I don't feel so lonely in the smaller space.'

At ten o'clock David looked at his watch again, but Nicky reached over to him, gently taking his wrist in her fingers. He had expected her touch all evening, knowing that when it came he would not refuse it. Nicky had begun an action to which he had already surrendered.

'David, please don't go. I still feel the same way I've always felt about you. Please, no one can ever know, no one can ever get hurt. Please stay with me tonight.'

He tried to convince himself that he wanted this, that it was somehow payment for what had been done to him, but he could not. It was simply that his spirit had grown tired, had lapsed into a kind of moral catatonia.

They went together into her bedroom and sat on the edge of the large bed. 'Look, Nicky, this might not be very good for you. I mean, at the best of times I don't last very long and — well, I haven't done this for quite a while.'

She looked at him for a moment, then said that it didn't matter, that it would be all right. Almost reluctantly he tried to undress her, pulling at the hem of her sweater.

'It's all right, I'll do it. You get undressed as well.'

Without its clothes her body disappointed him and he lied when he told her how nice she was. She unpinned her hair and it fell down, covering her flabby breasts and belly. When he lay beside her and put his hands upon her skin he was repelled by its coarseness, the slackened muscle underneath. He kissed her, moving his mouth across the failing flesh. The skin of her belly was marked by child-bearing, patterned like the green cardboard covers of the photograph album he had shown to Megumi such a long time before. He knew that then, at least, she had told the truth when she had said there was no escaping the past.

As soon as she took him inside her Nicky shuddered and began to moan, rolling her head from side to side as if in pain. David was frightened, asked if she was all right.

She said, 'It's because you're in me. I've wanted you in me for so long.'

He began to move, slowly, expecting what always happened now. For one moment he thought it was beginning, but then the sensation faded and there was nothing. Nicky gripped him hard and began to push herself against him, her breath harsh, like a runner's.

When at last he was finished, Nicky was astride him. Her face hanging above his in the tent of her hair was ugly, her heavy cheeks pulled down by the force of gravity. She kissed him on the mouth, and then slid away to take his numb and shrivelled cock between her lips, an act of gratitude.

'That never happened to me before,' she said. 'I knew a French girl once who used to call it *un col de perles*, you know, when a woman just keeps coming one time after another. Christ, I feel — I don't know what I feel.'

She got off the bed to wipe herself. David said it had never happened to him before either, but if she heard him she said nothing.

He left early the next morning. He had another interview at eleven o'clock and he needed to get back to the Y.M.C.A. to shave and change. Nicky said he could use the shaving things and underwear Jack kept in the apartment but he would not.

They arranged to meet later. She wanted to go with him to the Tate.

She was waiting on the steps of the gallery and greeted him affectionately. They went downstairs to eat lunch, joining the queue of tourists and suffering the lecture against pickpockets from the gallery attendant who walked up and down the line warning elderly American women to guard their handbags.

The exhibition was of works by the French Nouveaux Realistes. David and Nicky wandered through the hall past Tinguely's kinetic constructions, some early Christo, Cesar. The last pieces were two female torsos by Arman, moulded from clear plastic, one filled with shaving brushes, the other with old sanitary towels and boxes. David turned away, sickened.

In the Rothko room they sat before the vast canvases of sombre colour that so austerely delineated space. A couple came into the room, the girl was young, perhaps twenty years old. The man with her was in his late middle age. Her father, her lover? They held hands. David wondered, imagined, envied and wondered why.

'They're so full of hope,' the girl said. 'They contain so many possibilities.'

The man smiled, 'I don't think I know of a more depressing place anywhere in London.'

Nicky watched the two leave. 'I come here a lot, you know. I mean, to see these paintings. Rothko was like a god for me when I was at St Martin's. Today though all I can think about is how I want to be in a bed somewhere with you.'

She stood up and led him away. As they went out towards the foyer, David glimpsed the painting by Victor Pasmore he had looked at that day long ago before he left for Japan. It made him think of Megumi, and he regretted the woman whose hand held his.

They were together, naked in the darkness with no sounds but those of their breathing.

'Wait,' Nicky said. 'Put the lamp on. I want to see. Don't you want to see?'

He switched on the lamp by the bed, turning his head away from the face beneath his, the creased flesh, the hair fixed in sweat. She pulled him to her, pushing her mouth into his, hurting him. She began bucking with her hips and he felt her flesh tighten about him as the new spasm built itself.

'You come now. Let me get on top, I feel you better that way.'

They tried to move, with him still inside her, but he could not get her weight over the fulcrum of his thigh. Lifting himself, he came away from her and glanced down at his stiffened member to see it covered with blood. He cried out in horror, the first spontaneous sound he had made in that bed.

Blood had stained the sheet, and was smeared between Nicky's thighs and on her buttocks. 'It's okay,' she said. 'It's my period, that's all. Come back inside me, I want you to finish.'

She coaxed him until he was ready again and put him back into her. When his moment came Nicky yelped like a hurt dog, jerking herself up and down on him as she milked his seed. Afterwards, when she had stripped the stained sheet from the mattress and trailed it to the bathroom, she told him she had menstruated just ten days before.

'It's probably all right — I'm a bit irregular these days, but it — I thought perhaps you'd hurt me for a moment today — I know you didn't mean to, but I felt something.'

He stared at her. 'Why didn't you tell me? Why did you want to go on?'

'I don't know', she said. 'Sometimes desire is stronger than anything else. When I'm with you I just want you to fuck me. Would you stay again tonight? Just to sleep with me? I don't want to be alone here.'

They lay apart, but then Nicky turned to him and asked if he would hold her. As soon as she was in his embrace she began to move herself against his body, rubbing her wounded sex against him until he came on her belly. Afterwards she wept, saying, 'Dear God, I don't know myself with you.'

She asked him how long he could stay, 'I mean, I'd just like you to be with me. It feels right you sleeping next to me. I thought perhaps you could bring your things from the Y.M.C.A. today and stay for the weekend.'

David said that he had a last interview the next morning and then planned to fly back to Belfast in the evening.

'Couldn't you call your wife and say there was something you needed to do here, that you were staying over for a couple more days?'

'No,' he said. 'I think I should get back.'

She looked at him with saddened eyes, 'You don't have to worry, you know. I just wanted the weekend. I won't make any claims on you.'

The telephone rang as they were eating that night. When Nicky came back to the kitchen she said, 'That was my daughter. She's coming with a friend from university on Friday, so that settles things.'

In bed she made David come with her mouth and found her own pleasure by guiding his hand between her legs, and when they woke in the morning again she took him into her mouth, again used his fingers on herself.

She asked if he would come back to the apartment for lunch and spend the afternoon with her, but he said he had to be at the airport by six. She said she understood. In the hallway as he prepared to leave she kissed him, resting her head upon his shoulder.

'I won't ever see you again, will I?' She still held on to him, unwilling to let go. As he moved away from her she reached out to him again and said, 'Don't ever tell your wife about this — please.'

He had been back in Belfast for a week when the first letter came from Nicky. 'I'm sitting in a pub waiting for Jack. He came home yesterday — a surprise. I keep wishing it was you I was waiting for.

'I thought I'd feel a shit when I saw him again, but I don't feel anything at all. I'm numb with wanting you. You asked me once in Tokyo why I felt about you the way I did — do. It wasn't, isn't, something I could or can help. You seduced me. Your innocence and the hurt in your eyes seduced me. You will probably be thinking that you've fucked up my life for me. You haven't. The little time we were together was life enough, the rest doesn't matter.

'Last night I had a dream about us, and when I woke this morning it felt as if you were still there inside me, filling me up.'

The letter had come with the lunch-time post when he was alone in the house. He threw it in the fire. Two days later there was another. It arrived on a Saturday with some other mail and Kayoko, who was playing in the hall, picked the envelopes up and brought them to him. He knew Nicky's handwriting at once. Megumi was still asleep and, without opening the envelope he destroyed it.

That afternoon while he was up in the study pretending to work, the telephone rang. He knew he could not get to it before Megumi and he sat at his desk iced with fear. He heard her lift the receiver and give their number, there was a silence and she gave the number again, then put the speaker down. He called out, asking who it was and she said it was no one, a wrong number. He was sure the caller had been Nicky Stevens.

He wrote a postcard telling her to leave him alone, sealed it in an envelope. He made an excuse to get out of the house and posted the card with stamps he bought at a shop in Botanic Avenue. The next post delivered to the house contained only rejections from the three interviews he had been to.

Through the months of winter the hatred David Kennedy felt for himself and his life came to be focussed more and more on Megumi. When she was away from the house her absence angered him, and his imagination fed his heart with images of deception and betrayal, yet when she was around him, when she wanted to work in the kitchen, or help to clean the rooms, he resented her intrusion. He was cold to her, and her eyes told him that she knew he was slowly pushing her away from him. When they quarrelled openly, which they did more and more often, she would try to stand against him but with the knowledge that he must win, taking the strength from her with every accusation, every taunt or admonishment. Afterwards there would be a terrible silence in the house, which even Kayoko learned was not to be broken.

The days that followed these scenes were always the same, with Megumi staying more at home, nervous, obedient, like a chastened child. Then the tension would ease, she would go out more often and longer, his bitterness towards her beginning to build again.

There were times when, if Megumi was late coming home, he would imagine she was dead, swept out of his life in some accident or other. When a car slowed as it passed the house he half hoped it was the police coming to tell him she had been killed, the unwitting heralds of his freedom. Then he would suddenly stop, ashamed and fearful, like a child pulling faces in a mirror told by his mother that the wind will change and fix his face in its grotesque contortions for ever.

April came again, and then May with surprising days of hot weather. David worked in the garden without his shirt, and when Kayoko got back from school she would change into shorts and a little sun-top that left her skinny shoulders bare. Together they pulled weeds from the garden and the lawn, or washed the car, wiped the winter's dirt away from window-ledges. David's mood improved, there was a sudden rash of vacancies in the job columns, and he began again to know a sense of hope.

The heat continued into a second week, although the forecast was for rain by Thursday. He was in the garden at the back of the house, planting four dwarf azaleas he had bought that morning. The holes were dug, but he thought he would wait for Kayoko to come home. She liked to help him put plants into the ground, and the flower-beds were filled with evidence of where she had used her feet to firm down new stock. When the bushes were in he thought he might drive with her to the garden centre in Carrick to see if it had anything interesting. Kayoko liked Carrick, there was a place there that sold ice-cream, and she always asked him to take her into the castle so that she could look out across the sea from its high walls.

He stared at the four bushes, still in their containers on the lawn, remembering the first week he had spent in Japan. The azaleas would be in flower now in Tokyo. He thought of the paths around the campus of the National Womens' University, of how, that day when Asano had taken him there, they had filled so suddenly with the black-haired girls in their grey dresses.

So much remained with him from the years in Tokyo. When he bought the azaleas, he had taken only three to the cash-desk. The Japanese feared *shi*, the number four, and used another word for it; they would buy things in threes or fives. It was a habit even

Megumi retained. *Shi* was death. The girl in the shop, seeing the one remaining bush, gave it to him, saying she was unlikely to sell it. He took it, reasoning that having been given, the bush was separate from the others.

He was drinking tea in the sitting-room when the grey R.U.C. Landrover drew up outside the house. David watched the two policemen get out and position themselves with their F.N. rifles, a third walk up the short driveway to the door.

'Mr Kennedy, is it?' the policeman asked. He was young, with a strong moustache and the peak of his cap pulled low over his eyes like a guardsman. David thought he was the one who had come to the house the time the judge and his daughter had been shot. 'I'm sorry to say there's been a traffic accident involving your wee girl. She's been taken to the Royal Victoria and if you'd like to get your coat we'll have you down there in no time.'

David stared at him, 'My wife is at Queen's. I should — I should tell her.'

'There's no need for that, Mr Kennedy. We've already sent a patrol over to Queen's for her. She's probably at the hospital now.'

He told David that Susan Adamson's car had gone out of control on the dual carriageway into Belfast and crossed the central crash-barrier into the path of an oncoming vehicle. The police could not say how serious the injuries were.

He knew that Kayoko was dead as soon as he got to the hospital. A small group of people, a woman police officer, a doctor, Susan Adamson's husband, was waiting for him in the emergency treatment section. Kayoko had been pronounced dead on arrival, the doctor said. The Adamsons' youngest girl had also been killed. She and Kayoko were riding in the back seat of the car and had been badly thrown about during the collision. Susan and her other daugher, Jennifer, were both in intensive care, and described as 'very poorly' by the doctor.

He was told it would be necessary for him to identify Kayoko's body, and he was taken into the side-room where she had been placed. He had expected blood, disfigurement, but her face seemed simply to have been surprised by sleep, for her eyes were closed and her little mouth was open. He asked if he could be left alone with her, but the doctor said it was not possible, although he offered to wait in the room with him for as long as David wished to stay. More than anything he wanted to touch her, but he did not.

Finally he said he had seen enough, telling a lie in her presence for the first time, and she was covered again. He looked back once, trying to remember how she had been that morning, the shape of her pretty legs, her arms and hands, how far her fingers arched back from the tips when she bent them. It was all going from him so quickly. Outside Peter Adamson had been taken home and David sat with the policewoman to wait for Megumi. He looked at his watch; it was four-thirty.

He waited in the empty house for Megumi. The police who had gone to Queen's were told she had left, but no one knew where she had gone to. As soon as he heard, David called Martin Cassidy's house. There was no reply. He went home by taxi, and began telephoning Megumi's friends, but none of those he was able to reach had seen her.

When she did come back he went into the hall to meet her, 'Where have you been? I've been trying to find you. I was trying to find you because your daughter died this afternoon in a car accident.'

It seemed that she did not understand what he had said to her at first, but then the muscles around her mouth began to work, and her voice was ugly when she spoke, pushing the suddenly-foreign words from her tongue, 'I didn't know. I was at the hairdresser's with Rosslyn.'

As he looked he saw that her hair was no longer black but the peculiar rusty orange shade that Asian hair turns into when peroxide is applied to it. He swung at her from the shoulder then, his fist glancing her jaw and mouth. She went down and he saw blood start from her lips. He turned from her and walked through the kitchen to the garden.

They had Kayoko at home the night before her cremation and, together with the undertakers, made her ready for the coming day. She was set with her head to the north without a pillow, and covered by a white cloth. Megumi placed a silver paper-knife on her thin chest to guard her from evil. They used the coffee-table to bear the vase of white chrysanthemums David had searched the city for, the candles and incense, the bowls of water and rice.

The minister who was to bury the Adamsons' child had called on them to convey his condolences. He said he understood that they would not wish a Christian service for their daughter, but offered to put them in touch with someone from the Buddhist Fellowship of Northern Ireland who might be able to help them arrange a ceremony proper for her.

When it was over and they were back again in the house with the boxed plastic container holding the ashes of their daughter, David said he intended to go back to Japan, 'I'll write to people there. I think they could find me work. You understand there's nothing here for me now?

'If you want to you can come with me, or you can stay here. As long as we're married you have the right of residence, there's your job and this house. You could sell it, get something smaller. You could move in with Martin once I've gone. I'm sure you'd be happy with him.'

Megumi looked up at him. She had cut her hair back to the scalp and already it was showing specks of black at the roots. 'I know you think I was Martin's lover, but that is not true. He was seeing someone, someone who is my friend as well, who is married, and sometimes they asked me to tell lies for them, to do things to help them be together. But I promise you, David, I have never been not true to you. I would not.

'I think I have been a bad wife. I lived only my own life here, but you seemed — you and that little Kayoko — so complete, as if you did not need me. When I would try to be a part of that with you it felt like you pushed me away.'

That night they were sitting quietly in the kitchen, listening to the rain. David thought of it falling upon the streets of the city, and on the freshly-turned soil that covered the Adamson girl. It seemed wrong, putting dead children into the cold and unforgiving earth. He would not have done that with Kayoko.

Megumi broke the silence, saying, 'If you go back to Tokyo then I will come with you.'

LIFE
IN TOKYO

Megumi spent her days alone in the damp, dark house sifting through the box of things she had brought with her from Belfast: old magazines, photographs, a clipping of the article that had been written about her for *The Belfast Telegraph* when she had first taken up the post at Queen's, the catalogue from Martin's exhibition, all the paraphernalia of memories. Taking each item out and putting it away again formed a ritual through which she sought to retain some connection with her past, brief happiness, the life she had lost.

Sometimes there were letters from people she had known; Martin kept in touch with postcards, and Carol, who had left her husband to live with him, would usually put a page or two of news into the envelope. She kept all the letters. Among them was the one she had received from Nicky Stevens. It had never occurred to her that David would go with other women, but she remembered this *gaijin* with her long yellow hair and big breasts, and thought that, after all, it was understandable. Megumi wondered why he still kept her with him. She could not find an answer, she could only be grateful that it was so. Without him there was nothing and so she accepted the little he gave, on whatever terms, with gratitude.

She saw no one in Tokyo except David. She had met her mother just once since coming back to Japan. She had telephoned her early one morning when she thought her father would be at the public bath, and they arranged to meet. It was then she had told her mother about Kayoko's death. She would have liked to see her mother again, but acknowledged that this was not possible. From time to time, when her mother was at the house of a trusted friend, Megumi would receive a telephone call from her. It was the only contact the old woman dared have with her daughter.

When they first returned Megumi tried to continue the life she had in Belfast. She registered for work with an agency supplying translators to foreign businessmen. The job was important for more than selfish reasons; the post David had come back to was poorly paid. He received the same amount of money as a Japanese and there was practically no housing subsidy. Even with two extra part-time teaching jobs, he was still earning less than when he had last been in Japan.

Her first assignment was with a department store in Ginza. The store was having a special promotion of British goods to match the spirit of the prime minister's recently televised plea that everyone go out and buy at least one foreign product to help offset the country's embarrassing trade surplus. In this way it was hoped to circumvent the mood of protectionism in America and Europe, a mood which threatened Japan with tariffs and barriers almost as severe as those the Japanese employed themselves.

Megumi was part of a team of three girls sent to the store to act as guides and interpreters for the leaders of the British commercial group. Her English was far better than that of the other two girls, she knew that as soon as she heard them use the language, but somehow it was she who made the errors, who found herself engulfed in silence when she was expected to speak, who mislaid important papers and took her charges to the wrong offices in the wrong sections of the store. Somehow she survived the week, but she knew that, although her name remained on the agency's books, she would never again be given work, and she was not.

She hated the house they had rented in Iidabashi. It was cold in winter, hot in the summer, shut away from the world. There were no windows in any of the rooms; like so much else in the life to which she had returned, the white paper window screens were simply an effect, a meaningless gesture. If opened, these *shoji* revealed only a recess in the wall where a light-fitting gave an approximation of sunshine. She had not wanted to take such a place, but with David's new salary it was all they could afford. Even though they had sold the house in Belfast, it was still impossible for them to buy anything in Tokyo, and had they been able to do so, David would then have lost the meagre rent allowance from the university and become subject to property taxes he could not pay.

Yet for all that, the house, with its long, corridor-like rooms where the fluorescent lights burned all day, the smell of bad drains and old, mildewed *tatami*, was the place where she spent her time. Her fear of the world that lay once more beyond the door was stronger than her dislike of what lay behind it. The constant noise in the streets, where loudspeakers hung from lamp-posts, blaring a mixture of synthesized Mozart and old Beatles songs, the crowds of shouting boys, like so many cockroaches in their ugly black Prussian uniforms, the clicking steel of the *pachinko* parlours, the fascist vans that roared up and down assaulting the air with their propaganda, the sirens of police cars and ambulances, ate into her head until, once, she had run in near hysteria from the shop, where she had gone to buy vegetables, all the way back to the house. She had hidden in the darkness, had not moved or made a sound all through the long hours until David came back and found her crouched in the corner of the tiny hallway, as he had found her once before.

More and more it came to seem to her that Belfast had been a cruel trick. It was as if life, like some malevolent uncle, had given her something she found she liked more than she had ever liked anything before, and then snatched it away again. In the first few weeks after her return she found the old habits and conditions coming back to her. She began to sleep more and more, often not waking until eleven or twelve each day. She was haunted by fears and anxieties that she knew were illogical even while she cowered in terror before them. She began to smoke again. What did not return was the courage she had once had, the anger that had made her fight her demons.

The day Kayoko died, the moment her husband's fist had broken her flesh, something went from Megumi. She felt herself to be, finally, passive to her future, like a soldier shuffling towards the enemy with hands held above the head; the last act of self-volition before the descent into imprisonment, where all is resignation and the last exit is through the door of death.

For David, the return to Japan was no sweeter than it was for his wife. The city he had dreamed of so often during the years in Belfast was not the one to which he had returned. Tokyo was a nightmare to him; it was everything Jack Stevens had said it was, and worse. The green train for which he was waiting cut a circle through hell. And like a soul in the medieval inferno, David knew there was no escape; knew that here, in this city, married to a woman he was now convinced was utterly and irrevocably insane, he must enact his penance without hope of redemption.

One night, a few weeks after he had come back to Tokyo, he had waited for his train, tired from the long hours of teaching. Down the platform a drunk freed his cock from the tangle of his clothing and sent a stream of piss in a steaming arc over the tracks, adding to the accumulation of waste around the steel rails, the gobs of phlegm, the thousands of cigarette butts. The other passengers, invoking the solipsism which, more and more it seemed to him, was the essence of their culture, looked away, but David did not. He watched the flow diminish and stop, saw the clumsy hands push the other piece of flesh, still dripping, within the concealing cloth. At David's back was a poster showing the littered steps of a station, and underneath, printed in English, the legend 'This is Japan'.

He was lonelier than he had ever been. In the crowded streets he carried his isolation about with him as if it were a disease. He owed his job to Asano and Onizuka. The two men, who had met him at the airport when he had first come to Tokyo, had been the ones to answer the letters from Belfast. Both worked as part-time teachers at the university where David was now employed. There was a vacancy in the Department of Foreign Languages and Cultures and through their recommendation the position was offered to him whom the other faculty members had never seen. David had met both of them since his return, and Onizuka had said they must go out to a restaurant to celebrate, but he had not seen either of them again.

As well as the post at the university, Asano found him two part-time jobs. One was a day's teaching at another private institution, the junior college of a celebrated women's university in Ogikubo. The other was for two evenings a week at a culture centre.

With so much work and all the preparation it involved, David was hardly ever at the house in Iidabashi. He ate his meals in cheap restaurants and noodle-bars, or had the secretaries in his department send out for food for him. Even when he could have been at home he chose not to be, preferring the streets, the darkness of cinemas, a table in some coffee-shop. Megumi slept most of the time; she was never out of bed when he left in the morning and was there again when finally he came back at night. He had no way of knowing whether she had actually got up at all during his absence. He gave her money for housekeeping each week, but he did not whether she used it to feed herself for there was never any food in the house, other than the cartons of milk and packages of instant noodles he would buy in the all-night store on his way from the station.

He did not know if she ever went out, but he suspected she did not. Her hair grew lank and greasy because she seldom washed it. The clothes she had brought back with her remained in the closets where they had been put the day they moved into the house. When he did see her out of bed she would wander around in pyjamas, with a sweater over the top if the weather was cold. Some days, when she tried to make an effort, she put on jeans and one of his shirts, hiding her hair under a scarf.

They no longer slept together. Once, soon after he had started teaching again, when he tried to have sex with her, Megumi turned from him, weeping, saying she was too tired, that he should leave her alone. He had gone from her room to sleep in another part of the house and not returned. In the morning she came to him to say she was sorry, but he had heard her apologies too often before.

She had knelt in front of him and begun to weep again. She said she knew she was no good for him. 'I am ill. I don't know what to do. All I want to do is sleep, but when I wake I am more tired than I was before.'

He told her to see a doctor and went to leave the room. She crawled across the floor after him, pulling at his legs in supplication. 'Please, I know you are angry with me, and I don't blame you. What can I do to make you happy? Tell me and I promise I will try to do it. Only give me a little time, please, just a little time.'

He had looked at her, with her unkempt hair and dirty skin, the nightdress yellow with her sweat, and felt nothing. 'You cannot make me happy,' he told her. 'Just do your best to make me a little less unhappy.'

As he went into the bathroom she shouted, 'I did not kill Kayoko, and I cannot bring her back from the dead! If I could I would — I would — I would!'

He came back that night and was eating a pot of instant noodles in the tiny kitchen when Megumi came to him. 'Please, I know you do not love me, that you never loved me. I think though, once, the fact that I needed you and loved you was enough. It gave you something that made you good and kind to me, more than I ever deserved.

'I still need you, David. I promise I will try to be better. I will cook and clean for you, and be a companion in your bed, only I need a little time. It is so difficult for me being here again. If I promise to be good please say you won't leave me. Please say it.'

'I won't leave you,' he said, carrying his noodles to the room where he was to sleep.

The Department of Foreign Languages and Cultures held two staff parties each year. One, which took place just before the New Year festival, was for teachers and their wives. The other, in late June, was one to which wives never came. Why this was so, David did not know. There seemed no difference between the parties, affairs of carefully co-ordinated tedium with speeches, expensive bad Chinese food, formal toasts and stilted conversation.

On a hot summer evening David found himself in a room high above Shinjuku, holding a small glass of flat, warm beer and listening to the opening speech from the departmental chairman. The other teachers were ranged around the walls of the banquet hall, as it was called, facing their leader. He had already been talking for twenty minutes. On a long table in the centre of the room a variety of cooked food congealed in its sauces, and the colour of the fish in a huge basket of *sashimi* paled perceptibly.

David was the only foreign teacher there, the two others who taught full-time at the university always stayed away from these events. He was not in attendance by choice himself; as a new member of staff the party was, ostensibly, in his honour and, at the beginning of his speech, the chairman had referred to him by name, officially welcoming him.

He waited for another half-hour after the opening speeches were over before deciding that he could leave without insulting anyone. He approached the chairman and thanked him for his kind words, saying how much he had enjoyed himself but adding that he must go. As he moved towards the door one of his colleagues stopped him. David lingered, expecting another interchange of pleasantries. He was wrong, the man wanted him to stay until the end. There was to be a second party, one that would be more fun than this. He was expected to come.

David knew exactly what *nijikai*, a second party, was, and he had no wish to be involved in one. At the National Women's University such things had not existed because so many of the faculty members were female, *nijikai* were men only affairs. He said he had to get back to his home, but the other teachers who had begun to gather around him laughed, saying that Megumi would understand, she was Japanese. Again David declined the invitation, but he saw in the faces of the Japanese that a definite refusal would offend and so, as the neon gained the definition of the darkening night, he found himself being led through the crowds making for Kabukicho.

They went deep into the quarter, impervious to the din of music, the promises of the glowing signs and the barkers in the street. This was what the *mizu shobai*, the 'water business', had come to: coffee shops where the waitresses went without underwear over mirror-tiled floors, *nozoki gekijo*, rows of tiny cubicles for the customers to sit alone in with their box of paper tissues and watch through a window as girls writhed in a tired pretence of masturbation; massage parlours, assisted showers, all the tawdriness of the business that on such a summer night feeds upon the loneliness of men in the city, the desperation of women.

At last David followed the others into a modest-looking coffee house which seemed to sell nothing but coffee. Inside, two of the teachers talked with the cashier, seated by the door. The man, dressed in a tuxedo, his hair expensively curled, left his till to lead them up a flight of stairs to another floor, another world. They were in a place of sugar-pink upholstery, where ormolu mirrors hung upon the walls, and a chorus of girls sang out their welcome to the establishment; young girls, some in their teens, with strips of matching pink material about their waists, and pink rabbit-ears set into fluff-cut hair. Around their throats each wore a name-tag, with the English letters spelling Mariko or Fumiha or whatever the name was, traced in pink upon a white background, like the icing on a child's birthday cake. They were bare-breasted, and as each man passed along the line towards the pink-benched alcoves, one or other of the girls would offer a breast to be swiftly fondled.

There was no alcohol served, only cola or lemonade. The sweet fizzy drinks were appropriate, for what took place that evening was little more than a children's party for big boys. The man in the tuxedo played host in a series of games, and David watched his colleagues regress into a sexually precocious childhood.

They pushed the girls one by one on a swing, a *fête gallante* where the downward motion would ruffle the pink skirts to display for a moment a shaved and chubby pudenda. In another game a girl placed sweets into the mouths of the men, taking them out when they were sticky to mount them on her breasts. Then each man would nuzzle against her, seeking to claim back the candy with his tongue. All the time a girl sat with each of the men not taking part in the play, pouring his drink, encouraging when it was his turn to go out into the middle of the room, synpathizing if he was not chosen.

After almost an hour of this, the girl sitting by David put her hand on his fly, seeking to undo the zip. He stopped her. The girl, embarrassed, not knowing if the *gaijin* could understand her, asked if she displeased him. David said gently that it was not a question of her displeasing him, he did not wish what she offered. She blushed, lowering her head, and said in a whisper that if the honourable guest wished for something more they could retire to another part of the club, but there would be an extra charge for this 'great pleasure'. David shook his head, again the girl blushed.

The lights were down in the room now for the special cabaret. Two of the girls had changed their clothing for tiny *cache-sexe* in a shiny pink material. Following the beat of the music, they rolled with one another on the floor, convulsed in simulated ecstacy. David looked around him at the faces of the others, knowing well what was taking place beneath the concealing folds of each pink tablecloth.

As the men went down into the narrow streets again David found himself walking with Onizuka. Asano had not been at the party, and David understood why. Asano was a Christian, a Catholic from Nagasaki, active in the affairs of his local church. He would have no business in Kabukicho. But Onizuka was different. He asked David if it was the first time he had been to such a place. When David said that it was, Onizuka laughed, 'It is for children. One day you will come with me and I will show you how men amuse themselves.'

Onizuka kept his word sooner than David would have liked. He had not wanted to accept the invitation when it was made, but knew that if he declined the man this time there would be another, and another. He rode the train to Funabashi, where he was to meet Onizuka. It was an evening in early autumn, and warm still, although the maple leaves were already turning red along the river banks, as if the weather belied the season.

Onizuka was waiting for him on the platform, and together they left the station to walk into the city's pleasure quarter. It seemed the same as anywhere else in Japan to David, the same streets, the glare of neon, the noise. They came at last to the blank face of a screened house whose refined austerity described the centuries of winnowing down, of shedding ornament, to arrive at this precise anonymity.

Onizuka spoke his name, and they were shown into a large *tatami* room where there were some twenty other men. After being seated at a low table, drinks were served by a woman in a kimono, who stayed, kneeling at their table, to fill their glasses whenever they were empty.

They waited for perhaps an hour, and then the lights were dimmed, except for a bright spot that lit a small stage at the far end of the room onto which another girl in a kimono walked, her small feet in their white socks pointing inwards with each tiny step. Koto music played, and the girl began to unwind the long *obi* from her waist. She turned, presenting her back to the men in the room, and slowly, delicately bared her shoulders, letting the silk fall until at last it lay in folds about her ankles and she was naked.

She turned again to display the front of her body before the eyes that watched from the darkness, and moved to the edge of the stage. Like the girls David had seen in Kabukicho her pubis was shaved clean of hair, but unlike those chubby, milk-fed children, this girl had a beauty that cried out against what she was doing. He wanted to look away from her, but he could not.

The lights thrown onto the stage grew brighter now and the girl squatted at the very edge. With her arms behind her, she slowly lowered herself onto the glazed wood until she was on her back, then she raised her knees and opened her legs, pulling back the folds of the labia with her fingers the more completely to expose herself.

A man moved towards her, and then another. David turned to Onizuka, questioning him. The Japanese smiled, 'They are going to fuck her. Or at least, they will try. Watch.'

There were five men on the stage now, pulling at their belts. One of them had moved the girl so that she lay sideways to the audience. The man, his trousers about his ankles, tried to mount her. David watched as more of the men went up to the stage, roaring one another on in their efforts, drunkenly shoving and pushing for their turn, as if they were one of the senseless crowd on a station platform waiting to mount a train. Few of them penetrated her, mostly they fell between her legs, desperately poking their flaccid cocks at her body, their mouths drooling spittle onto her face and breasts. Once, when one was actually in her, the girl turned her head to the side, and it seemed to David her eyes met his across the darkened space.

At last it was over, the men went back to their seats, applauded by their companions and the hostesses at their tables. The girl on the stage knelt, bowing her head before them, her body coated in a slime of sweat and spit and semen.

From the darkness he heard Onizuka speak to him, 'That too was the children's hour, but have patience, we shall have a more fitting entertainment.'

Soon the room began to empty, men were shown to the door by the women who had served them, but David and Onizuka sat on, as did the men at one of the other tables. The Japanese said he had made appointments for them. 'I trust you will enjoy your companion.'

An older woman came to the table where David sat with

Onizuka and motioned to them. David, Onizuka and the girl who had sat with them, followed her to a long corridor on the second storey of the house. The girl opened the door to one of the rooms leading off the corridor and Onizuka, turning to David, said, 'Now I shall leave you. Enjoy yourself.'

The older woman took David along the corridor to another room and showed him inside. Kneeling by a *futon* spread with white sheets, naked, her forehead on the *tatami*, was a girl. As he moved into the room she lifted her head and he saw it was the girl he had watched on stage a little before.

He knelt by her and she moved towards him. He told her he did not want what it was she waited in the room for, but she took no notice of him. She worked at his clothes and moved her hands about his body until at last he took her. It was done in minutes.

It was late when they got to the street again, drunken men and boys fell about in the gutters, staggered towards the station with their comatose companions. Trains would take them home to women who waited to bathe and feed them, put them to bed and in the morning dress them in clean clothes to send them back out into the world again. Onizuka, though, was not in any mood for his home. He said he was hungry and told David he must come with him to a restaurant where he was known, where, in spite of the lateness of the hour, food would be made ready for them.

The restaurant, when they came to it, was empty, the owners preparing to close for the night, but when Onizuka asked if they would prepare food for him and his friend, it was done.

They were seated, and an old woman put a match to a small gas ring set in the middle of the table. She unwrapped a large cake of *tofu*, and setting it at the bottom of a deep cast-iron tureen, emptied a jar of water over it. She put the tureen aside and went off to the kitchens, returning with a plastic container in which David could make out several small shapes moving. He asked Onizuka what they were.

'It is a special kind of eel, fresh-water; I am not sure but perhaps in English the word is "loach". She will put the eels into the pot and begin to cook. As the water boils the eels will seek coolness and burrow into the cake of *tofu*, thinking it is the mud of the river-bed perhaps. When they are cooked, we remove the *tofu* and eat. It is a good food for men who have spent the night as we have.'

'You cook them alive?'

'Of course, how else would we attain the mixture of fish and curd?'

The woman put the eels into the pot with a strainer, and David watched the glistening brown bodies contort in the restricting mesh for a moment before they fell into the other water, sliding through the unaccustomed space after the narrow confines of the jar. Then the lid was put in place and the tureen lowered over the hissing flames.

Onizuka ordered a brown rice *sake*, chilled like white wine, while he waited for the tureen to boil. Then, when it was ready, he served David with broken chunks of the fish and white bean curd. David hesitated before he put the food into his mouth and Onizuka scolded him, so he opened his lips, took the cooked flesh on his tongue and swallowed. Onizuka poured *genmaishu* into the tiny beaker, pushed it up to his companion's face, urging him to drink. David drank.

They were too late for the trains by the time they got back into the streets, and David took a taxi back to Tokyo. His head swam with liquor and the images of the night. He kept seeing the body of the girl on the stage, and the lithe shapes of the eels swimming in the pot. He remembered how she had looked at him, and how her eyes had been like Megumi's the day he had taken her out of the hotel in Shibuya to the waiting taxi; the day Kayoko had screamed out and Megumi had looked at him, utterly defeated, with nowhere to go, but with him, seeking his protection as the loaches had sought the coolness of the *tofu*. At one point on the journey he felt that he would vomit and he had to stop the taxi. He was not sick, once out in the night air he kept it down. He kept it all down.

He answered the telephone and heard his sister's voice speaking to him, 'Brendan, I mean David, is that you? It's Deidrie. I've been trying to reach you for two days. Does nobody answer the telephone in your house?'

'Daddy's passed away. It was very sudden. He went to sleep in his chair, and when Mammy tried to wake him for his tea he was gone. There's going to be an inquest and all that sort of thing because, you know, it was so unexpected.'

'How's Mammy taking it?' David asked.

'Very badly. She's staying with us, she won't go back to the house at all. Look, do you think you could get over here for the funeral? It won't be for at least a week. I know it's a lot to ask but it's for Mammy.'

He said he would come if he could, and promised to telephone when he knew for certain whether or not he could make the journey. He sat for a long time in the silent house wondering why it was that death had become such a familiar to him. It was later, as he stooped over the wash-basin in the bathroom that he found this new loss charging him with sorrow.

The next morning he made his arrangements. The university gave him a two-week leave of absence on compassionate grounds, and then he had some luck with a travel agent, securing a reasonably cheap ticket to London via Moscow on Aeroflot. He would leave Tokyo and arrive in England on the same day.

He got back to the house in Iidabashi early and woke Megumi to tell her that he must travel to London and the reason why. She seemed not to understand him at first, and so he repeated himself in Japanese and she nodded her head, her eyes heavy still with the sleep that followed the sedatives she took. She said nothing, and David watched as she slowly lay back in her bedding.

The flight was on a Saturday. He finished his Friday classes early and was in Iidabashi by three o'clock. As he let himself into the house he found Megumi up and dressed. She was in the kitchen, ironing.

'See, I did these for you,' she said, pointing to the slacks and shirts that were hanging from the cupboard door. 'Now I'm getting my own things ready.'

She had washed her hair and tried to mask the darkened skin about her eyes with make-up. David fought his desire to move towards her, because he knew it would do no good. The comfort he wanted to give her would do nothing to ease the effect of his words. He said he was sorry, that she must have misunderstood, but he was going alone.

She had been smoothing the creases from a blouse she used to wear a lot in Belfast, now she lifted it from the square board she had on the kitchen table and began to fold it. Her shoulders were sloped forward so that her hair fell over her face; he could not see her eyes but he knew she was crying.

'I'm sorry,' he said. 'I had to get the cheapest flight I could find. I just didn't think —'

'It's all right,' Megumi said, picking up the other clothes she had on the back of one of the kitchen chairs. 'I didn't understand you. I think I'll sleep now. I'm very tired.'

He asked if she would like him to make her something to eat, but she shook her head. 'No thank you. I'm not hungry, just very tired. I'll see you tomorrow before you go.'

Later, as he ate the food he had prepared for himself, he could hear the sounds of her weeping. He closed the kitchen door but still they came to his ears. Finally, he went out to one of the neighbourhood bars. He stopped at a florist's shop, its lights burning brightly in the night, only the empty cans that had once held flowers testifying to the lateness of the hour. He bought the only blooms that were left, a dozen or so freesias. The flowers were for Megumi, but even as he paid for them he asked himself how such a gesture could possibly ease her sorrow. The house was quiet again by the time he got home, he put the flowers into a tall glass, and filled it with water.

He thought she would still be sleeping when he left for the airport the next day, and so he placed the money he had taken from the bank in an envelope, together with his cash-card and a note giving their card number, and his sister's telephone number. He put the envelope on the kitchen table with the flowers. He was wrong in thinking he would not see Megumi, as he made ready to go she came into the hallway. She was dressed and held one of their small suitcases in her hand.

'Megumi, what is this?' he asked.

'I want to come with you. I am your wife, I should be with you. You shame me going to your father's funeral alone. We can buy a ticket at the airport.'

He was already late. 'We cannot buy another ticket at the airport. I don't have enough money and anyway there are no seats on the flight. I got the last one, it was a cancellation.'

'You have money. There is money in the kitchen, a lot of money. We still have credit card from Britain.'

'Look, to buy a ticket at the airport is very expensive and — oh Jesus, I can't take you with me. I'll be gone for ten days, that's all.'

Megumi put down the suitcase, 'No, now you go away I know

you won't come back. Please, please take me with you. I promise
I will be good. I will do anything you want, but please take me
with you.'

'Stop this,' he said. 'I can't take you. I'm going because my
father is dead. I have to go. I'll be back in ten days time, sooner if
I can.'

She took hold of him, falling over the luggage that lay between
them so that as she went down she pulled him with her. Again
and again she begged to be allowed to go with him.

'Will you stop this!' he shouted, tearing his coat free. 'I'll call
you from the airport, and I'll call you when I get to London. I'll
call you every day.'

There was nothing else he could say, and so he turned from her
and got out of the house. At Narita he telephoned, as he had said
he would, but she did not answer. Then he did something that
had been in his mind from the moment he had decided to go to
England: he called her mother. He was prepared to hang up if he
heard a man's voice, but it was a woman who answered and he
asked to speak to Mrs Iwase. A few moments later she came to
the 'phone and he explained who he was and why he was calling.
He told her he had to go overseas on family business, but that he
was very worried about leaving Megumi. As he had hoped, the
mother said she would take care of her daughter. He put the
receiver down and got ready to dial his own number again when
he heard his flight being called.

He was in London by early evening and caught a train to Loxley
from St Pancras. He was one of only three people in the First
Class compartment, but from time to time the automatic door
would swish open to let through a procession of football
supporters, young boys and girls, their heavy accents marking
them as readily as the blue and white scarves most of them wore.
Loxley had been playing Chelsea and the newspaper David had
bought in the station carried a story and pictures of the fighting
that had gone on outside the ground. A Loxley boy had been
stabbed and was in serious condition, forty supporters were
being held by the police on various charges. The headlines on the
front of the paper warned, 'LIBYAN TERROR THREAT'.

Deidrie met him at the station. 'I'm glad you could come.

Sinead's here and Danae arrives tomorrow. How's Megumi these days, all right?'

David said she was fine. He asked his sister where he would sleep.

'In Beeby Street, if that's all right. Sinead's going to stay there as well. Mammy still won't go near the place. I'll take you home first though, get you something to eat, and I'm sure you'll want to see Mammy.'

They drove in silence, and then Deidrie said, 'Mammy's asked Jean to the funeral and I think she's going to come. They've always kept in contact, well, you know how Mammy felt about her. I didn't tell you when I spoke on the 'phone because I was sure you'd stay away if you knew.'

His father was buried on the following Wednesday. Jean Kennedy, who had kept her married name, travelled up from London and David borrowed his sister's car to collect her from the station. When they met they shook hands like familiar strangers.

After the funeral, the mourners returned to Deidrie's house for the wake. Although David's father had been the youngest of his family, he was survived by a brother and two sisters. The house was crowded with aunts and uncles, cousins, friends of his father David had not seen since his childhood. For all the sobriety of the bereaved families' clothing, the afternoon quickly became an occasion for reaffirming contact with the living rather than remembering the so newly-buried dead.

A little after four, when David had again tried to telephone Megumi, Jean came over to him. She was leaving to catch her train. He said he would drive her to the station, but she already had a ride. 'I should like to see you though, David, if you could manage a day in London before you go back. I'm very free at work, so if you give me a ring we could meet. I think we need to settle a couple of things, or at least, I do. Maybe I just want to tell you how sorry I am for what I did.'

'You already have,' he said bitterly, and turned away from her.

Jean followed him, 'Here's my number anyway, just in case.'

She gave him a small business card. 'The work number is good from around ten until six, after that I'm at home. It was nice seeing you again. I needed to, I'm just sorry it couldn't have been under happier circumstances.'

He stayed with his family for another two days and then arranged to take the Sunday flight back to Tokyo. His sisters were busy planning his mother's life. She had decided she did not want to return to the small terraced house in which she had spent the years of her marriage. It was not certain where she would make her permanent home, but for the immediate future she was to go with Danae to California as soon as she could get a visa. David spent his time wandering through the streets of the town in which he had grown up, lingering there because he knew he would not return. Deidrie hated it and, if her mother decided to settle permanently in America, would leave as soon as a suitable job for her husband became available. He was a science teacher and David had heard his sister say more than once that staying in Loxley had damaged his career.

Because the flight left Heathrow in the morning he decided to spend the Saturday in London. He thought he would go round the galleries, and try to pick up a ticket for the theatre in the evening, but on the train he decided to call Jean, not sure why he had changed his mind about seeing her again. As soon as he got to St Pancras he dialled her home number. She sounded surprised, but said she would meet him for lunch at a trattoria they both knew near the Victoria and Albert Museum.

She worked in the City, in the overseas section of an important merchant bank. Her clothes were expensive; she had her own house in Kilburn. He had always thought of her as beautiful, but now her slim figure, her shining hair and skin, had an elegance that spoke of money. She and David ate together and then went to the museum, finding themselves in the section housing the Japanese collection.

'I try to imagine you out there, you know. There's an awful lot of programmes about Japan on the television just now, and I always watch them. I wish now I'd come out to you that summer. Are you happy there?'

He was looking at the exhibit of *netsuke*, 'It's a place like any other. It's just the distance that lends the mystique. Were you happy in Fez?'

They walked back to the trattoria for a cup of tea. Jean asked where he was staying that night. He told her he had a room in a hotel near Victoria.

'I was just wondering if — if you wanted to stay at my place for the night. I've a spare bed and everything. I don't know why, I just want you to see where I live. Still, if you've a room — ' She was not as good at this as Nicky Stevens.

'What about you, are you seeing anyone at the moment?' he asked.

She shook her head. 'No, not really, nothing serious. Sometimes men in the office ask me out, but I don't want to get involved with anyone, to tell you the truth. I was seeing this chap about a year ago, it was stupid. He was very serious about it and I wasn't.

'Look, don't get angry with me, David, but I really miss you. I know I hurt you very badly, but I hurt myself even more. If I could turn back time and have things as they were between us, I'd do it, no matter what it cost me. I didn't realize how much I had, until it was gone.'

Jean paid the bill and together they went through the darkening afternoon to the underground. She asked if he had time to come and see her house, 'I'd just like to show it to you. I mean, we might not be together again. You know how things are.'

When they got to Kilburn David said he was surprised she would buy a house there. 'I thought you wanted to get away from the Irish.' She laughed and slipped her arm through his as they went into the street. Later, when she asked him to stay and eat with her, he said yes.

The ground floor of Jean's house had been converted to form one large room, with the open kitchen set to one side against the party wall. Jean had the radio turned on while she prepared the food. A disc jockey whose voice David recalled from his youth announced a listener's request. Jethro Tull began to sing 'Living in the Past'.

David admired the room.

'It was Cairns' idea. He did all the designs for it. We were going to live here together at one time, but it didn't work out in the end. We sort of broke up and I moved down here. Then we got back together again, and broke up again. It just wouldn't work in the long run. He's with his wife again now.'

They ate at a round white table overlooking the back garden, where the leaf-stripped trees stood outlined in silhouette against the orange glare of the London night. Neither of them had very much to say.

She made coffee. 'How was the food, all right?'

'It was good,' he said. 'You always cooked well.'

'What about your wife? She must cook you a lot of Japanese food.'

'No, she — she doesn't really like to cook.'

Jean seemed nervous, going to pour more coffee into a cup that was still full. 'How are things with your marriage, David? I was very sorry to hear that you lost your little girl.'

'How did you know? Did my mother tell you? Deidrie?'

'No, it was — it was Martin Cassidy in fact. We met again and we've kept in touch since.'

Annoyed, he asked what else Martin had told her.

'He said that things weren't going too well for you. He gave me the impression that he and your wife were very close when you were all in Belfast, and I think she writes to him now and again. Look, this isn't any of my business really, I'm sorry I brought it up.'

David ran his finger around the smooth rim of the cup she had served his coffee in. 'Well, the truth is, things aren't very good between us. It isn't her fault. She's ill and I'm not much of a husband to her. I tried to be, I really did. When Kayoko, my daugher, died, something — I don't know.

'I couldn't take any more. I felt as if God had specifically picked me out to shit on. I loved the child so much. She was so beautiful, like a little doll that walked and talked. She was the best thing that ever happened to me and for no reason she was taken away. Now my father — I don't have very much left to lose.'

He was quiet for a long time. Finally he said, 'She — Megumi — always used to tell me how different she was from everyone else. It isn't true. She's very Japanese really, she cultivates her sorrow, tends it like a garden.'

Jean looked at him and said, 'Then you obviously have a lot in common.'

His anger flared suddenly and he shouted at her, 'I don't have to cultivate my sorrow, it grows well enough on its own, and it has ever since you planted the seed.'

'David, stop feeling so sorry for yourself. It hasn't been easy for me either. I know exactly what I put you through, because Cairns did the same to me. But it's all in the past, it's over, all of it. You have to deal with it, and put it behind you or else the past is all you have, it poisons the present.'

'Exactly, Jean. The past is all I have. The past is my present and my fucking future.'

He sat staring out into the night until, finally, he said, 'I can't go back. I'm so tired of it all.'

Jean took his hand, saying she could not bear to see him so sad. 'I made a lot of mistakes, and I hurt you. I wish I hadn't done what I did, but I did. I pay for it every day, believe me.

'You seem to have made mistakes as well, for the best reasons, but they're still mistakes. It ought to be possible for us, together, to do something about all of this, don't you think?'

'Such as what?' he asked. 'Us getting back together again? Is that what you're saying?'

He pulled his hand away from her. 'And how would that solve any problems, Jean? I'm married, I can't just get rid of my wife, throw her out like something I don't need any more. However difficult it is, she depends on me. I don't know why, but she does. And even without that, if I came back here to you — I wouldn't have a job, it would be the same situation all over again.'

'Look, first of all, you don't need a job. I earn so much money from my work that — the money's not important, all right? As for your wife, from what Martin said both of you are really miserable. He told me himself she's an extremely unstable person. What can you do for her? She doesn't need you, she needs proper care. I just feel that, for some twisted reason, you're the one carrying the guilt for our break-up and it's all come to be focussed on her. As if being unhappy with her for the rest of your life is your punishment or something.

'I'm just trying to say that it doesn't have to be like that, that it might be better for her as well as you — I really want you back, David. I need you too. I'm begging you, you know?'

Late in the night he called the airline to cancel his flight and reserved a seat for the following Monday. He stayed with Jean through the rest of the weekend.

Megumi sat in the hallway for a long time after David left. She heard the telephone ring, but did not answer it. When it rang again, and kept ringing, she stood, her legs stiff from being folded under her for so long on the hard floor, and went into the kitchen. She took the receiver and let it fall from her hands to swing against the greasy wall, then cut the connection by jabbing the cradle down once with her fingers. After a minute or so the noise coming from the receiver changed from the rhythmical beeping of the engaged tone to a consistent hum.

She carried the suitcase she had packed so carefully back into her room, and slowly started to take the clothes out again, but stopped, leaving a creamy Aran sweater she had bought in Donegal spilled onto the *tatami*. She went to the cupboard to get her box of souvenirs and placed it next to the suitcase.

For some time since their return to Japan Megumi had been receiving medication for depression. She kept the pills in the kitchen so that she would remember to take them when she ate. Now she went to get them. In the same cupboard was a bottle of valium she had been given by her doctor in Belfast just after Kayoko had died. She emptied it into a small bowl with her other tablets. She began to put the drugs into her mouth, swallowing them with mouthfuls of water. It took ten minutes to get them down. Because she had not eaten that day she was afraid of vomiting, so she found some bread and ate it with a little milk before going back into the room where she slept.

She smiled as she took the envelope of photographs from the box and spread the pictures on the floor: they were little frozen moments of happiness, Martin in the house in Castlerock, Martin and Stephanie, Megumi with Carol and Rosslyn at a restaurant they had driven to in Carlingford, Kayoko and David in the garden. Not once did she think of what she was doing to herself. There was nothing to think about. David had left her, she had known that as soon as he told her he was going to England alone. His assurances assured her only that he would not come back. Now the only thing left for her was to die. There was nothing to think about.

Jean took the morning off from her work to go with David to Heathrow. When the flight was called she held him tightly, kissing his mouth. As he turned from her to go through passport control she called out to him, 'See you soon.'

He walked down the long corridor towards the gate where his aircraft was boarding. The space seemed to stretch before him for ever, a long tunnel from which, if he missed his turning, there was no escape.

He knew how difficult it would be when he got back to Tokyo, but he was sure that what he intended to do was the best thing, the best thing, not just for himself, but for Megumi as well. She was ill and unhappy. She needed care of a kind he could not give her. She needed to be with her family again. Her mother, when he had spoken to her from Narita, had said as much. A divorce was not immediately necessary, Jean didn't care whether they were married or not, as long as they were together. It would be easier on Megumi to wait until she was stronger. Perhaps one day she would understand. Like an impetuous swimmer he had dived into waters too deep to save someone beyond rescue and, caught by frantic hands, he was being pulled to his own death. It was time to break free.

As David took his seat in the aircraft he thought of what he was returning to. The house would be filthy, filled with the odour of dead flowers in stagnant water.